MAYBE SECOND TIME'S A CHARM

SAQUIB AHMAD

To the girl I loved,

Let this book be our last goodbye.

Contents

Contents

Acknowledgements

Writing this novel has been a journey of discovery, growth, and unwavering support. I am incredibly grateful to everyone, who has contributed, whether in ways big or small, to bringing this book to life.

To my family, and especially my sister, my fiercest supporter and most honest critic. Thank you for believing in me even when I struggled to belive in myself. Your faith and presence have meant more than words can express.

To my friends, Sameer and Chandan, thank you for reading early drafts and offering thoughtful insights that helped shape this story. Your encouragement and feedback made me a better writer.

A heartfelt thank you to my publisher, Notion Press. Thank you for believing in this story from the very beginning. Your professionalism and dedication has made this journey smoother and infinitely more rewarding.

And finally, to you, dear readers, thank you for your curiosity, and for taking a chance on this story. Without you, none of this would be possible. I am endlessly grateful.

This book is for all of you.

1

Chapter One

The month paints a beautiful scene with its cloudy mornings and refreshing cool breezes. In the background, the distant noises of hawker calls and occasional car honks fill the surroundings.

A cool breeze of air flows in through the open window and brush against my face. A shiver ran through my body waking me up.

The clock showed 6 AM. With a mixed feeling of sleeping a little more or walking towards the balcony to feel the soothing chills that the breeze carried with it, I choose the latter.

The cold floor felt good beneath my feet as I walk towards the balcony. A gentle gush of air flew in as I pulled the drapes to a corner, carrying freshness along with it. The sky was slowly turning into a lighter shade of blue, sunlight shimmering on the ocean waves, while I breathe the fresh air.

I love slow mornings. It makes me feel smaller, like there's a world out there where everyone is so busy in their own lives, unbeknownst to others and their problems.

A good place to live was always my priority, a place where you can feel at ease after a long day. Though finding an apartment in Mumbai wasn't an easy task. Either your balcony opens up in the face of your neighbour or you don't get a balcony at all. I love my home very much. An apartment with a balcony that opened up to a sea was quite expensive and hard to find. It took a chunk out of my salary but it's worth it. On clear days, you could watch the sun set in the sea, although it's rare that I'm home before sunset to watch it, but the idea of a cup of coffee, a really good book and sunset sounds nice.

After being there in the balcony for a while, I make my way towards the bathroom to finish my morning routine. It wasn't raining outside, so I quickly put on my running gear and made my way to the door. I've always loved running, my go to exercise when I'm trying to stay fit and over the years it has become more of habit than fitness. Nothing clears your head more than a good few kilometers. Maybe a long shower, but close.

Some of the shops were opening while others still had some time left to open. There were people returning from their night shifts, the hawkers selling their stuff from the back of their bicycles. I turn towards the narrow lane that led to the sea, navigating past other couples who were walking on the aisle of the road.

ᠣᠣᠣ

I enter my apartment after jogging for approximately thirty minutes. The clock showed seven thirty, which meant I still had some time left before finally getting ready for work, so I brew a cup of coffee and then on my way to the balcony, I grab the book that I was reading last night before sleeping. With a warm mug in my hand, I settle on the edge of the balcony.

Romance is and always have been my go to genre and the more the story makes me cry, the more I am in love with the book. Stories in which the protagonist are always happy and luck always favours them—like they are god's favourite child and somehow the universe seems to conspire to bring them together like some sort of fairy tale—seems very delusional to me. I agree that love isn't black and white, but it isn't golden either. It has shades of warm yellow sun, crimsons of the dusk and the darkest blues of the midnight.

The real world doesn't work like this. Love isn't as effortless as they show it in movies. Falling in love is easy but staying in love requires constant efforts, without giving up on each other and making sure it works out. And when two people refuse to surrender without a fight, in spite of knowing that there's a good chance that they might fall apart in the end, but they still cling on to a hope is really fascinating. There's something about forbidden love that makes it more enthralling.

After reading for a while, I get ready, have my breakfast and then leave for work at nine thirty.

ꝓꝓꝓ

I place my bag on the side of my desk and then start my computer. As a management consultant, the first thing I do when I reach at work is to create a to-do list before resuming my work so that I don't miss out on anything important.

"Good Morning." Shruti greets, slumping on the desk. She soon hops on to the desk and sits beside the monitor.

"Good Morning." I greet her back.

"Let's go somewhere tonight. It's the weekend and it has been a very stressful week. I just want a getaway." She sighs. "Just four of us. I've already asked Khushi and she agreed."

"Oka-ay." I respond, my voice laced with confusion, as I try to make sense of what's going on in her head.

"I am not asking you. I am telling you that you're coming with us. I've told Khushi that you're coming and she must have already convinced Rohan by now. So you are coming with us and that's final."

"Easy woman. At least take a breath and relax. I'll come with you guys. I was just gathering my thoughts before your getaway came out of the blue. Some of us actually do our job here in the morning, you know."

"Haha, very funny." She says with a grin on her face. "You better get your ducks in a row and make sure everything gets done on time. I don't want any last minute excuses."

"Thank god, you aren't my boss or you would have made me miserable on deadlines." I chuckle.

"Whatever."

ꝓꝓꝓ

"Come on. They're waiting for us downstairs. Wrap up fast." Shruti shouts from the door.

"In a second." I shut off my computer and rush towards the door. Shruti had already called the elevator. She had placed her hand on the elevator's door as I hurried towards it. I step inside and press the ground floor.

"So, where are we going for your awaited getaway?" I ask her with a hint of tease in my voice.

"I have no idea, but I've been eagerly waiting for it since I woke up. It's not like I wanna do something special. I just wanna go to a place where I can bitch about everything that happened this week until my heart finds peace."

"Until your heart finds peace." I laugh as we do a fist bump. She slumps back on the elevator's wall with a grin.

"Yeah, it's exhausting being an adult. Always on your own, with tons of responsibilities." She sighs.

"Responsible Shruti? Who's she and why haven't you introduced me to her?" I tease to which she scowls but as she was about to say something the elevator pings and the door opens only to show that Rohan and Khushi weren't there.

"They must be in the parking lot." Shruti shrugs and we head towards the basement parking.

As we enter the parking lot, we see Khushi sitting on Rohan's bike and Rohan stood in front of her, holding her hands. He has a fond look on his face as he whispers something in her ear, while continuing to rub her knuckles with his thumb.

"Walk softly." Shruti whispers, then moves ahead of me, sneakily walking closer to them.

"Ahmm... Ahmm" Shruti does it loudly on purpose, clearly having fun teasing them. Rohan immediately leaves Khushi's hands as he sees us and starts to scratch the back of his head with a flushed smile on his face.

"We didn't mean to interrupt, but you know we kind of had plans for tonight. But if you guys have other plans, we totally understand.

I mean it's kinda rude to bail on friends but we don't mind as long as you promise to tell us the details tomorrow." She nudges Khushi with her shoulder, making her lose her balance a bit, but she manages to stay put.

I burst into laughter. "Okay-okay, let's decide where to go. We are already late."

"You are a killjoy, you know that right? Anyway, let's decide." Shruti says.

"How about bowling?" Khushi says and Rohan's face lightens up immediately. He really loves bowling and she knows it.

I look towards Shruti and she nods in agreement. "Okay then, let's go to the Game Palacio. There we can do bowling and if anyone wants to punch something to relieve their frustration," I look at Shruti "there are plenty of options there, and also Khow Chow is nearby, so we can have dinner there."

"So it's done? Bowling and then dinner. We should leave soon. It's Mumbai, it can rain anytime." Shruti says and we hurry to the Game Palacio as in this city, at one moment, the weather would be pleasant and within no time dark clouds would cover the sky and begin to rain.

As we were about to reach the Game Palacio, it started to drizzle. So I park my car as fast as I could and then we ran towards the entrance to prevent ourselves from getting soaked.

ᗁᗁᗁ

Bowling was fun as always and Rohan played it the best. Like every other bowling plan we had made before, he had scored above a hundred and fifty points. The weather has become pleasant after a light rain. Cool breeze brushed our faces as they passed through our hairs, making them sway in its direction. Since Khow Chow wasn't far away, we decided to walk there.

Shruti wraps her hands around her, slowly moving her palms. "You okay? I think I have a sweatshirt in my car. I can get that if you're too cold." Without waiting for her reply, I turn around towards the parking, but Shruti holds my wrist and stops me.

"No, I am fine. The weather is so pleasant here." She says, still continuing to rub her palms around her.

"Are you sure?" I ask her again. She nods. We start to walk towards Khow Chow. Rohan and Khushi were walking ahead us. "So, how do you feel after whacking that little mole?"

"Okay, I guess. At first I was trying to hit it and the more times I missed, the more I got frustrated, so I started hitting the machine. And then I felt better."

"Oh that I figured." I laugh. "Why are you so frustrated all of a sudden with the job?"

"I don't know. It feels like I am complaining too much but sometimes it gets overwhelmingly stressful, and I know there's good money in the job but still, sometimes I feel, things would be nicer if it all slowed down a little bit." She says in a low tone.

"No, you're not complaining at all. I feel it too, sometimes."

"Hmm. We joined this company, like literally together and it has been more than a year and half for us being in this job but there has always been something. There's always something, projects, deadlines. And I know we can take leaves, but I don't wanna take a sabbatical after a project. What am I gonna do all day at home, alone."

"I totally understand what you're saying. You know what I feel sometimes, that I don't get to see the end result of something for which I worked my ass off for months. It may be different for other people, but I like it when I get to know if the strategy we made worked well." I say as we slowly walk towards the hotel since it was nearby and it hasn't started to rain again.

"Dude, you took words out of my mouth. I totally wanna know too. That is one of the reasons I am not liking my job."

"Do you hate consulting or just the job?" I ask her.

"No, I don't hate consulting. It's only the few aspects of the job, which I don't like." She replies.

"Okay, so don't tell anyone about this. I've always thought of starting my own consulting, at some point of time. Not too late. I've been waiting for a right moment. Would you be interested?"

"What? As partners?"

"Yeah. As partners. I am not going to make any big promises. We can start slow and then grow it big, and also mould it to our liking, so it doesn't make us frustrated again. So, what say?"

"Oh, it's on partner." She smiles and we shake hands as a gesture.

ᑭᑭᑭ

It was already eleven by the time we had our dinner. Rohan was dropping Khushi to her apartment.

"I'll drop you." I say to Shruti.

"It's okay, I'll take a cab." She takes out her phone from her purse and started searching for cabs.

"It is late already. Get in the car, I'll drop you." She was still on her phone, searching. "C'mon, don't be a child."

"Okay fine." She finally agrees. I open the door for her and she gets in the front seat. The traffic was less than usual. It took us around twenty minutes to reach her apartment.

"Wait here. I'll bring your charger. I keep forgetting to put it in my bag every day." She says as she climbs out of the car.

"Don't worry about it. It was a spare."

"No, just give me two minutes. I'll bring it." She shouts over her shoulder as she rushes towards the elevator.

"Wait, I will come with you." I step out of the car and shut the door behind me and start following her to the elevator. The elevator opens at the seventh floor and we walk out of it. She moves ahead and knock on the apartment 703.

Her roommate opens the door and a familiar face appears before my eyes. Shruti gets inside her apartment to bring the charger, while I stand there looking at the person holding the door open. Our eyes meet and it felt like all the blood has drained from my face. My mouth goes dry and the words stuck in my throat creating a lump.

"Here's your charger." Shruti comes back and hands me the charger. I turn to look at Shurti as she hands me the charger. Her roommate was still holding the door. I swallow the lump formed in my throat.

"Thanks" was all I could manage to mumble.

"Oh yeah, let me introduce you both. Anya, this is Aahil, my friend from work, and Aahil, this is Anya, my roommate and my girlfriend." Shruti says and wraps her hand around Anya. Anya smiles, but the smile seemed forced.

"Hey, nice to meet you." There's so much awkwardness in every word.

"Hi, same." She replies lowly, her voice barely above a whisper.

"Ah... I better go. It's getting late." I hate how my voice cracks a bit, an obvious stutter visible in my words.

"Yeah, sure and thank you for the ride. Good Night." Shruti cheerfully says.

"No problem. Good night." I reply to Shruti and then take a last look at the door before turning towards the elevator.

I get inside the car, frustrated, I hit the steering wheel with my palm. The sheer coincidence of her turning out to be the roommate of my colleague feels almost unbelievable. What are the odds of this happening? It was so unexpected to see her after these years. Why does everything have to come back to a circle? A straight line would've been fine for once.

"Don't irritate me by calling again and again. If you cannot make it easier, at least don't make it hard for me. And if you cannot get this thing in your head then I think it is for the best that we are ending this relationship. If you really love me as you say and you want to see me happy, never try to contact me again."

2

Chapter Two

It was a slow tuesday morning at work. Even though the day had just begun, there was nothing much to do as the internet was lagging severely, making it hard to send a single file, and not even our internal server was accessible. I was staring at my computer aimlessly whilst fiddling with the pencil.

"I'll find a way, please trust me. Please don't give up on us."

Words I remember saying to her, echo in my mind every now and then, every word haunting me to this day. I vividly remember the moments when I was saying, rather begging her to stay, promising her that I'll make everything right, but she chose to walk away, turn her back on me, and on everything we built together and on the endless love she told she had for me. Maybe, we can never know someone fully, their every secret, their every habit or how cruel they can be when they need to protect themselves.

"Hey, no daydreaming during office hours." Shruti interrupts placing her hand on my shoulder, bringing me back from my thoughts. "What happened? Everything okay?" Her tone changes into a voice of concern.

She moves towards the desk and with her arms crossed, she slumps on the desk. "Yeah, I'm fine." I say, but she doesn't look convinced with it. Her expression doesn't change and she keep staring at me with a stern glare, wanting to know the real reason. "Was just thinking about the book I was reading at home."

The expressions on her face change. "What is the matter with you? Why do you read such books when they affect you so much?"

"Um, there is something about these books. Anyway, do you need something?"

"Oh yes. Can you take a look at this report and check if everything looks fine? I don't wanna make a fool of myself in front of boss in the meeting. She already has plenty of reasons to be mad at me."

"Yeah sure. Let me get a chair first."

As I turned to grab a chair, she stops me by holding my wrist. "Hey, are you really okay?"

"Yeah, totally." I say with a smile.

"Doesn't feel like it. No snarky comments, no leg pulling. You are behaving differently today. This can't be because of a book."

I hold the back of the chair, guiding it towards my desk. "Oh, so you like being bullied."

"You making fun of me gives me the opportunity to make double fun of you. So in a way you are ripping me of this opportunity by being nice to me."

"Don't worry. I am fine. Anyway, show me your report fast. You don't wanna give her another reason to be mad at you." I say.

She sits on my chair and inserts a flash drive in my computer while I sit on the chair next to her. Once she opens the report, she passes me the mouse to take a quick overview of the report.

"Everything looks fine... Yeah, everything's okay. Breathe and just be yourself. You have nothing to worry about.

She takes a deep breath. "Be myself." She repeats the affirmation.

"Yeah, not too much." I smirk and immediately she punches my hand. "Don't worry." I say. She takes a deep breath again before walking towards the conference room.

I lean back on my chair and my gaze falls on the broken pencil on my desk. Confused as to its state, I shrug, assuming I pressed it too hard or something and start fiddling with it again.

Does Shruti know about it? They are roommates and it's common for girls to share everything with each other. But then again, if she knew, she would've dropped hints about it, but she hasn't. Maybe, Anya hasn't told her about it, yet, so asking her about Anya would really be a bad idea.

The ring from the landline interrupts my chain of thoughts. "Hello." "Please ask him to wait in conference room six. I'll be there in a minute."

"Hello Mr. Shrivastav. How are you?" I said as I enter the conference room. He stands up from his chair even though I gestured him not to. We shake hands and then I take a seat opposite to him.

"Hello Aahil sir. I am good and this is for you." He responds ever so cheerfully, then hands me a box of sweets.

As I hold the box of sweets in my hand, I remembered that he was in such a hurry to compile the product costing data because his wife was expecting a child and he had to come to office for a few days to compile the data during his paternity leave. "Is it a boy or a girl?" I asked him.

"A girl." He replied, with an obvious hint of happiness in his voice. "Thank you so much Aahil sir for staying up late with me."

I smile at him. "Don't mention it. And congratulations." I say. "You are a lucky man. Girls are a blessing from god. Do you have a photo of her?"

He takes out his phone from his pocket and shows me the photo of her daughter. "She looks so adorable, like a beautiful little angel."

"Thank you. Ah, I better go. Thank you again for everything." He gets up and starts to leave.

"Congratulations again." I smile at him. He smiles back, then nod before leaving. I hold the box in my hand, then take it back to my desk.

I place the box on the desk. My gaze falls on the computer screen which showed the email I sent in the morning was still sitting in the outbox. The internet issue hasn't been resolved yet. Leaning back in my chair, I grab my phone from the pocket. "Tea?" I send a text to Rohan.

"That's not even a question." His text appears almost instantly as if he had been waiting for the message. So I get up from the chair and head towards the cafeteria.

It is raining heavily. The shed attached to the rooftop made loud noises as they kept flapping when the wind relentlessly collided with it. I pour tea in two mugs and hand one to Rohan.

The chairs near the edge of the shed were completely soaked as the rain fell on them, with the wind constantly shifting its direction. We take a seat near the wall to prevent ourselves from getting soaked.

"The internet won't work anytime soon." Rohan says looking at the rain.

"I really wish it doesn't work today and the boss says, guys, it is raining heavily, let's all go home before the roads get blocked with water. I will really love a lazy day like this, sitting in cosiness of my home with some hot tea and enjoy the weather."

"Now I wish that too. Let me check the news." He says. He takes out his phone from the pocket and opens the local news app while I sip my tea. "Water has clogged in the harbour line track and it is just a few inches away from getting submerged. The local trains are going to stop anytime now. All we have to do now is wait for the good news." He extends his right hand forward and we do a fist bump. Although it's cruel to be happy for something that is causing misery in the lives of many people but the people in Mumbai are used to heavy rains. We judge the intensity of rain by number of days it can get us holidays or half days.

Rohan's phone rings. "Hey." "In the canteen." He hung up the phone and look towards me. "Seems like your wish has been granted."

I drink the whole tea in one sip, then rise from the chair. "Hurry up, finish fast. Oh god, I burnt my tongue." I blow out air to cool it down. I always get excited on the thought of reaching home early. It gives me some extra hours for my freelance work. I like being all by myself, and do whatever I want and just not care.

I keep the box of sweets in my bag and head towards Rohan's desk. Khushi was already there, standing next to his desk and checking her watch. She too seemed to be eager to go home judging by the way she kept tapping her fingers on the desk repetitively.

Rohan finishes wrapping up his work. "Where is Shruti?" He asks.

"Damn, she's probably with her team lead in the meeting." I say. "Khushi, can you call her and ask if she'll be there for long?"

Khushi calls her. "She isn't picking up." Khushi says but her phone vibrates immediately. "The meeting's gonna end in twenty minutes." She says, while looking at the phone.

We grab the chairs around and pull it closer to Rohan's desk and sit. "Here." I take out the box of sweets from my bag and pass it to them.

"What's the occasion?" Rohan asks as he takes one from the box.

"Shrivastav had a girl, so he dropped by to give me the box." I say.

"Shrivastav, the accountant, right?" Rohan asks while he passes the box to Khushi.

"Who's Shrivastav?" Khushi asks.

"He works as a cost accountant in Ahluwalia group." I reply.

"You should've heard his voice during the time he had to come during his leave. He really didn't wanted to come." Rohan chuckles. I smile.

"How do you know him?" Khushi asks Rohan.

"I heard him talk to Aahil while we were drinking tea in the canteen."

"I see." Khushi passes the box to me without taking any sweets from it.

"You can take some, Rohan will still love you even if you gain a little weight. Won't you Rohan?" I chuckle.

"You know you'll still be beautiful." Rohan says as Khushi looks at him. I pass the box to her.

"No-no, thank you. I am saving for tomorrow. Shruti won't let me go without making me eat like a panda on her birthday." She passes the box back.

I take out a sweet on the box, then place it on the desk.

"You'll be the cutest panda." Rohan envelopes her palm between his and caresses her knuckles.

"You don't need to butter me up." She says but still a blush was evident on her cheeks.

"Aren't you guys the cutest." I smile at them. "Hey look, she's done." I say as Shruti walks out of the conference room.

"Sorry-sorry, just give a minute more. I'll go grab my stuff." She doesn't wait for us to say something as she walks towards her desk in a hurry. She returns back quickly grabbing her bag.

I pass her the box. She takes out a sweet. "Why? Don't tell me, you finally found a girl?"

"No. Why?"

"You're straight, right? You can tell me. I won't judge." Shruti chuckles. Everyone laughs.

"Can we go now? The roads will be blocked if we don't hurry. And I am straight."

"Yeah-yeah, we can definitely go." Shruti says and we stand up from the chair and start walking towards the exit. "If you're straight, why haven't I seen you with a girl in two years?"

"I don't have time for that?"

"Ah, classic excuse." She laughs as we get in the elevator.

ᐳᐳᐳ

I serve my lunch on a plate and place it in the microwave to heat it, then open the refrigerator and pour some juice in a glass. The microwave pings. Holding the glass in other hand, I walk towards the balcony to eat alongside watching as the rain fell on the sea waves. It was still raining heavily outside and everyone was coming back to their homes.

After I finish eating, I leave the plate in the sink and on my way back to the balcony, I pick up the book I was reading from the table.

As I read the last page of the book, I could feel my eyes tearing up. Gently, I slide my thumb and wipe a tear that fell from the side of my eye, then keep the book aside. Shifting my gaze to the view outside the balcony, to the clouds, the rain, the sea and the waves as they gushed on the shore, I think about the series of events in the book. I wonder what I would do if I was the doctor holding my love in my arms, and I had to stand there, helpless, and watch her take her last breaths, crying that I tried my best but it still wasn't enough.

Almost immediately, I feel an ache in my heart, a void, as the memory of how happy I was five years ago flashed in front of my eyes.

"Ask me anything you want and I'll give it to you." Anya says.

"Anything." I ask.

"Yes, anything." She says again.

"I don't want anything right now but I want it in the future. When I take my last few breaths, don't look at my face, just bury it in your chest and hug me, tightly. I want to take my last breath wrapped in your arms."

I remember telling her this, when we were together. I really wish things would have been different. Those few years that we were together, I haven't been happier than that. Suddenly the ache in my heart is back and my eyes start to well up again and I am not sure whether the tears are because of the book I just read or the memory that I just remembered.

I lean back a little against the wall with my gaze fixed on the vast expanse of sea which mirrored the turmoil in my heart.

3

Chapter Three

❦

September 8th, 2019

There are days when the air feels heavy as I open my eyes. My lungs struggle to breathe and between them is my aching heart which is getting heavier with each passing second.

I was sitting beneath a tree with tears rolling down my eyes. I tried to scream as loud as I can, but the burden of her words muffled my voice and turned it into a cry. My head weighed like I was having a hangover but there was no one around to support it. She was my destiny, or at least that was what I believed.

An Hour Before...

"Aahil, mom won't accept our relationship. I tried to tell her everything about us, even about our future, our dreams together, but she declined. I tried to reason with her in every damn way possible but she didn't listen to a single word, like this isn't open for discussion at all. I tried to plea that you would do something great and become successful, but she dismissed it, saying that you belonged to a different class of society. She said, if the two of us still want to be together, we can do it after she dies. As long as she's alive, she'll never accept us together.

I don't want to give you any false hope Aahil, please, don't dream of us together, no one will ever accept us together, neither my parents, nor yours. You worry about yourself and take care, okay? I wish you all the best for your future."

I was on my way back to my apartment when I hear the message ping on my phone. A chill ran through my body as I read her message. I tighten my grip on my phone to ground myself as I wasn't prepared for this, there's no way I could've been prepared for something like this. The realization hit me like a ton of bricks and my eyes started to water.

"This couldn't be happening." I keep saying it over and over inside my head. Shaking my head, I wipe my eyes and started walking even though every step I took felt heavy. No amount of air that I breathe seems to reach my lungs. My legs starting to give out, trembling too much to stay upright. I lean against a tree near the pavement, my hand still clutching the phone tight. I sit beneath the tree as my legs couldn't hold up any longer, and squeeze my eyes shut, praying, that this is all just a nightmare and all I needed to do to end this pain is to wake up.

My phone started to ring, and I picked up without looking, knowing who it would be.

"Hello" my voiced cracked a little and I hated it. It gave away every bit of agony that I was feeling.

"Hey! Everything alright? Why is your voice shaking?" She replied.

I resist my urge to hang up the phone on her audacity to ask if everything's alright after sending me that message. How can she break up everything we built together and then have the nerve to ask if everything's alright?

"Why would you send me that message all of a sudden? Your mother knew about us for a while now, then how the hell did this happen? And if that cursed message is a part of one of your pranks, then you've messed up really bad this time, cause it's not funny."

"Please try to understand Aahil, we cannot live together. I tried to convince my mother in every way I could but she didn't budge from her decision. Please understand Aahil." She pleads.

"Okay, for a moment, let's hypothetically say that we don't end up together in the future, does that mean we should give up right now?

Throw everything down the drain over a possibility that may or may not come true? Why should we give up our present for a future that is so far away?" I reason her.

"Then what do you suggest we do? Go behind everyone's back, continue with our relationship. But until when? What about when we want to marry each other and we have to tell our parents. You know what they'll say? A big fat no. What are we going to do then? I won't be able to take that no. Aahil, I'll end my life if that happens." Her tone is cold, lacking its usual warmth, her voice devoid of any emotion. I couldn't believe what she had just said. Ending her life? God, I don't even want to think about a life in which she isn't there, let alone live in a world she isn't a part of.

"Anya, love, I'm trying to understand you but meet me in the middle, please. You're right, okay, I agree that what we want seems impossible and we cannot find a way, but you can't do this to us Anya. You can't give up now. Right now, we are just teens. We aren't wise enough, but we know our destination, right? It's you and me, together, till we are old and grey and I know this all seems so difficult right now but love, shouldn't we take small steps until our paths become clearer? We can worry about the rest later."

"Aahil, I request you, please don't make it more difficult for me than it already is. I love you so much. But I can't see you wasting your time on me. We can't be together. We are destined to get apart." She starts to sob.

"Please don't cry. I'll find a way. Just trust me. Don't give up on us like this."

"Aahil..." The pain in her voice was unlike anything I had ever heard before. "Listen to me Aahil." She says, trying to breathe. "Aahil, I know I'm hurting you. I know I am hurting you so bad..." Her voice breaks again in a cry, but somehow she's trying to control herself. "I don't want to hold on to a hope that isn't there. Aahil, this is not me giving up on us. I tried... so damn hard, but I failed. I failed... I want a life with you Aahil. I really do. I love you so freaking much." She takes a deep breath. "I really wish to see our dreams come true, but it's time for us to part. I'll always be there for you. You own my heart and only you'll own it forever. Goodbye. I know, right now it hurts so much but it'll heal soon. Don't let your past

stop you from moving ahead. I know you'll do something extraordinary. I trust you." She breathes. "Please don't try to contact me, ever. I love you and will always love you, till my last breath." She was crying but her last words sounded determined. I wish I had a quarter of the strength she seemed to have.

"But I want to take my last breath with you." I wanted to say, but she had already hung up the phone, for the final time. I sat there, not knowing whether I'd get to hear from her again or not.

Her words kept repeating again and again in my head. It all seemed too unreal. My life had turned upside down in a matter of minutes. But unlike her, I couldn't give up on us like this. I still had to convince her that we can make it together. So I called her, but the call disconnected automatically after a ring. I was blocked. Not even her display picture appeared when I tried to check her whatsapp and neither did her profile appeared on instagram. I was blocked there and every other place we used to talk.

I call her, again and again, in hopes that if she sees enough notifications of my calls, she'd call me back. But, she didn't.

Never in my wildest dreams did I think that a day would come when this had to end. I didn't want it to end. I wanted to look at her, dwell in her eyes, her beautiful face like the way I did. I wanted to hear her laugh, again. I wanted to wait for her on the phone while she forgot that she had called me, then come back giggling and saying 'Oops, I completely forgot I had called you.' I wanted to hug her, and kiss her. I wanna hold her hands and feel how warm they feel between mine. I wanted to wrap her in my arms, while we lay on the bed, our heads resting on the same pillow, lost in each other. I wanted to take my last breath, wrapped in her arms, feeling safe, even in the moments of death, but here I was, all alone, lifeless like a bird without wings, with a love destined to be torn apart.

I sat there clueless, not sure for how long. My tears kept falling freely. She didn't just leave me, but she took a part of me with her. She broke her promise to stay with me forever. Never did I imagine that betrayal would cut so deep.

4

Chapter Four

I rummaged through my closet, pulling out one shirt after the other, unable to decide what to wear for the party. I really envy those people who can think of a whole outfit for any occasion in their head. It's not that I have a bad dressing sense, rather it's just that I can't think of multiple layer of dresses and accessories. I think girls are better at it. Anyway, Shruti was hosting her birthday party at her apartment, so I had to get ready fast as I was already late.

After going back and forth, I finally decide to wear a plain maroon shirt, pairing it with black jeans. This would look good, I say to myself and start keeping the other shirts back in the closet.

Just as I was about to wear the maroon shirt, it occurred to me that *she* would be there at the party. And this sudden realisation made me rethink my decision of wearing the maroon shirt as I had to look good. Not that I am dressing for her, but it's a party and one should look good when they go in a party.

So, there I was again, back in the same spot as I was a couple minutes ago, staring at my closet. "Screw it." I say as I pull all of my shirts out of the closet.

I keep on switching shirts after shirt, until I find a plain white shirt. You cannot go wrong with the classic combination of white shirt and black jeans. Before putting on the shirt, I do a few quick push-ups so that the shirt fits nicely, and then slip on the white shirt. Rolling the sleeves up to rest above my forearms, I then pull out my trusty white sneakers.

As I stood outside Shruti's apartment, I could hear the music outside. I press the doorbell and take a step back from the door, waiting for Shruti to open.

She opens the door and the music hits me like a wave–it was way louder than I thought it would be. She was on her phone, talking to someone, but she shortens the conversation immediately and hung up the phone.

"Happy Birthday. This is for you." I wish her while giving a side hug and hand her a box of her favourite chocolates.

"Thank you so much." She says gleefully and leads me inside the hall where some of her friends were sitting. "Everyone, this is Aahil, and Aahil she's Nisha, Diya and he's Abhi." She introduces us, and I shake hands with Abhi while I wave a hand, saying hello to Nisha and Diya.

"Make yourself comfortable, I'll bring you something to drink." Shruti says and walks inside, and I look around, smile, and then excuse myself and sit on a nearby couch while her friends were busy talking with each other, and I kept wondering where in the world are Rohan and Khushi. Shruti brings and hands me a coke before excusing herself to greet other friends.

More of Shruti's friends were arriving at the party one after another and she greeted everyone with the same level of excitement. She would hug every one of them as they enter and welcome them in. Compared to me who has only three friends whom I can call if I had a party, she really has plenty. I have friends from school but we don't talk on a daily basis or rather we go on for weeks without talking, and it isn't like we have a grudge or something. It's just we all work in different fields, some of us are in different cities too, so we all kind of phased out of each other's life.

On the side conscious of my mind, I was wondering where Anya is. I let my eyes wander around the room. While they did not land on her, I saw Rohan and Khushi enter the apartment, making them last of Shruti's friends to arrive at the party.

I stand as Rohan finds me in the crowd and they make their way towards me. "I have never missed you guys as much as I have in last twenty minutes." I say in lieu of greeting and they start laughing.

The lights dim around us and the music fades from an upbeat to a soft melody. I turn around and I see Anya walk in the room with cake in her hands. The only prominent light in the room came from the candles that were on the cake. As she made her way towards the table, the soft glow of the candles cast a golden hue on her face. She walked steadily, ensuring that the flames of the candles doesn't blow out before reaching the table.

She passes right by me, too focused on the candles to notice me there. My heart skips a beat. My eyes follow her as she walks gracefully towards the middle of the crowd, to place the cake on the centre of the table.

She turns around after placing the cake. Her eyes meet mine, for a moment, but then she looks away from me and glances at Shruti and with a smile on her face she gestures Shruti to come at the centre while she takes a step to the side. Shruti stands at the centre with a big smile, looking around the room at other smiling faces, she smirks and blows all of the candles in one go, as if she had been saving up air just to do this. Everyone starts clapping. Some of her friends take out their phones to take snaps while she cuts the cake and the upbeat music was back in full volume.

With the change in music, the floors thrummed with the beats and everyone starts dancing. My friends dragged me in to dance and Shruti joined us soon after. I try to mimic what others were doing, though they did not looked like they knew what they were doing.

"You guys continue, I am gonna find some coke." I shouted for Rohan to hear. Shruti was now dancing with her other friends. I excuse myself and take a deep breath of relief before heading towards the kitchen.

"I really need to find a place away from this loud music." I thought to myself. Looking back at the people dancing as I walked towards the kitchen, I accidently bump into someone. "I am sorry." I immediately blurt out in a reflex.

"It's okay." A voice says. As I look towards the source of the voice, I see her. Anya. And as cliché as it may sound, time stops for a moment. Everything I had to say, every question I had thought of asking her when I meet her again, nothing came out, and instead I was at a loss of words and all I could mutter was "Hey."

It has been years since we last spoke and here we are, standing, looking at each other, yet everything feels totally different from what it felt five years ago. The warmth, happiness and love have been replaced with awkwardness, bitterness and grudges. She still is beautiful as ever but the weight of unresolved emotion have maimed the beauty of it all.

"Hi. Do you need something?" She says looking at me. I let my gaze wander around the kitchen, anywhere but her.

"Umm, yeah. I was looking for some coke." I look at her for a moment, only to turn away the next moment. A palpable sense of awkwardness and tension filled the room.

"Oh." She says, then turns around and open the refrigerator to take out the bottle of coke and poured me a glass.

"Thanks." I say forcing a small smile on my face. She gives a small nod and before anyone of us says or does something, I turn to leave the kitchen, eager to escape suffocating awkwardness of this situation.

I walked back to where Rohan and Khushi were dancing, but this time, they were dancing close to each other. Rohan sees me coming and takes a step back and distances himself from Khushi. "What took you so long?" He asks.

"Looks like you wouldn't have minded few more minutes." I chuckle. "I was finding the bottle. Anyway, you guys continue, I will be on the couch." I say and walk towards the couch.

It hasn't even been a minute I sat on the couch, Shruti comes and pulls me up to dance. "You've sat enough, it's my birthday, so screw you and your 'I-don't-like-loud-music-and-all' and come with me." She had no intentions of hearing anything so I give up and dance with her.

"Now don't sit." Shruti says after we have danced for a while. She excuses herself and walks towards the kitchen as the food were about to be served.

The music goes loud again after everyone had something to eat, but I slowly excuse myself out again and stand in a corner, sometimes moving my head with the beats to not look excluded, pretending to dance but at the same time having a safe space from the crowd, and I wasn't sitting so Shruti can't be mad either. Some of Shruti's friends are starting to leave as it was getting late already.

"Here." I hear a voice and turn. Anya was holding two glasses of coke and she passes one to me. "I know it isn't healthy but I guess you can make an exception today."

"Thanks." I hold the glass and smile at her.

"Why aren't you dancing? You still don't like it?"

"I was, a minute ago. Taking a short break." I say looking at her.

"Break from?"

"Bobbing my head here and there with the beats and pretending to dance." I say in playful tone. She laughs, instantly awakening a nostalgic feeling. I didn't realise how much I missed it all those years until now. "I haven't seen you dance either." I ask in an attempt to keep the conversation going.

"Shruti has to be there with her friends, so I am kind of looking at the arrangements." She says with a tiny smile, then takes a sip of coke. Contrary to the loud music in the room, a silence settles between us and no one speaks for a while.

"Sorry about that day. It was totally unexpected to see you like that, I wasn't prepared." I finally break the silence, hoping to make amends or something, I wasn't sure, but now that she was standing next to me, it was too much to bear. There has been nothing but radio silence for a long while. She looked at me intently like she wanted to hear more.

"Your face looked so pale, like you saw a ghost, but to tell you the truth, I was equally shocked to see you too. I didn't knew how to react, so I stood there." She smiles and take another sip.

"I was." I say, looking at the glass, and rubbing it with my thumb. "It has been a while, hasn't it?"

She didn't say anything for a while. She kept looking at the glass she was holding and finally let out a deep sigh. "Yep, it has been long." She says, shifting her gaze from the glass to me.

"So graphic designing, right?" I try to change the topic knowing full well where our conversation can head to. As much as I would like to get some answers, I know there's no point in bringing stuff up right now. Sometimes the band-aid needs to stay put because there's no point opening an old wound. It'll just open the scars and nothing less.

"Yup, a graphic designer at Excel marketing solutions."

"Oh, I think I've heard of them. That sounds cool."

"Yeah, it is good. So you and Shruti are colleagues?"

"Yes." I nod and smile.

Shruti comes looking for Anya. "There you are, come with me. You haven't enjoyed the party at all." Then she notices me standing next to her. "Unless you are busy here." She chuckles and elbows Anya. "Do you mind, if I take my girlfriend with me?" She was grinning ear to ear.

Anya half hid her face with the glass pretending to take a sip, but mostly hiding the laugh behind it. "No, not at all busy. Let's go." Anya smirks.

They turn towards the dance group. "Thanks for the coke." I call out and Anya looks back and smiles over her shoulder but then they join the dance floor.

There was contentment visible on Anya's face, the way she moved around freely with the rhythm of the music. Her hair flew around her, the strands she had curled bounced on her shoulders, occasionally hitting on her face as she danced with the group. She looked lost in a bubble, or maybe I was, lost, in admiring the beauty that beheld me in the moment. Nothing else mattered in that moment, the past seemed to blur in the background as I stood there with a smile on my face. Just because the end was bitter doesn't mean what we had wasn't good. There were a lot of storms but the rainbows outweighed them all.

ϸϸϸ

I open the door of my apartment, ready to pass out, exhaustion hitting me with full force. It's been a long week at work already and the Shruti's birthday party, a couple days ago, I had gotten only a few hours of good sleep. I pick the first pyjamas I see and quickly change into them, then fall on to my bed, my eyes drooping from sleep.

Just as I was about to slip into unconsciousness, my phone pings with a notification. "_anya started following you."

5

Chapter Five

❦

March 21ˢᵗ, 2016

"Anya accepted your friend request." My phone pings and a notification pops up as I connect my phone to the wi-fi. I click on the pop up which opens her facebook profile.

She has a photo with her friend as her profile picture and I have no clue, who among the two would Anya be as I haven't met and to be honest I didn't know her before. Her cover photo was of a quote, so no luck there. So, I scroll down her feed to find any photo of her but her profile photo was the only picture she had uploaded of her.

I click on the message button on her profile, then typed "Hey", unsure what else to send. I have never texted a random girl before and to the ones I know, I have only talked to them on stuff about notes and assignments. They think of me as a studious guy and their belief only gets stronger because I usually get good grades.

There is nothing to lose. I do not know this girl anyway and with that reassurance, I hit the send button. The messenger showed active thirty minutes ago beneath her name. I cannot explain it but somehow I had mixed feelings, seeing her offline. For one, I feel relieved that I'll have some time to think how not to screw up, and on the other hand, I don't know how long would I have to wait before she replies me, if she even choses to.

I keep my phone aside and take out my books to prepare for the test next day when my phone pings and a notification pops up showing a message from Anya. "Hi." I read the message from the notification. I did not want her to think of me as someone who has seen the message and is ignoring, or to be seen typing and erasing again and again and to be honest, the latter would be more embarrassing. Although I had just sent her a message a minute ago and not replying instantly does give a rude impression but it isn't like I am not trying to think of something fast but my inexperience made everything complicated and made me overthink everything.

"How are you?" I send her as if we were friends who are catching up after a long time but this is the best I can think of at the moment. Although, who are you would have been a better question at this time. How is it so easy for Yash? He talks to a lot of girls and that too at the same time. He is probably one of the reasons I sent her the friend request. I was fed up of him showing off to me about the number of girls he talks to and for a change I wanna show him that I am not a total loser.

"I am good. WBU?" Her message appears almost instantaneously. What the hell is WBU? I google the meaning of WBU. 'What 'bout you?'

"I am also good." What next? I ask myself as soon as I hit the send button. Can't she just ask something first? But then who am I to expect. I start brainstorming ideas for my next message but boy-oh-boy, did I fail miserably. I curse myself for not developing a tiniest bit of communication skill in sixteen years of my life.

"You both study in the same school." My inner self spoke to rescue me. Oh yes, she studies in the same school as I do, so she must be having a test tomorrow. It felt like a mini achievement to me. "Prepared for tomorrow's test?" I type the message and send her as fast as I could but the message does not deliver. The messenger showed active five minutes ago beneath her name. I didn't realise that I have been thinking for over five minutes. Shit! I curse myself for not doing it better.

ᗧᗧᗧ

I rub my eyes a bit, trying to clear my vision. To say I wasn't expecting this would be an understatement. I thought she'd let it fizzle out, whatever conversation we had. It's not like her to initiate conversations, but what do I know anymore?

I click on the notification and it takes me to her instagram profile. The only thing I could see was her small, circular profile picture which had a sun kissed photo of her wearing a hat, maybe from some resort. I hit the follow back button.

I refresh her profile once again and all of her photos start to appear along with the message button adjacent to the following button. I hit the message button before I see any of her photos as I was not sure how long my drowsy eyes are ready to cooperate with me.

"Hey." I message her. The memories of our first conversation come right in front of my eyes. It was definitely not the first message on the chat box but this message was after a long time. I ignore the older messages.

"Hi." She messages back.

"How was your day?" It did not take much of brainstorming unlike my first interaction with her, even though we were talking after five long years, with the exception of the birthday party. Maybe we were past the feeling of stress of framing appropriate questions. Even though the awkwardness is still there but it is quite different from what we or to be accurate I had in the beginning.

"It was tiring but overall good. How was yours?"

"I guess no matter the field, all jobs are tiring, but that is what makes weekends more relaxing." I text her back.

"Yeah, maybe." The typing animation still appeared so I wait for her to send the next message. "So, what do you when you get home?"

"Nothing special. Cook myself dinner and relax."

"Don't you ever feel lonely living all by yourself in the apartment?"

How does she know that I live alone? She must have asked from Shruti about me. "Umm I have company." I send the message, then click a photo of the sea view from my balcony and send her. "This takes away everything." I add.

"God, it's beautiful."

"IK, and on a full moon day, it becomes even more enchanting when the moon light reflects on the waves. It's as if, no matter how bad the day has been, all you need to do is lay on the bed, gaze at this mesmerising sight and it will gradually take all of your stress away."

"Okay, now you're showing off. I was already jealous looking at the photo but now you're just adding salt to my wound. I wish I could be there." Her message catches me off guard with the possibility that she might want to be here at my apartment. Yet, I quickly dismiss the thoughts, rationalising that she was probably expressing her desire to see the view in person and not mean anything else.

"Oh, but for that you have to spend the night at my apartment." I send it with a few laughing emojis, to make it sound casual.

"Haha, only if you make me paneer tikka for dinner." She plays along. "Okay I have to go. Bye."

"Done. Good night."

"Good night."

I click on her profile and scroll through her photos on her feed before keeping the phone aside. She doesn't post a lot. There weren't many photos of her. A few photos were from some resort, the same place from where her profile picture was, wearing a white floral dress and a hat. A couple of them were with friends in some restaurants and then there were some quotes on life which I think she wrote.

Fate has a weird way of messing up your life. I was doing fine until I met her two weeks ago and now, the only thing I can think of when I am alone is her. At times, the bitter memories would play out in front of my eyes, making my heart burn with anger and resentment but then on other times, it would be sweet memories that flash before me, making me miss her even more. More often than not, I wanna re-live that feeling of talking our hearts out with each other. Never in my wildest dreams did I imagine that after all these years, I would meet her again, and what hurts even more is that I don't know if our paths have crossed again, only to drift apart once more.

I keep my phone aside and take a deep breath. This isn't the way thing should have been in the first place. Can I really do this to myself? I barely survived the first time it happened. Can I handle it again? Part of me wants to tell her how happy I am to see her again, ask her to forget everything and start again from the beginning but am I prepared for it? Those years were not easy. I had come to terms with everything and for once I was doing okay in my life, if not happy.

I look outside towards the infinite sea, with small tides gushing, taking water with it as they move forward and then fall back. The weather was pleasant outside with gusts of wind making the curtains flow in the air occasionally.

The fact that she didn't have trust and faith in our love has kept on eating me since then. I remember how my heart ached when the pain went unbearable. I remember the time when I would scream for her, to help me and bring my heart at peace, but instead, she was the one causing it. Can I really bear another heartbreak? Do I have enough strength to pick up the pieces again? I don't know, maybe no one does. The thoughts keep running on my mind as I drift off to sleep.

ꗞꗞꗞ

Either the time slows its pace after lunch or it is just that I start to feel lazy, but minutes feel like hours now. I was on my computer, working, when my phone vibrates. "Hey, can we meet somewhere?" I was from Anya. I pick up the phone from the table and click on the message.

"Sure, I'll be free by eight." I text her.

"Have you seen the café near our apartment?"

"Yeah. I'll be there by eight fifteen."

"Okay. But please don't tell Shruti about it."

"Okay." I reply and keep my phone aside. What does she want to talk about? Maybe she wants to catch up after all these years. Maybe she's gonna tell me what the real reason was because I am not buying the reason she gave me. Maybe I'll get the answers I've been waiting for all these years. Or maybe I'm being too presumptuous, and it could totally be nothing.

Ever since the day I picked the last piece of myself, I've been wanting to ask her for an explanation. Ever since, I've been framing questions that I'll ask her when we meet, but today, when we could actually talk about it, I feel unprepared. I never wanted to hurt her, nor do I want to now, but there are things that are to be resolved for the sake of my own mental well-being.

6

Chapter Six

I reach the café by eight ten and reserve a corner table for two. As I settle on the chair, I look around the ambience of the café. Although it was my first time here, I have seen some the graphitic designs on the wall in Shruti's stories. The café wasn't big but the owner really nailed the vibe. There were these warm light bulbs hanging from the ceiling in caged holders, not too bright, casting a gentle glow and the curtains totally added layers to the whole aesthetic.

I was looking at the door when she walked in the café, her eyes scanning the room until she finds me. "I'm sorry, you had to wait." She says as she approaches the table.

I get up for her. "It's all good. I got here a few minutes ago." I assure her, gesturing towards the chair. She takes a seat. "You okay?" I ask because she seemed flustered.

"Yeah-yeah, I'm fine." She replies, but her eyes said otherwise as her gaze was fixed on my shirt instead of looking at me.

A few moments pass where neither of us say anything. Maybe she was thinking of a way to tell me what exactly happened between us and I was just waiting for her to say something. "What would you like to have?" I ask her as the silence grew unbearable.

"A cold coffee. Thanks." She mumbles, her gaze momentarily shifting to my face then she glances down at the table. I get up from my seat and walk towards the counter to place the order.

"Two cold coffees please." I request from the barista then turn around towards our table, but my feet comes to a pause as my eyes fall on her and I notice her visibly sigh. She had her hands crossed and her elbows rested on the table. Her gaze was fixed on the oregano jar in front of her although she was distracted. Her face reflected her obvious sadness, but also a struggle to contain her thoughts and the turmoil inside her.

Looking at her fighting her battles alone was the last thing I would have ever wanted but the fate has its own weird timings. While she is fighting, I am standing here at the counter looking at her, incapable of walking up to her and asking her not to worry, assuring her that I'll fix it for her because to be honest, I am not sure whether this conversation we are about to have will embark a new beginning for us or we'll get the closure we needed. This conversation is long overdue and has to be done for the sake of our mental sanity. I don't want to be haunted by a '*why*' for the rest of my life.

I've always wanted to be with her, and those three years we spent together were the happiest years of my life. I still wish for a future in which we could be together but I cannot risk building the foundation of our relationship without trusting each other. That is exactly why we need to have this conversation—sometimes a wound needs to be reopened before it can truly heal.

"Sir, your cold coffees." The voice brings me back from my thoughts and I realise I've been standing at the counter ever since my eyes fell on her. I lift the mugs from the counter and walk towards our table.

"Here's your coffee." My voice startles her and I don't think she had noticed that I was at the counter for past few minutes. I place one of the mugs on the table then settle down in front of her.

"Thanks." She says with a stiff smile. She holds the mug between her hands, just staring at it. Clearly she was having trouble choosing the right words to start, so I wait for her as she gathers her thoughts. The moments of silence that passed between us were like the calm before the storm, except they were just quiet, and not calm.

"You okay?" I ask even though I knew the answer, but I had to say something as the silence was growing unbearable. She looks up and nods.

"I know you hate me for what I did and I know you won't believe me, but the reason I did what I did was that I couldn't see you getting hurt." Her words hang in the air. After all this time, these are the words she chose, like really? I feel a surge of anger rising within me. I take a sip to calm down.

"So you are saying, that you took away the one thing I loved the most to *protect me.*"

"I know my parents Aahil and the last conversation before our break up with my mother crushed any remaining hope of us being together. I couldn't see you wasting any more of your time on me." She gulps, supposedly a lump and then speaks again. "I knew you would never leave me and if we discussed it, you would've talked me out of it, so I ended up things with you."

I listen to her as every word of hers weighs heavy on my heart like a rock. "Who were you to take decisions of my life?" I say, barely suppressing my anger.

"I loved you. I couldn't see you getting hurt because of me." A tear slide from the side of her eye as she looked down at the table.

"So you decided to hurt me yourself. Look, I don't see this conversation going anywhere good. It is making me angry. You live nearby and I don't wanna make a scene here." She looks at me, her eyes pleading, silently urging to understand her, but this isn't what I hoped that she'd say. And what hurts me to the bones is that she still doesn't have the courage to tell me the truth. She wipes the tear that fell out of her eyes with her thumb and rises up from the seat.

With a mixed feeling of anger and betrayal, I stand and make my way towards the door, moving ahead of her. No matter how much I wanted to storm out of the door and never look back, I hold the door open for her to walk out and then I stride towards the basement where I parked my car. She walked a few steps behind me.

"Would you please listen to me once for god sake?" She shouts at me once we reach the basement as there was no one around.

"Listen to you? You know when I would've listened to you, inside the café and on the day when you decided to hurt me because *you didn't want me to get hurt*. You know, all these years I always thought that there must have been some other reason that left you no choice but to leave me, or else you'd never leave my side. And right now, you took that away from me. So tell me, why should I listen to you Anya when you don't even have a least bit of decency to tell me the truth? That day, has been haunting me for five years and right now I feel like I lost those years for nothing. Maybe you just didn't love me enough or trusted me." I could feel all that built-up pain spilling out, completely blinding me that I didn't even notice that she had started crying.

"Don't you dare question how much I loved you." I hear her voice breaking, and as her crying face appears in front of me, a sudden realisation of guilt hits me hard, subduing all my anger. *What have I done?* In this moment, I would give up anything in this world to take my words back. I take a step towards her to console her but she steps back. "Don't." She says and I stop.

"You wanna know the real reason, my father caught me talking to you and he said it won't just be a warning this time. I know my father and I didn't want you get hurt, so I left you." She says then turns towards the exit and starts walking.

I felt like someone just pulled a rug out from under my feet. I run towards her and hold her wrist to stop her. "Anya, wait. Here me once."

"I don't think there's anything left to hear. You've already said it all. You blame me that I don't trust you but you don't trust me either. You say you lost your five years, and after what you said, I think I lost eight years of my life." She didn't even blink her eyes, but they reflected the pain she had buried in her heart for all those years. She looks at my hand which still held her wrist. "You were not the only one who was hurting." Those words cut deep into me and I let go of her wrist. She looks right into my eyes before turning away.

I couldn't let her go, not this time. I wanted her back in my life and if I let her walk away, I'm never gonna get her back, so I reach forward and hold her wrist again but she doesn't turn back instead she looks at me from over her shoulder. "How would you feel, if I did the same thing to you?" I could feel her body tense at my words, but she doesn't turn back towards me.

My heart couldn't bear it anymore. "You made the decision to leave me, without even giving me a chance to explain, with just a message, yet I am here, aren't I? I kept on telling myself that you'd have done it for a reason and you told me the actual reason now, but I've kept my trust in you for all those years." She turns towards me as I say, but my eyes were too welled up to see her clearly.

"I am sorry." Her voice barely above a whisper. "I am sorry for everything you had to go through because of me. I know I should've handled it better but I couldn't think of anything else at the moment." Her voice turns into sobs, so I take a step towards her and this time she doesn't step back, instead she clutches my shirt and bury her face on my chest.

She was crying uncontrollably while I stand there, thinking about my place in her life, stuck in a dilemma of whether I should hug her to provide comfort or should I stay put. If it was the time when we were together, I would have wrapped my arms around her, holding her tightly until her heart was at peace, but things are different now.

But despite everything, I cannot see her cry and do nothing, so I gather up courage and wrap my arms around her, with one hand supporting the back of her head. She didn't flinch, taking the nervousness away from me, I gently caress the back of her head. "I missed you so much." She mumbles on my chest, then adjusts her face, opening her clutched hands and wrapping them around me in an actual hug. I tighten my arm around her as I feel a familiar feeling that I've been missing for so long. I keep on caressing the back of her head, she keeps on sobbing for a while and we stand there in each other's embrace.

"Hey." I say as she calms down. She looks up, her hands still clutching the back of my shirt. "There is something I wanna say to you but let's get out of here first. Come with me." I take a step back from her. Then, reaching out for her hand, I intertwine my fingers with hers and lead her to my car.

I open the door of the car for her and she slides in the front seat. I shut the door gently then climb on to the driver seat, then take out the water bottle from my bag which lay on the back seat and hand it to her.

"You have time?" I ask. She looks at me for a moment, then nods. I drive the car out of the parking.

"Where are we going?" She asks.

"Ice-cream." I say. "You still like it, don't you?"

"Uhuh."

ᗡᗡᗡ

"Why are we here?" She asks looking at the infinite sea on her left, as I drive towards the parking lot.

"To get some ice-cream." I say.

"No, but it's a half-hour drive."

"Yeah, I know." I park the car and then quickly walk to the other side and open the door for her. "But I also know that you like sea." We walk on the aisle of the road of the marine drive at Nariman point, towards the ice-cream parlour.

The nights at Nariman point are captivating, with a glowing marine drive on one side and an expansive sea on the other. Cool breeze brushed against our skin as the waves crashed against the walls. Due to recent rains, the waves were bigger than usual but not alarmingly so and luckily it wasn't raining at the moment, so it was pretty nice out here. I extend my hand for her to hold as we navigate through the street to sit on the platform on the edge of the sea.

I hold her hand tight, as she climbs on the platform and sit, facing towards the sea. I sit next to her with our ice-creams in our hand, looking at the vast sea in front of us. Except for the few lights that twinkled at a distance, the sea was dark, like our sight just melted away into nothing. The only noise that surrounded us was of the waves that crashed against the wall.

While our feet dangled over the sea as if we were sitting on a cliffside, a comfortable silence settles between us as we didn't say much for a while, our gaze shifting from the sea to the ice-cream in our hands. We'd take a bite and then look back out at the water.

I steal a glance at her from the corner of my eye. Strands of her hair sway as the breeze brushed against them, and all I could notice was the small details, like how her earrings complemented her dress and also matched with her watch. I really don't get how someone can pay so much attention to every little detail of their outfit and still look like it's all effortless.

"You were going to say something." Her voice interrupts my thoughts and I subtly shift my gaze towards the sea as she looks at me to avoid appearing like a creep. I don't want her to know that I've been looking at her this whole time.

"Yeah, it can wait." I shrug, because I am kind of unsure that asking her what I really want to is a good idea, since I don't know much about her life these past few years. "You okay?"

She looks at me. "I think I'll be, especially after today." She takes a deep breath and slowly lets it out. "It feels lighter today." Her cheeks curve into a half-hearted forced smile continued with a few more moments of silence.

A powerful gust of wind slams into us, followed by a wave that's bigger than all the previous ones. I hold her hand tightly as a reflex, but not because I was scared. Okay, a little scared, but mostly worried about her. "Do you wanna get on the other side?" I ask.

"No, it's fine." She replies. I was still holding her hand, but she didn't seemed to mind.

"Your girlfriend would be really pissed at you when she'll find out you're with your ex, eating ice-cream."

I look at her with a knowing smile, but she kept looking at the waves, trying to avoid any eye contact. "She would've been, but I'd need a girlfriend for that to happen." I say and she shifts her gaze on me.

"Do you have someone?" With fingers crossed, I gather up courage to ask her.

"Nope." She shakes her head.

I take a glance at my hand, the one with which I was holding hers, then look at the sea and take a deep breath. She doesn't say anything, but I know there is a hint of smile on her face. "Hey." I say and she turns her face towards me. "Do you remember the time when we used to talk at night for hours about things we'd do, and places we'd go once we had jobs?"

She smiles, and that wasn't forced, it was like how she used to smile before, the one I fell in for. "That used to be the best moments in my day. And I also remember that I always wanted to hear more." She glances away for a moment, then turns back to me. "I couldn't get enough of that."

"Yeah. You know, by now, we would've ticked off a few things from our bucket list." I immediately realise that I shouldn't have said it because I could see her smile fade away.

"I wish." She lets out a sigh. I keep looking at her as she gathers all her hair and moves it to the other side with her other hand. She kept holding my hand, I mean, she could've, but she didn't. That means something, right?

She was beautiful. She is beautiful and right now, while I sit next to her, holding her hand, I wonder which one is more serene, the sea or her. "You look beautiful." I say. She blushes and the smile that faded is back on her face, making my heart skip a beat for her.

"Ah, only if you had a guitar here, it would've been perfect. You still sing, right?" She asks.

I shake my head in disagreement. I don't remember the last time I held the guitar in my hand except for that one time, when I shifted it to the storage room, but I think that doesn't count. "You weren't there. Who would I sing for?"

"Why would you do this to yourself?"

"Ah, nothing. Forget I said anything. I can't help but blurt out stupid things that end up bringing down our mood. But to tell you the truth, I am happy today—maybe happier than I've been in a couple years."

"Yeah. Me too."

"C'mon, let's take a walk. The waves are getting bigger anyway." I say and she nods in agreement. I climb down from the platform first, then give her a hand to make sure she gets down without losing her balance. Even though I was holding her, she stumbles because of her heels, and I instantly support her with both hands. She looks up right in my eyes. This is the closest we've stood to each other in five years, aside from that hug today.

"But you really loved singing." She says, not breaking the eye contact, her eyes asking for a reply, and at the same time trying to hold back her emotions.

"I loved you more. In fact, I never stopped loving you." I hold her hand as we start to walk.

"So, why did you ask me not to tell Shruti? She doesn't know about us?" I ask, trying to change the topic of our conversation to anything but our past.

"She knows but she doesn't know that it's you. I haven't told her your name. So I have to be the one she knows from." She replies but her steps started to slow down.

I look at her. "You okay?"

"Can we go to the car? Please." She says, her voice low. Her eyes looked like they'd give up to the storm of emotions she's been holding in her heart.

"Yeah-yeah." We walk back to the parking. I open the door for her and she slips in the front seat. I walk to the other side and as I climb inside the car in the driving seat, she wraps her hands around my neck and bury her face on my shoulder.

"I'm sorry." Her voice muffled by her sobs. "I am really sorry for what I did. But I loved you, I loved you so much that I couldn't let anything or anyone hurt you Aahil. I know I should've done better, but I didn't and I'm sorry." I hold her with my right hand and hold my seat with my left hand to maintain balance. "I am sorry—I can't control my tears but I am happy that I got to meet you again and when you hugged me today, it felt like a huge burden was lifted from my shoulder. I missed it so damn much, your love, your songs and simply you."

I hug her back tightly. "It's okay Anya, let it out, everything. You don't need to hold back anymore emotions. And I too am sorry for everything you had to go through because of me. I am really sorry for what I said and also for not being there for you when you needed me the most, but you don't have to be strong as you've been all those years. Let it out."

"I am not strong Aahil. There were times when I wondered whether I did the right thing. I always wondered how you were doing but then I remembered your eyes when you came to my classes to talk to me and then guilt would take over me. That moment has haunted me ever since and I didn't have the courage to face you."

I gently caress the top of her head. "Anya." I say. She looks up and I cradle her face between my palms. "Don't you ever think that way." I say, wiping her tears with my thumb. "I love you Anya. I love you so fucking much and nothing in the world can change that. As far as I remember my life, the best thing I've ever done is falling in love with you."

"I love you too." She whispers.

I let my hands slide from her face, and then taking her hands in mine, I kiss her palms. "I loved you every day, every second of it but I missed loving you so fucking much. I know you didn't mean to hurt and you did what you thought was best but I still missed you. I still miss you every day, when it's with your thoughts I have to sleep to and not your voice." I clutch her hands tight. "I love you Anya and I'll love you even in the darkest phases of our lives. I want you in my life, more than anything in this world. I wanna spend every moment ahead, with you in my life and it is killing me inside to say it but things haven't changed much since we left off. There are still high chances that our parents wouldn't agree and we won't end up together. I promise you that I'll do my fucking best so that we can be together but I just want you to promise me that even after everything we do, if we fall apart, we'll do it together, cause the last time we talked, you said that you'd end your life and I cannot let that happen and c'mon, we aren't eighteen anymore."

She slumps back to her seat, her gaze fixed at the dashboard. I know she's trying to process everything. "Hey." I say. She looks at me but doesn't say anything. "I love you and I promise you that I'll never give up on our love but please no suicidal thoughts." She nods and looks away. "Hey." I say again and she looks back towards me. I don't know if, what I am about to say is going to backfire but at least I'll be sure that she's going to fight with me. "I know it is a lot and you can take as much time as you want, but don't say it just yet. Please reply me back only if you can promise me this."

She nods, then looks away.

7
Chapter Seven

Anya

September 7th, 2019

"Don't make me laugh, someone will hear." I whisper into the phone, trying to hold back my laughter as I cover my mouth with my hand.

"Okay-okay. I'll stop, but I love how you giggle. When we start to live together, I'm gonna tickle you so hard if you don't laugh on my jokes like this."

"I can always run away." Just the thought of us living together makes my cheeks turn red, and I don't even have to look in the mirror to know that.

"You can try, but I won't let you go." I can literally see the smirk on his face right in front of my eyes.

"I can always bat my eyelashes on you and escape." And now I can see his jaw dropping. It has been three years since we've been together but he still has this effect on me. It's like time flies when I am with him and the best thing about him is somehow he manages to make me feel the same rush that we have during the first few months of the relationship. I can't imagine anything I wouldn't give up just to be with him.

"You saying stuff like that makes me wanna kiss you."

"Uhum."

"I love you Ana." He says and I can feel him smiling on the other end.

"I love-hold on, there's someone at the door." The door knob turns and I hear someone enter the room. I quickly hide my face in the blanket and shove my phone under the pillow, pressing the end call button. I somehow manage to keep the screen from flashing too much, as the room was dark and if anyone sees even a hint of light, I am definitely screwed.

"Please god, don't let it be dad. Please." I prayed. My eyes were shut but all of my senses were heightened. I can hear the footsteps and I know for sure that there are more than one person, but I didn't dare to peak my head out and confirm.

"I told you she's asleep. She wasn't talking to someone." I hear my mother's voice, saying to the other person, who I guess is my father. How could he hear me talking? Was I really too loud? Please god, get me out of this mess and I promise I'll be more careful next time. Aahil, please don't call back now or we are definitely screwed.

"I heard her talking with someone while I was passing by her room." And there it is—his voice, and I don't need any confirmation to know I'm in serious trouble and I'll need all the luck of my life to get out it alive.

"She must be sleep talking. She does sometimes." I hear my mother say. God, I have the best mother in the world.

"Are you sure she isn't talking to that boy she used to. Because if she is, then this time I won't be leaving him with just a warning. This is against our principles." My father was so loud that even if I had been asleep, I would have woken up. Still I chose to keep my head under the blanket and my mouth buried in the pillow, muffling any voice that can come out.

"No they haven't been speaking since the day you talked to him. She must be sleep talking. Let's not wake her up." Mom says and I think dad agrees with her because I could hear the footsteps fading out as they walked out of the room.

"Can't talk now, good night. Don't reply." I text Aahil as soon as I hear the door lock and then started to delete all the call logs and messages and shove the phone back under the pillow. I don't know I've escaped it or it has only postponed until tomorrow. My heart kept racing out of fear, my mouth getting dry but I didn't have a least bit of courage to peek out of the blanket. My mind overthinking every possible scenarios of what could happen tomorrow, but at least I have my mother on my side to cover for me.

ᐯᐯᐯ

"I need to talk to you." My mother says as she enters my room. "I know you were talking to Aahil last night when your father overheard you."

She's mad, very mad. "No I wasn't." I lie.

"Don't bullshit me. He still is suspicious that you are talking to Aahil and I am done hiding it from him. I cannot lie anymore. Better cut it off right now or I am telling your father today and you clearly know how much he hates it when someone breaks his principles. It won't be good for you, both of you."

I look at her, dumbstruck, like how can she be the same mother who was on my side last night. Yesterday, I was so happy that I have world's best mother and today she wants to take everything from me.

"Why do you have to tell him anything?"

"Excuse me?"

"I'm not asking you to lie for me. Just don't say anything about it. I'll try to be more careful next time. I promise." I say but she looked really pissed.

"The attachment you are building will take you nowhere. It will only hurt you and our family, because we are not going to accept this whatever you call it, not now, not ever. So better cut it off right now."

"Whoa." Where did that come from? "And why are you so irritated about it all of a sudden? It's not like you haven't known about it for a while now and you were okay with it."

"I was never okay with it and I've made it clear already that I don't like you talking to him."

"Okay, but why do you want to tell dad all of a sudden?" Finally I lose my cool and retaliate.

"Because I know what would happen if he finds out again. He has already made it very clear that it is against our principles. And think carefully what you're asking. You want me to keep secrets from my *husband." Her voice filled with anger.*

"You have been keeping this a secret from your husband for a while now. And fuck such principles where..." My head snaps to a side, my feet stumbling, my eyes filling up with tears as I place my palm on the cheek on which my mother just slapped. Yes slapped, for the first time that I remember. "Mom..." I say but then my voice trails off.

I'm looking down at my feet, I'm breathing but I don't say anything. Somehow I was feeling betrayed, by my own mother. "Ana I'm sorry." I hear but I don't look up, instead I take a step back. I feel her hands, wrapping around me, pulling me closer. "I'm sorry Ana." She says again and her voice is filled with regret and guilt, and somehow there's a strange feeling that what just happened, she isn't the one to blame, but I still feel betrayed.

"You don't get to do that, mom. You don't get to hit me and then say you're sorry." I say, my voice low.

"I know, I know. I'm sorry." She says and places her palms on my cheeks. I look up, in her eyes which were filled with tears. She kisses my cheeks and my forehead, then hugs me, tightly.

"Mom please, I beg you. Please don't do this to us. We really love each other. Please. He's really good, mom. And I promise you that he'll do something so great that you won't even have to think twice in giving him your blessing. Mom, he looks after me, my problems concern him. He's happy when I am happy and he's sad when I am sad, but he always knows how to lift me up and make me happy again. He keeps me happy mom. He's also smart in studies. He's everything you'll look for me. Please mom, don't do this to us." I start to cry. "I promise, I won't ask you anything ever. Just this."

She makes me sit on the bed and then sits beside me. "Ana, baby I believe you, but this can't happen. No matter how extraordinary he'd be, we cannot accept this relationship, not now, not ever." Tears fell uncontrollably from my eyes but this didn't stop her. "And let's just say that I and your father agree to it but the society and people around. They won't accept this. They won't accept us."

"I don't care about society." I say.

"But you do care about your father, right? And he cares a lot about his reputation. People praise your father that he is a man of his words and how would you feel if the same people start to talk negatively about him. He'll also lose business."

I shift away from her. She looks at me with a visible sigh on her face and then places her palm on my thigh. "The fact is that even we would not accept this marriage and if you do care about us then you better end this now. Don't act like a child Ana."

"Please don't make me do this mom. I'll do anything, but not this." My voice started to choke.

"I don't want to see you get hurt Ana and I know you heard what your father said last night. Do you want him to get hurt?" Her words hang in the air. Do-you-want-him-to-get-hurt? Air seemed to have lost its way to my lungs. My voice choking up, and even my cries came out muffled.

"This was the last time I have said this and I think I've made myself very clear to you. End this right now or I will be telling your father tonight and if you still want to be with him, you can do it after our deaths." She says and stands up. "Here, take your phone and end it."

I take my phone from her hands. "I hope you are happy." I say without bothering to look at her.

"I am." She says and walks out of the room.

I look at his photo on whatsapp, maybe for the last time, maybe this is it, the end. The life we thought to live together, crumbling in front of my eyes, with each pieces piercing my heart. I wanna scream so loud but I can't. I don't think I've known pain until today. It hurts so much but I have to do it. I cannot let him get hurt, not now, not ever.

I wipe the tears from my eyes and started to type a message with my trembling hands. "Aahil, mom won't accept our relationship. I tried to tell her everything about us, even about our future, our dreams together, but she declined..."

As I send the message, I look at his photo, and kiss my screen as if I was kissing him. Now I know what I can't give up to be with him and knowing that hurts badly.

He's seen the message. I know he doesn't have anyone he'd tell. I have to talk to him, maybe one last time. I have to be strong. I have to be strong. I am not strong. I try to control my tears but my eyes won't just listen. I have to be strong.

I wipe my tears and press the call button.

8
Chapter Eight

I change into something comfortable as soon as I get home then walk towards the balcony and slide the door open. The cool breezes sweeps in, making the curtains sway back and forth. Thank god it didn't rain until now, or it would've spoiled whatever little time we got to sit there watching sea.

I won't lie, it felt so good to hug her after so long. And knowing that she still loves me makes me so happy—I can't even put it into words. If anyone would've seen me, they'd probably think I'm crazy with the goofy smile I couldn't shake off. Although there's a small part of me that is still anxious about what her decision will be. I know that I asked her to take as much time as she wants to think but for me, every passing second only adds to my anxiety.

It was a lovely weather outside, and to make it better, I poured myself a coke and on my way back to the balcony, I grabbed my wallet and a blanket. I wrapped the blanket around me snugly, then settle in comfortably because I wasn't ready to leave the balcony anytime soon.

I hold the wallet in my hand and pressed it along its width to access a secret section, where I kept her photograph and her last letter. I take out her photograph and the letter and then keep the wallet aside.

I hold her photograph with my fingers on its edges, caressing her face with my thumb as if it isn't her photograph but her face. I have a couple of letters from her but this is the only photo I have of her. Although it is completely my fault that this is the only one I have and I remember how angry I was with myself when I did it but it's okay, because she's pretty in all of her pictures and if things go well, I can have plenty of her photos again.

For a while, I look at her photograph. She was wearing a green polo t-shirt from some sports camp. Her hairs tied in a ponytail and she was smiling with her cheeks and her eyes. Those beautiful eyes, were once the only place I'd dwell in when everything was falling apart.

I keep the photo aside and take the letter in my hand, and coke on the other.

ꕤꕤꕤ

Dear life…
Hey. You might be wondering why, even though we talk every day, I am writing you this letter. Well, there are some things I wanna say to you and I don't want to talk about it in already little time we get over the phone.

Here's the thing, you have a big exam coming up and I am way more concerned about your exam. I know you are already anxious about it and I am telling you that you'll do great in it. Just don't put unnecessary pressure on yourself and panic. I know that the stakes are high, but how are you going to give your best if you are panicking over other things.

We are going to live together, unless you've found someone else ;-).

Aahil, I know you love me so much, and you prioritize me over everything and even when I fight with you, you still are so sweet to me. I love you too and the mere fact that there is a chance that we might not be able to live together is unbearable to me. I know that we are dangling on with a hope, clinging to the belief that if we do our best then maybe somehow, fate will conspire in our favour, so that we can live together.

I really want to live with you, but it's only possible if we do our best. You need to understand that you are only prioritizing me by working harder. Some small fights may happen between us and I won't lie, I like the way you pamper me till we sort it out, but dear, it takes a big chunk of your time. I promise that I'll try and be a good girl, won't eat anything that would make my tummy hurt, or do anything stupid, but you've got to promise me that if something does happen, please prioritize your studies. I'll totally understand everything and be good by the morning. Please, I want you to swear it on our love that you'll try harder.

One more thing, don't get used to me being a good girl. I'll not behave well for long—only till your exams, and after that I'll do all sorts of stupid things, eat whatever I like and annoy you like hell. And I want all the pampering that I missed during these days with compound interest. So be ready for it because you know how much I love to annoy you.

I love you so much.

I do not appreciate it as much as I should in front of you but you are the best person in the world. Ever since you came in my life, my life has blossomed. You made me feel incredibly special. You took all my sorrows as if they were your own and, in return bringing me joy and happiness. I really hope I never lose you and I hope it never ends. You're so precious that I'mma keep you close to my heart forever.

Please throw it away as soon as you've read it.
Love Anya x.

þþþ

I smile as a wave of nostalgia hits me. Moments of her teasing and trying to annoy me flashed before my eyes, as if they were happening all over again. She has always been dramatic. To others, she would appear all smart and intellectual but only I knew the child in her. Only I've seen how her eyes sparkled with mischief, how she'd giggle on the silliest of thing, or throw tantrums to get her way.

With all these emotions running through my head like blood runs through veins, I suddenly had this strong urge to talk to her. So I grabbed my phone in hopes that she would've made her decision already and there would be a message from her, waiting. But there wasn't.

I can't blame her for my impatience. It has only been two hours since I dropped her at her apartment but somehow I am getting restless with each second passing.

I rest my head on the wall, my gaze fixed at the trees which sway with the wind. It was raining heavily, so I wrapped the sheets tightly around me.

ϷϷϷ

I was leaning back on my chair with my hands behind clasped behind my head, just staring at the computer screen.

"Coming for lunch?" Shruti asks, as she walks towards my table.

"What time is it?" I ask but instead of waiting for her answer, I glance the time on the bottom of the screen. "Shit bro! It is already quarter past to one."

"How long have you been staring at it?" She asks, standing beside my chair and leaning towards the computer screen. "Still stuck on that?"

"I don't know. Maybe half hour or a little more than that."

"But you do have a decent enough strategy for it. Why are you wasting time?"

"I know it's decent enough. I just know I can make it better. I just need to give it a bit more thought, and I'm sure I can come up with a better idea."

"You and your obsessions. Anyway, are you coming, or are you still gonna sit here romanticising the screen."

"I could use a break." I grab my lunch box and we head towards the cafeteria.

"So, tell me something new?" Shruti asks.

"Like what?"

"Anything new you wanna share until we get to the cafeteria."

"Umm, I can't think of anything. It's the same old boring days. What about you?"

"Yeah same here." She says. "I have to go to Delhi next week."

"Meeting someone special? Might as well recreate the scene from Baghban." I chuckle.

"Haha, if only I was that lucky. For work. And guess who's gonna be there too. Jay."

"Dude!" I laugh.

"Yeah! That bastard is no fun and all work."

"Still, that's no reason not to have fun. There are really nice places to have fun, and I mean real fun."

"I don't know about that man."

"Okay, so don't tell anyone. He goes from being sober to being a total drunkard in two pegs, and then he tells stuff."

"Oh my god. You are not a good friend." She laughs as she says. "By the way how do you know? You don't even drink."

"Exactly that is why I know. I am being a good friend to you." I laugh.

"Two pegs only." She mouths dramatically as we join Rohan and Khushi at the table.

"What are you guys talking about?" Khushi asks.

"Jay." I reply.

"Oh, the infamous two-peg story." Rohan chuckles.

"Oh, so it looks like everyone knows." Shruti says. "How do you know?"

Rohan points at me, and Shruti gives me a look that says, "Seriously?"

"What?" I respond. "Is it my fault I was the only one sober? And don't tell me you didn't enjoy hearing it." I say with a grin and everyone bursts into laughter.

"You are a sick man." Shruti says. "What's in your lunch that smells so delicious?"

Shruti takes a spoonful of lady fingers to her plate. "This is the reason I wait for you on lunch. These are delicious."

"Mumma's recipe." I proudly exclaim with a smile spreading across my face.

"These are really good dude. How do you even find time to cook in the morning? I'm barely awake enough to make coffee for myself." Khushi takes as she takes another spoonful.

"You guys are such terrible friends. Find me someone so I don't have to get up early." I playfully complain. "I wish I could sleep in until late morning too. I only get weekends to catch up on sleep."

"Believe me when I say it, you'll have to cook for two." Rohan chuckles. "Once Khushi brought momos which apparently she made. Eating them was the hardest thing I've ever done in my life. God knows how her parents would've eaten it." I nudge Rohan just as he bursts into laughter, oblivious of the punch heading for him.

"Ouch." Rohan winces as Khushi punches his biceps.

"In my defence, I made those for the first time." Khushi says and we laugh— everyone except for Rohan. He just pats Khushi on her shoulder.

"If you are that miserable, I can send our cook to your apartment. She'll cook and then you won't have to worry about waking up early."

"Uhm, is she beautiful?" I smirk.

"Depends on what type you're into." Khushi replies with a smirk.

"Good one."

Shruti elbows me. "How about I fix you up with my roommate. She's beautiful and single and you've already met her."

"Anya! Right?" She exclaims. "There you go. Now you can't complain that we didn't find you someone if she doesn't like you."

I involuntarily choke on hearing her name. "Water." I manage to say and Rohan passes me the bottle.

"Look his cheeks are getting red just by hearing her name." Khushi teases.

"No, it's not. I choked on food." I say, trying to hide my flushed expression, but then it hits me—Shruti asking about anything new in my life and now bringing up Anya here. I think Anya has told her about us. But then again, it has been four days since I met Anya but Shruti hasn't acted differently at all and knowing her, if she even had the slightest of idea of it, she'd start pulling my leg the next moment, and she hasn't. Maybe I'm overthinking it.

I shift my gaze towards Shruti. "So, your roommate can cook." I say, deliberately skipping Anya's name.

"So inquisitive." Shruti smirks and there you go. She starts teasing and I am not sure if she's playing along with Khushi or if she's actually teasing me for real because she knows. "Besides, she can make maggie, tea, coffee, warm already made food and boil water. What more do you want?" She chuckles.

Rohan places his hand on my shoulder and says "I told ya, you'll have to cook for two." And we all burst into laughter.

ᕼᕼᕼ

It wasn't exactly a slow morning, but I definitely felt sluggish as I hit the snooze button the second my phone alarm went off, hoping for a few more minutes of sleep. I'd crashed on the couch after working late, and I couldn't even remember when I'd fallen asleep. It's been almost a week since I last saw Anya, and I haven't heard from her at all. I didn't expect this when I told her to take as much time as she needed. It has just made me more anxious and to be honest, I've lost the count of how many times I've checked my phone, just waiting for a text from her.

The timer ends and the alarm rings again. My eyes still refusing to open, I try to find my laptop, one to make sure it didn't fall off my lap when I fell asleep and the other to know where it is so that I don't step on it. I sigh out of relief as my hands touch the laptop because the screen was shut, which meant I've kept it on the floor. I reached out for my phone and my eyes finally open when the screen showed eight forty five and without wasting another moment, I got up in a hurry as I was definitely going to be late for work if I didn't. I took a quick bath and then ran towards the kitchen. I place a pan on the stove to make an omelette and kept the bread on the toaster then run towards the room to change.

I grab a navy blue pant and a light blue shirt from the closet. As I was trying to button up my shirt as fast as I can, I also run to the kitchen to prevent the omelette from burning and then place it between the bread. With barely any time to think, I stuffed the bread omelette in my mouth while also tying the shoe lace, I left for work.

ᐳᐳᐳ

Another day is almost over and I am sitting on my chair wondering why haven't she said anything? I know I was the one who told her to take as much time but this is really pushing it. I mean it is either a yes or a no, then why is she taking so much time?

Now that I know the reason why she broke up, I don't blame her because she was a teen and I know she was scared, but still, instead of ending everything with a message, she should've trusted that we'd find a way out of it. If she truly believed we'd make it together, would she have really ended things the way she did? Is she still not sure about us making it to the end? Maybe that's the reason she is taking so much of time and if that's the case, maybe it's okay the way things are.

The realisation of her still not believing that we can make it to the end this time is making my stomach turn into knots. But, something that scares me more is whether I believe, that we can make it this time, or not. Am I just tethered to this belief by a single strand of hope that can snap at any time? I know I have this job and I have my other work but I still don't think I'm far off from where we were when things ended.

"How many times am I gonna catch you day dreaming?" Shruti's voice startles me. I was so engrossed in my thoughts that I didn't notice Shruti sneaking in and standing beside me.

"Dear lord. You scared the crap out of me." I say.

"So what were you thinking about this time?"

"Umm, nothing."

"Yeah, that's what I thought you'd say. I mean why would you tell me anything?"

"When have I ever kept anything from you?" I counter.

"Oh, how about this." She places the envelope on my desk and then slump against it with her arms crossed.

I reach out for the envelope. "*I've sent you plenty of these. Haven't I?*" It read and merely looking at it unleashed a flood of emotions, overwhelming me and the way it's written, it's definitely a good news. I take a deep breath to calm myself down and regain my composure before looking back at Shruti.

"Now when were you going to tell me about it? Out of all people, you guys were the one who kept secrets from me. I didn't expect this from you." She says with a stern look on her face.

I get up from my seat and gesture to sit. "I can explain."

"Yeah. So explain."

"I wasn't sure until—never mind, I can't. I am really sorry for keeping it from you. Let me make it up to you."

"I don't want you to make it up to me or anything. I just want you to tell me things, at least big stuff. Right now, I feel like I don't really know you." She says in a low tone.

"I'm sorry."

"It's okay. Now let's go." She gets up from the chair.

"Where?"

"If only you stopped your day dreaming, you'd notice that everyone's already gone."

I look around and no one was really there. So, I take out all the things from the front section of my bag in a rush and stuff them here and there, making space for the envelope, which I place very carefully in it, then wrap up other things. "Let's go." I say.

"So, when did she tell you about us?" I ask her while we wait for the elevator.

"Sunday night. She ordered my favourite food, brought some drink and when I ate my heart out, she says 'Remember the boy I told you about, with whom I was in a relationship with? He is Aahil.' I almost spilled the drink on her."

The elevator pings and the door opens. "You'd have been the first one I would've told but I wasn't sure, until now." I say as we enter the elevator.

"Who said you can be so sure about it? I haven't read the letter." My face falls immediately. "Look at your face. But really, I don't know what's in it." She's grinning from ear to ear.

"Shut up! Someday you're gonna be in my shoes and then I'll tease the hell out of you."

"Still, it's so fun to tease you." She says and starts laughing.

We walk out of the elevator. "Come, I'll drop you."

"No-no, its fine. You don't need to be extra nice just because you're feeling guilty."

"Hold on, that's not true. When have I ever not been nice to you? And seriously, it's all good—I'll drop you off. No worries."

"Nu-uh, it's okay. Anyway, you have to read that letter. So hurry and go home. I'll take a cab."

"You sure."

"What's there to be sure in it? I always take a cab."

"Umm okay."

"You give up so easy. You should've said 'No Shruti I'll drop you and I won't listen anything.' But—its okay never mind."

"That is so not fair."

"Ahh, I'm messing with you." She laughs and gives me a side hug. "I'm so happy for you guys."

"Thank you. Let me walk you to the cab at least."

"Okay." She says and we start walking towards road. "You aren't gonna hurt her. Are you?"

"No, why?"

"Because if you do, remember you'll have to face me."

"Sure thing, I'll try not to." I smile at her. "There's your cab."

"Yup. Good night." She says as she gets in the cab.

9
Chapter Nine

I hold the envelope in my hand, which shivered a bit out of excitement. I know Shruti was just messing with me because I have a strong feeling that it will be a 'yes'. So without wasting any second, I carefully open it and I see her handwriting. Oh, I've missed it so much.

Dear Aahil

I've written you many letters before, but I don't think I have enough words in this one to truly express how I feel about you. And since I'm writing a letter after a long time, I might ramble a bit here and there. So please bear with me.

I still remember how madly we were in love with each other, how we couldn't think of a day without the other. I remember my friends being fed up of how much I used to talk about you and I can't blame myself because you were perfect. Now that I think of it, it seems hard to believe, that we were able to hold ourselves together, or maybe not.

Ever since I said those things to you, I've been dying a little every passing day. The guilt inside me kept bottling up to the point that I felt scared to face you again. Never in my life did I imagine myself hurting someone I loved, but I did and no matter what the reason was, I hurt you so much, so much that I can't even ask for your forgiveness, and still you were so kind to me (except for the two sentences you said at the café), you held me when I was crying, you made sure I was okay, and you still wanna be with me, after what I did.

I remember the look in your eyes the last time I saw you outside my class. I don't wanna relive it, but I can't forget what I did—it felt like someone had ripped my heart out, but I had to do it because in my mind, I was trying to protect you and if I had to make the same choice again, I wouldn't think twice before doing it. But still, knowing that you are out there, crying and hurting and all I could do was nothing but cry felt like someone was stabbing a knife in me and then pulling it out to stab it back again.

When I first saw you the day you came by to drop Shruti, my heart raced like I had just finished a marathon. I stood there, looking at you, trying to find out how much do you hate me, but instead your face was pale. I thought maybe you didn't want me to see you dropping Shruti, or maybe you just didn't wanna see me. I wouldn't lie but for a moment I thought you and Shruti were together, because why would someone drop a girl to her apartment so late in the night and that too to her door and I don't know why but apart from the usual hurt that I felt, I felt betrayed too. So I looked at you again and you looked like you wanted to say something or rather a lot of things but then you turned away.

I really wished you had said something. Even a nod would've been enough to tell me that there was nothing to worry about, because while I stood there watching you, I had to hold the door with all my strength or I would've ended up falling. You might have saved Shruti from a lot of teasing too because I had to tease her a lot about you that night to actually know about you guys. But then she said you were her friend and I'm not proud of it but I was so relieved and happy hearing that.

You must be thinking why am I telling you this? I just want you to know and I know that I'll be too shy to ever admit it in front of you, so I'm writing it to you. But really, what a nightmare it would've been if you guys were together.

The day when I handed you your glass of coke, your fingers brushed against mine and it was after so long I felt your skin and all I could remember was about the time when we

started dating and you were too shy to hold my hand, so you'd
brush your fingers against mine. I wouldn't say that I felt
the warmth of your skin just from that, but it was the most I
had in these five years until I hugged you in the café.
Although you took your sweet time to hug me back.

You still can't see me cry, can you? I would really wanna
know if me batting my eyelashes still works on you ;).

Anyway, when you told me you still loved me, I was so
overwhelmed that I wanted to fall into your arms, bury my
face in your chest and stay there forever, just like we used
to. Thinking of it, it was such a beautiful time when you'd
hug me tight and I'd clutch your shirt, laugh on your chest
and you'd caress the strands of my hair, give a peck on my
temple and hug me back, tightly.

So, you might be wondering why it took me so long to send
this to you.

When you asked me reply only if I could promise to never
give up, I felt like you don't trust me. But then again, you
were right. Promising you that without truly believing is us
would be like building something on quicksand. And I don't
want us to fall apart.

So here I say.

I love you Aahil, with all my heart. I want to spend
every moment of my life with you and this time I won't give
up so easy and I also promise to do anything stupid which
would make you regret this new beginning.

And also, I'm really sorry you had to wait so long.

I love you…

Anya x.

ʚʚʚ

An exhilarating rush courses through me as I read the letter again
and again, my hands visibly shivering as they couldn't contain my
excitement. I turn around and my eyes fall on the clock on the

wall— it was almost nine. I need to hurry or the shops will be closed soon. We have already lost so much of our time and I cannot bear to lose any more. So I grab my car keys and walk out of my apartment.

Thank god *Archies* is open. I walk past the door in a hurry towards the cards section. I wasn't looking for anything glittery or flashy. I wanted a card that was simple yet beautiful, so I could let her know I received her letter and tell her how much I'm missing her. So I search high and low through the cards placed on the shelves until my eyes fall on a small beige colour card which had a glass jar tilted and the word love fell from it letter by letter.

"I'd be lying if I said I missed you a little because I have been told that first love lasts forever...

I'll pick you up at eight, tomorrow. Love you." I write the lines in the card, then put the card in the envelope. "I can never have enough of these." I write on the envelope, then place it on the passenger seat as I drive the car towards their apartment.

"Hey, can you come down at the main gate. Please." I text Shruti instead of Anya because the next time I want her to see me is when I pick her tomorrow.

I hold the envelope in my hand and climb out of my car as I spot Shruti at the entrance of their apartment. She notices me and walks towards me.

"So, what's this?" She asks when she notices the envelope in my hand. "Dude seriously, you drove all the way here to give her your letter? Could've just given me at the office."

"It isn't a letter. I didn't have time to write one, because someone gave me the letter moments before we were about to leave. And about that, why? You could've given me the letter in the morning."

"I meant you could've given me tomorrow in office. And about that, you're lucky I made you wait only a day after your betrayal of friendship." She rolls her eyes.

"So will you give this envelope to her right now? I've brought your favourite chocolate for you."

A grin appears on her face as she takes the envelope and the chocolate from my hand. "This isn't over with just a chocolate. You owe me a goddamn party."

"Sure. Any day, but after tomorrow."

"I see. Tomorrow is your date night."

"Yup," I say, trying hard not to blush.

"I hope you brought another one for Anya, cause I'm not sharing mine." She smirks.

"It's in there." I gesture towards the envelope with a flushed smile on my face, then scratch the back of my head.

"Okay then, good night." She says.

"Good night."

ᚦᚦᚦ

It has been a really long time since I've played anything on my guitar. I think the last time I touched it was when I moved in this apartment a year ago and that too during the shifting process and since then, it has been locked in the store room.

Thank god the fret board is okay. I hold the guitar in my hand, cleaning it with a cloth and then tuning the strings before taking it to the bed to play. As I hold it in my lap, a long familiar feeling consumes me but my hands have become way too rusty to switch between chords swiftly. So I took a few extra pauses between lines to transition as I hummed *This Love by Taylor Swift*.

My fingertips started to ache after a while from the strings, so I leave the guitar adjacent to the bed and grab my phone to set a reminder to make a reservation at the hotel.

I lie down on the bed wide awake, my eyes fixed on the ceiling above as I try to curb down my excitement. "It's gonna be great tomorrow." I whisper, trying to reassure my pounding heart as it was completely overwhelmed by a strong feeling of nervousness, the good kind, like the one you feel on a first date. I pull a pillow close to me and squeeze my eyes shut in hopes of getting some sleep but it feels miles away as my mind is reluctant to calm down.

Time changes and so do the things attached to it. I remember the time when the only thing I did was wander here and there, mindlessly scrolling phones and gossip, thinking it was cool. But then I started talking to her for fun but little did I know that I was going to fall for her so hard that it would completely change the direction of my life. Before I met her, I didn't have any purpose in life, no reason to push myself out of my comfort zone. My grades were decent, my parents were satisfied, so there was nothing that would drive me to work harder. But when I met her and fell in love with her, I had to work harder if I wanted to have her in my life because her parents were loaded and I belonged to a middle class background. So soon she started to be the only thing that mattered to me.

"You asked who is my 'somebody' in the song Somebody's me. It is you. I love you. Will you be my somebody?" I text Anya. The messenger showed typing animation but then it would disappear and as seconds passed, I grew impatient and anxious. Impatient to know what her reply would be and anxious because I don't want to lose our friendship.

"Can you give me some time to think?" Her message appears. I know she'll talk to Maya about it before saying anything, but why does she have to ask her best friend before doing anything?

"Okay." I text her back. What else can I say? She knows I like her. It's not like I asked her out of blue. I've been flirting with her for a while now and instead of asking me to stop, she seemed to enjoy it and even played along with it.

The typing animation appears again but disappears within seconds. Maybe she's trying to find the right words. "It will likely be a yes. But till then, I like you." *Her text appears at last.*

We were each other's first love, and it wasn't like we were the most perfect couple, like the ones they show in movies, but we had a lot to learn. All I am saying is that we had our fair share of fights, but we grew together. And you know what the best part was, even if we were fighting or not talking to each other, our hearts were still connected and we still wanted to be together.

ᗞᗞᗞ

My entire wardrobe lay scattered on my bed, but I was yet to find something to wear. I have been trying shirts after shirts, in search of a perfect attire for the date for past hour. I had already made a reservation for eight thirty at the hotel, but I have to pick up Anya by eight o'clock and that leaves me with just two hours to finalize my outfit and also reach her apartment.

So instead of wasting time in my indecisiveness, I put on a crisp black shirt, rolling up the sleeves to rest below my elbow, and paired it with black trousers. It's a classic look that never fails. Then I run my fingers through my hair to give it a final touch, apply some cologne, and finish off with a black metallic watch and a pair of black shoes.

I walk up to the mirror to take a good look at myself, then with a few long breaths to steady myself, I walk out of the apartment.

ᠵᠵᠵ

Shruti opens the door. "Hey, you're early. That's odd. So eager to meet your childhood love."

"Do I look fine?" I ask her, seeking her validation as if I had a backup if she said no.

She steps back and takes a look at me from head to toe, and then glances up at me again. "You look good, real good."

"Thanks, but you took your own sweet time checking me out."

"It was you who wanted to know. But really why don't you dress up like this every day?"

"Oh someone's sad because they missed their shot at me." I chuckle.

"You definitely think a lot of yourself, don't you?"

"A little self-obsession doesn't harm anyone."

"Some might call you narcissist. Hope you don't mind."

I was about to say something when Anya came out of her room and the world around me literally went in slow motion. She was searching something in her handbag, or maybe double checking things, slowly walking towards me or it felt this way in my head. She walked with grace wearing a creamy white jump suit, strands of her hair crashing over her shoulder while other kept dangling at her back.

"Yes." I say as Shruti pokes me and I look at her only to realise that nothing was in slow motion.

"You seem lost." She teases. A flushed smile appears on my face as I look at Anya. She too was smiling.

"You look amazing." I say and give her a long stemmed red rose which I had been holding behind my back.

"Thank you." She blushes, then turns towards Shruti for a quick hug before walking over to me. I extend my hand, and she places her fingers on my palm. I gently place my thumb over her knuckles as we walk towards the elevator.

"Have a good time." Shruti calls from behind as the elevator door open and Anya waves her back.

A patent smile ran on my face as we stand close to each other in the elevator. Neither of us speak, simply enjoying the silence which surrounded us. I steal a quick glance at her beautiful face. She too was trying to suppress her smile by pressing her lips together. A loose strand of her hair falls on her cheek which she tucks back, showing her matching rose gold ear rings and wrist watch.

I lean a little towards her. "Checkmate." I whisper on her shoulder. Her cheeks grew red as she blushed, trying to hide her smile with the back of her hand in which she was holding the rose.

10

Chapter Ten

The doorman holds the door open for us. As we walking inside the restaurant, I reach for her hand, intertwining my fingers with hers. She smiles as we walk close towards our table. I pull out her chair with my free hand, helping her as she takes a seat, then take one across from her. A waiter approaches our table and fills our glasses with water, then place two menus, each in front of us.

She takes a sip of water while I watch her as the soft glow of the candles in front of us fall on her beautiful face, making her features shimmer gently. She looks up with a questioning nod and I shake my head with a smile. "You look beautiful." I say and she blushes, placing the glass down. She hold the menu in her hand.

"So, what would you like to have?" I ask. Her eyes still scanning the menu.

"Um, I'm thinking about having alfredo fettuccine. What about you?"

"Oh, I haven't even looked at the menu. I'm just... uh, enjoying the view."

"Enjoying the view, huh? You think of me as a dish."

"Definitely not a dish. You're the whole meal." Shit I didn't just say that. She smirks, rolling her tongue against the inside of her cheek.

The waiter arrives at our table. "Sir, your order?"

"Ah yes, one alfredo fettuccine and a spinach ricotta cannelloni." I look up to the waiter and say, then shift my gaze on Anya. "Um for appetizers, how about mushroom risotto balls?" I ask her.

"No, I don't like mushrooms anymore." She says and places the menu at the table.

"Cottage cheese croquettes?" I ask and she nods. "And for drinks... Strawberry?" I suggest, recalling that she used to love strawberry drinks, although she loved mushrooms too.

"Some things don't change." She smiles.

"A strawberry daiquiri and a virgin margarita. Thank you." The waiter notes down the order and heads back.

"What?" I ask her as she was smiling goofily.

"Nothing." She says but her smile widens.

"C'mon, tell me."

"Look at you being all fancy."

"Oh, I've been practicing it every night before going to bed." I chuckle and she laughs. "But I really gotta say that I'm relieved that you stopped eating mushrooms. When did this happen?"

"It's not that I hate them, but I rarely eat them now. I think it was just a phase."

"Two years is not just a phase. You? Not eating mushrooms? I need to check your pulse to see if you're actually okay." I reach for her hand, gently enveloping her palm in mine and caress her knuckles.

"Where, on my knuckles? You would've been an awful doctor." She chuckles but doesn't take her hand away.

"I can't feel your heartbeat here but I can definitely make you skip a few here and there." Lifting her palm, I lean towards her and place a gentle kiss on her knuckles. She can't stop blushing and I love that.

She pulls her hand and intertwines her fingers with mine. "You look happy."

"I am. I don't think I've been this happy in years." I gently squeeze her fingers. "Thank you for coming back in my life."

"Me too."

The waiter brings the appetizer along with the drinks. I leave her hand after an assuring squeeze. I do not know what it meant to her but the squeeze meant more of a reassurance to me.

She lifts her daiquiri, fixing her gaze on me over her glass as she takes a sip and all I do is look at her in awe.

"Aren't these just paneer balls?" I say putting a fork on one of the croquette.

"Saying paneer balls is too middle class, say cottage cheese croquettes." She mocks and I laugh.

"Shit! It's hot." I immediately cover my mouth with the back of my hand and blow air on it to cool down the burning sensation while she continues to laugh at my misery.

The waiter then serves the main course as we finish the appetizer.

ᐅᐅᐅ

"You still have time, don't you?" I ask her as we walk out of the hotel, holding hands.

"Yeah, why?"

"Well, we could walk along the beach. I mean what's the point of booking a sea-view hotel for dinner if we are not going to actually *see* the sea?"

"Um, I'm wearing heels, does that count as a point?"

"I have extra slip-ons."

"Hmm, what if it rains?"

"I have an umbrella in the car. But, if you don't want then its fine, we could go somewhere else."

"Nuh-uh, I was messing with you."

"I see." I intertwine my fingers with hers and pull them closer and kiss them. "These little quirks of yours are so adorable." I say and we walk towards my car.

I pull out the umbrella from the backseat. "Do you want to change your heels with slip-ons?"

She gestures with her hand to come closer. "How about we walk barefoot?" She whispers in my ear, then starts laughing.

I look at her and smile. "You really ready for that. Sounds like a big commitment to me, and that too on our first date. I mean walking barefoot, that's the stuff hard-core lovers do." I say in a dramatic voice.

"Huh, you afraid of big commitments?"

I pull her close. "With you, I ain't afraid of nothing." She smiles. "Okay, but you sure about walking barefoot? You're wearing white."

"Yeah. But it's not every day that I get to go on a first date with you." She says and turns around towards the car playfully, while I look at her, mesmerised, wondering how can such small things about her makes me fall for her all over again.

I open the front door for her, and she slips into the seat, kicking off her heels right away while I stand outside, grabbing the roof of the car to keep my balance as I take off my shoes. Once done, I offer her my arm as she hops out.

The wind blew her hair, strands falling across her face, giving me a perfect excuse to touch her face. So before she could fix it, I gently put my fingers on her cheek. Our eyes lock in the moment as I softly trace her cheek and tuck the hair behind her ear. "You look *breathtakingly beautiful.*"

Despite all these years of trying to find the right words, I still can't fully express how beautiful she is. I mean, right now, instead of thinking of a future with her, I am thinking that if ever I had to walk down a road knowing I wouldn't return, I'd take a snap of this moment and keep it in my wallet as I walk until my soul leaves my body. Don't get me wrong, I want nothing more than to share every moment of my life with her, but it's just that, at this very instant, she looks unbelievably beautiful.

A tear slide from the side of her eye but she doesn't break our eye contact. I nod my head up, asking her the reason to which she shakes her head. Surrounded by the sound of the waves gushing at the shore and the wind blowing, we were oblivious of the people around us, being too lost in each other to care. I envelope her face in my palms and wipe the tears with my thumb.

"Tell me." I say.

She shakes her head again, and instead of saying anything she clutches my shirt and buries her face on my chest. I wrap my arms around her. "Hey, you okay?" I ask her.

"Yeah. It's just the way you were looking at me, I missed it." She says, snuggling her face against my chest. "Although you took your sweet time in saying I look beautiful."

"Hey, look at me." She looks up and I cup her face in palm again. Leaning down, I kiss her forehead. "I'm sorry. I was busy being jealous with your curls because they get to kiss your cheeks anytime they want." I say as I run my fingers through her curls before pressing a soft kiss on her cheeks. "I was also jealous of the spoons because they get to touch your lips while I could only hold your hand." I say, then lean and place a soft kiss on her lips. "I was busy believing that you're mine. I was busy being lost in your eyes, trying to etch the way you blush into my memory. You aren't just breathtakingly beautiful, you are heavenly or something even more enchanting. I just couldn't find the right words."

She lifts up on her toes a little and kiss my cheek. "Well, when you put it that way." She says, snuggling and wrapping her hands around me. I wrap my hands around her and squeeze her a little in my arms. "You look really handsome too."

"Oh do I? That's the first time you've said it today."

"It's not my fault that you didn't pick up on the cues." She say, burying her face, and I caress her back while we stand there for a while.

She looks up at me, taking a slow, deliberate step back to free herself our hug. Smiling, she slips her arm around mine, intertwining her fingers with mine as we start walking side by side. Placing her other palm on my bicep, she leans her head a little towards me. "I was waiting for your call yesterday. Do not tell me you don't have my number anymore." She says, slightly shifting her gaze towards me.

"I thought it might stir up some angst. I've read it in books that a little bit of angst actually makes you feel even better."

"So five years weren't enough for you?"

"Oh, they were long. But this, it's different. How do I say it? Um, there's this wide spectrum of emotions on a first date, say for example feeling restless and excited at the same time, maybe also anxious knowing that you're gonna meet the person in a few hours." I scratch the back of my head. "Was it too childish? I just wanted it to be perfect." She smiles and shakes her head.

"You've changed." She looks at me trying to hide her smile.

"Good change or bad change?" I shift my gaze towards her as we stop walking.

"No, I mean, you used to yell at me for eating junk and today you're the one who ordered pasta and paneer balls."

"That is so not true. I never stopped you from eating anything. It was just that you didn't just eat junk, you devoured it like a racoon and that made your stomach hurt. Had you eaten like a human being, I would've had absolutely zero problems with it."

"No I didn't. And you called me a racoon on our first date. It's okay. I mean other people get showered with compliments of how beautiful they are and how the world is blessed because they are in it and my date calls me a racoon. It's fine, totally cool."

"Oh c'mon, that's not what I meant." I say, mimicking her voice. "I was talking about the past you, not this you."

"Still me."

"I was saying that you ate like one, you are not... I should probably stop saying." I look at her and pull her closer by her waist. "I know what you did here."

She smiles goofily as she wraps her arms my neck. "I won't stop eating, even now."

"I wouldn't want it any other way."

"So, what do we do now?"

"I was thinking about lifting you up and spinning you around, but since we ate a little while ago, maybe I'll hold off on that idea a little longer."

"Uh-huh, how about this?" She says, then bats her eyelashes. I'm momentarily stunned while she playfully wriggles free and tries to run off.

I barely catch her by her wrist and then pull her close, slipping her arms around my neck and wrapping mine around her waist. "I'm not letting you go this time." I lean towards her and whisper in her ear. She blushes and hides her face on my chest.

We start to walk again. "So how were your days after, you know?" I wanted to know about hers, because I knew mine were shitty.

"Hmm, I think saying bad would be an understatement. Although dad was happy. He thought I was getting focused towards studies as I never left the room." She chuckles. "Mom was there. I remember yelling at her, not eating anything for days but she was very patient with me. I kinda feel sad for her, but I was so mad and she knew it, so she was always there, helping me with it." She pauses for a moment. "There was this one time when I got so frustrated, I started throwing everything in my room on the floor, she almost lost her cool and was about to raise a hand on me, but she didn't, instead she sat next to me. She had tears in her eyes and after that day, I never threw any tantrums on her. I never yelled at her again."

I stop, clasping her hands in mine and lifting them, I kiss her knuckles, then look into her eyes. She meets my gaze, and I give a subtle nod, silently asking if she's okay.

"Yeah. Don't worry it's all in the past." She says, shrugging it off and we start to walk. "But I kinda deserved that slap. Anyway, Maya was also there for me and I am really grateful to her for not hanging up on me when all I did was cry to her on the phone. She'd come to check if I was okay, take me out to places, movies and stuff and keep me distracted. So yeah, they helped me keep my sanity." She says, then shifts her gaze on me. "How were yours? Your parents didn't knew about us, right? And I remember you used to live in a separate apartment than your parents with Yash."

"I knew you'd come back. So I handled it pretty well." I wave hand in the air, trying to appear as nonchalant as possible.

"Then why are you looking away." She pauses. "Look at me Aahil." Her voice getting lower with each word.

She places her hand on my face, guiding my gaze towards her. I try to force a smile. "Did you tell anyone? At least your mom." She asks, her voice filled with concern.

"Yeah-yeah. It was all fine." I say and look away.

"So, you'll lie too on our first date."

"No. it's not like that." I say.

"Then look me in the eye and tell me—did you tell anyone?"

I look at her but I didn't know what to say, so I stand there, still, without saying anything but my body tenses as all the memories which haunted me for years flash in front of my eyes.

She covers her mouth with the back of her hand, her eyes welling up. She didn't ask me about Yash, she didn't have to. She knew it way before I realised it, that he was never a good friend. So instead of saying anything, she places her palms on my cheeks and lifts herself on her toes. I could feel her breath on my face. Her lips touches mine. Her tears travelled down her eyes to meet my cheeks as she kissed. I wrap my arms around her and kiss her back.

11

Chapter Eleven

September 8th, 2019

Not sure how long I've been sitting under this tree. So I pick my bag up and dust myself before heading towards my apartment. But before I start to walk, I grab my bottle from my bag and splash some water on my face in hopes that it would wash away the glumness off my face. I don't want to invite any stares or questions. I start walking, but my feet feel heavy. Her words have drained every last ounce of strength from my soul.

I open the door and turn the lights on as I walk inside my apartment. Yash wasn't there, that's a relief. It's kind of better this way. I have other things to deal with than my roommate making fun of my life.

As I walk inside my room, I collapse on the bed, leaving my bag on the floor. Since the day I fell in love with her, I always imagined a forever with her. In spite of the possibility of us being together seemed to be slim, never did I ever imagine living a day without her. Maybe it was my faith in her, in our love or maybe I was just delusional as fuck, but I had never prepared myself for the day when she'd leave me. I never thought she would. And even if I had, I don't think any amount of preparation would've been enough to face this.

I slam my fist into the floor in frustration, then roll onto my back and stare at the ceiling above. It was getting harder to breathe. I place my palm on my chest as a sharp ache rises in my chest. I am gasping for breath. Tears well up in my eyes and I'm blink my eyes, trying to force the tears to fall away. I can't get my mind off her and all I want to do is call her. Even if there's a slight chance that she'd listen to me, I want to sort it out with her. It just cannot end like this.

So I reach for my phone and dial her number. "The number you've called is currently busy." The operator says as the call got rejected after one ring. I still was blocked but I knew it in my heart that if I called her again and again, she'd call me back. I know she still loves me. So I call her again, then again and again.

"Stop irritating me with your calls. If you cannot make it easier, at least don't make it hard for me. And if you can't get this thing in your head then maybe it's best that we are ending this relationship. If you really love as you claim and you wanna see me happy, just don't contact me ever again. Stop bothering me now." I read her text and the tears start to fall uncontrollably, my vision completely blurred but I still press the call button.

"The number you're calling is currently switched off." The operator says. I toss my phone away on the bed and close my eyes. I just couldn't take it anymore.

ᐅᐅᐅ

I wake up to the sound of the alarm, my head hurting like someone's been hammering it. I didn't remember falling asleep. The last thing I remember was that she switched off her phone and I closed my eyes because I couldn't watch my hopes lying shattered in front of me. I try to find my phone with my half open eyes to check if there was any message from Anya. There was none.

I stand in the shower with my eyes open, not wanting to close them because I fear I'd see her face. I always thought that a cold shower can always calm me but today, it didn't. Then again, I haven't ever felt pain like this. I walk out of the shower and change in some clean clothes for my class, then walk out of my apartment.

A strong feeling of numbness takes over me as I walk through the same street where I first read her message. I wanted to run back to my room as soon as I stepped out of it but I don't want to face Yash, let alone *his questions. So I keep walking. Somehow, I still find it hard to believe that this is actually happening. And with this realisation, I feel a hope rising within me from a corner in my heart.*

Maybe it was merely a hope, but it was helping me gather up my strength. I just can't give up on us, not yet. So, I paced towards her classes instead of mine. Although we studied in the same college our subjects weren't same. In fact, her classes were located at the complete opposite end of the campus from mine.

I pace back and forth in the corridor, scanning every corner, trying to find her in every face around me but she is nowhere to be found. As the bell nears, I try to peek in her classroom but I still can't spot her. So with a heavy heart, I sprint to my own class just as the bell rings. Maybe she didn't come today.

Sitting in the class was pointless as I couldn't concentrate on anything except for her. Her words flashed in my mind in a loop, my eyes trying their best to hold up. I try to shrug the thoughts away and keep my head low. I don't want to attract any attention.

Finally, the last bell rings after what felt like an eternity. Immediately, I run out of the class, but not towards my apartment instead towards Anya's class. Even if there's a slight chance that she did come today and was hiding from me—something she's already good at—I don't want to take any chances, so I run as fast as I could.

Despite all my efforts, I could only make it to the walkaway in front of her corridor entrance. At least I have a clear view of the gate so if she did come, I'll be able to spot her.

I tried hard to keep my eyes on the gate, but I was completely out of breath from all the running. So when I couldn't even stand straight anymore, I lean down, gripping my knees and gulping air in while still trying to watch the entrance.

My eyes finally spot her walking out of the entrance with Maya, chatting casually with her, as if it was just another ordinary day for her. Maya tells her something and I watch Anya's face, closely. She didn't just smile, it was more than a smile. She was laughing with her, but somehow the laugh which used to make my heart melt for her a day ago didn't feel the same, instead it was infuriating me.

While I was rushing here, I had planned to walk up to her the moment I saw her and try to clear things up. But after seeing her laughing with her friend, I just stand there, waiting for her notice me. I just couldn't think straight. I could feel that glimmer of hope I had in the morning crumbling in front of my eyes. Didn't she expect me to be here? Is she even trying to look for me? Or am I just a chapter she's turned the page on already?

I keep watching her while she and Maya remain completely engrossed in their conversation which from where I was, seemed much more important than the dangling state of our relationship. I was getting impatient with each passing moment and was about to give up and confront her when her eyes meet mine and she stops.

For a moment I thought, it was all going to be okay now but as I was about to take a step towards her, she looks away. A thousand stabs wouldn't have butchered my heart like this. I watch her as she walks past me without even bothering to look at me even for a moment. My eyes follow her to the car she enters while I remain frozen to the same spot watching the car fading into the distance. A turmoil of emotions whirl inside me, a storm so chaotic and baffling that it leaves me completely paralyzed.

I'm strong. I'm strong. I won't cry, I won't... I look down and start walking, walking away from the crowd, walking away until no one sees me. I am holding my breath so it doesn't give away the agony in my heart. I keeping my head down as I walk because my eyes can't holdback anymore tears. I won't cry. I put on my headphones, because I don't want to feel alone. I've walked away from the crowd. I wanted to be strong but I can't, anymore. My legs can't hold my weight anymore so I fall on my knees. I can't stop the tears from falling. I couldn't stop her from going. I am not strong.

My phone rings and I can't see nothing, so I wipe my face on my sleeve instantly and reach for my phone hoping that it would be her call. It was mom. I let the phone ring until it automatically disconnects.

The phone rings again, so I decide to pick it up. "Hey mom." I say, trying to be as normal as I could.

"Where are you? And why weren't you picking up your phone?"

"I'm on my way home and the phone was on silent. Everything okay?"

"Everything's fine. Are you okay?"

"Yeah. Why do you ask?"

"Nothing. I just didn't feel good. Come home today."

"I'm fine mom. Don't worry. There's an important class tomorrow. How about I come home on the weekend?" I felt bad lying to her. There isn't any important class tomorrow, but I can't go home today. I can barely keep my emotions in check and I don't want them to know. I don't want them to be worried.

"Okay, but I won't hear any excuses on weekend."

"Okay." I say, but I really wished to tell her everything, share my heart out with her, but I can't. I just have to be strong. "I love you mom." Tears start to flow freely from my eyes.

"I love you too Aahil." My mom says and I immediately hang up the phone.

ᗡᗡᗡ

I lie on the edge of the bed, my stomach pressed against the sheets with one leg dangling off the side. My face is resting on the back of my hand as I let my thoughts wander. It has been three weeks since our breakup, my tears are all dried up and I am damn sure she didn't receive my messages because she has blocked my number but she must have received my mails and the notifications of my calls but she hasn't called back or replied to any of my mails.

Nothing has been same since we broke up. I don't feel like doing anything. Sometimes I get so frustrated that I start punching walls or my mattress. I've lost my appetite in the process, in fact I've been living majorly on caffeine. While Yash has been so oblivious that he didn't even notice any change in me, or maybe he just doesn't care enough. So, I haven't told him either. What's the point? So here I am lying alone with my earphones plugged in my ears.

"I'm borrowing this shirt." Yash nudges on my shoulder.

I pull out the earphone from my left ear and look at him, puzzled. He was holding my maroon shirt. "Yeah sure." I say. "So, another date?"

"Oh yeah. I've been talking to this girl on instagram for about a week now and I'm meeting her at Sams." He says without bothering to look, busy getting ready for his date.

"Huh, what about that girl you went on a date with the day before yesterday?"

"We're still talking."

"Hmm. What's special in this shirt? You always go on dates wearing it."

"This shirt is like my lucky charm for date; every time I wear it, everything goes perfectly as I want it to be. If everything goes well today, maybe I could take her some place nice after Sams." He winks at me and I know very well what some place nice means.

"But if she lashes out on you, make sure my shirt is safe. She can do whatever the hell she wants to do with you." I fake a smile and he waves his hand and leaves.

"Sick bastard." I mumble to myself not sure whether I said it because he is a pervert or he doesn't care. I get up and lock the main door then turn off all the lights in the apartment. Finally, I was alone.

I've never really wanted to be around people, but I've also never wanted to feel completely alone. But during these days, I think I've learned to live with this lonely feeling. I never thought my heart would find its solace in the dark, but maybe because it blends perfectly with my cloudy life, I like it here. At least here, I don't have to wear a mask to avoid unwanted attention.

I fall on my bed, the place where I'm spending most of the time these days and disconnect my earphone. Scrolling through the apps, I open the vault in my phone. There were two folders in it. One having pictures of Anya and the other folder has few screenshots of our chats. Every time we had a fight, I would take a screenshot of the lines which hurt me the most, not because I wanted to rub that lines on her face later but those were the lines that really hurt me. Although she'd apologise for it, but I needed time to get over it, so I'd save the screenshot and read it again and again until I get over it and then delete it. I've saved her last message too in this folder but I don't want to look at it.

"Can you do me a favour and bring a bottle of poison tomorrow? After all you'd be happy having one of your problems gone permanently." A screenshot read, making my heart ache more but my eyes were too tired to cry anymore tears. I swiped to the next screenshot and then to the next and those screenshots did nothing less than making my heart ache more and my blood boil up, so I open the next folder.

The folder had a little over four thousand photos of her, some of them were of us together but mostly hers. There were photos of her looking carefree, laughing, making funny faces, photos of her looking at me, looking away, of our video calls, of her wearing ethnic, and in western.

I open a photo of ours in which I was sitting on a bench and she had wrapped her hands around me from the back and her chin was on my right shoulder and she was pouting for our selfie. I swipe to the next photo and it was from the same place, but instead of her standing behind me, she was sitting beside me with her head resting on my shoulder and mine resting on her head, our fingers intertwined. "I'll always be there with you, until death do us apart. And I wish to die first because I can't bear living without you." I remember her saying.

Everything seems to be fake now, phony emotions, fake promises because if they were true then, where are they now? But the moments that we had weren't imaginary but they were definitely momentary, because all the memories of them lie shattered in front of me.

You're a liar Anya, you're a bloody goddamn liar and I'm so stupid to fall for all your lies. You were the one who accused me of not loving you enough, so where are you now, the oh-so-madly-in-love-queen. Those letter you used to send me were nothing but a bunch of lies. How can you say such miserable things to me and still have the audacity to complain about my love? You didn't love me enough and that is why you are not here. "You're a liar Anya. You're a liar." I scream as anger takes over my mind and blinded by my rage I press the delete button on the folder.

My heart sank, my hands trembling. "Shit!" I scream. The screen showed 'No folders'. "Shit! Shit! Shit!" I bury my hands in my hair, unable to believe what I've done.

I'm screaming, I'm crying, I'm punching the wall and now I'm holding my phone again with an empty screen. I'm gasping for air but *at the same time I'm burning with rage. My heart is aching, my brain couldn't think straight and I'm looking at the empty screen again. I see my phone flying and hitting the wall, shattering into several pieces.*

"Shit!" I scream as I'm getting back to my senses. I don't understand what I am doing. I'm picking up the pieces of the phone, but it's getting harder to breathe. I look around in the room to find something to hold to but my heads spinning. I am panicking. "Shi..." my eyes shut.

12

Chapter Twelve

I open up the umbrella as the first drops of rain fall on us. "You can't run away from me now." I chuckle.

"You've really thought this through." She laughs. "But it's fine. Since you've been alone all this time, I'll let you walk close to me."

"Uh-huh! You know there's a much better way to make up for that." I lean in closer, my voice low and playful.

"I cannot think of anything at the moment." She grins.

"Umm, there's rain and then there's us, in love, standing so close under an umbrella. There's one thing that could make this moment even more perfect than it already is."

"Oh yeah!" She says and briefly hugs me. "Feeling better?"

"Oh, so that's how you wanna play?" I'm grinning with her.

"Should I not?" She says, drawing out each word with a playful tease.

"You definitely can, but let's get to the car first." I say and pull her closer by her shoulder as we walk towards the parking.

"I love you." She looks up at me and mouths silently.

I gently squeeze her and then place a kiss on her forehead. "Mhm, I can feel the makeup on my lips." I laugh, teasing her to which she playfully nudges me. "I'm kidding."

I open the door for her and she slides in the front seat. I close the door and walk to the other side and get in the driving seat. "So, someone wanted to play." I hold her wrist and pull her a little towards me. "I think we should pick up right where we left off."

"Oh right! The hug." She leans in, then suddenly tickles me, laughing as she falls back onto her side.

"Hey! You're not playing it fair."

"Everything's fair in love and war." Her voice dripping with playful mischief.

"Oh, then you shall have no problem with me doing this." I lean towards her, wrapping my arm around her waist, I pull her close. Our eyes lock in for a few moments until I place my palm on her face. She closes her eyes as I caress her cheek with my thumb, slowly sliding the strands of her hair and tucking them behind her ear. "Hey." I say, gently rubbing her chin. She opens her eyes slowly, or at least that was how it looked from my perspective. She leans in, our eyes locked. We could feel each other breathing, our hearts visibly racing and our faces inches away.

Our lips brush for a few brief breaths before we rest our forehead against each other. She wraps her arms around my neck as I pull her closer holding her waist. Our lips meet in a kiss so intense that everything around us start to turn into a blur. Maybe it was the years of pent-up angst or perhaps a reflection of how happy we were, but in the moment, we were utterly lost in each other, oblivious everything else.

Our lips part and we rest our foreheads together, trying to catch our breaths, her hands still at the nape of my neck and mine wrapped around her. I tilt my face slightly, pressing a gentle kiss on her forehead before sinking back a little. I take her hands in mine, and place a kiss on each palm, then cradling her hands together, I envelope them in mine.

"I love you so much Anya. I really missed you. I don't wanna lose you, ever again." I whisper.

She leans forward and rests her face on my shoulder. "I love you too Aahil and I'm never gonna leave you. Never." She says, her voice breathy.

ᐅᐅᐅ

I pull a pillow on my side as I fall on the bed, not bothering to change the shirt I was wearing when I was with her as it had a faint scent of her from all the hugs. I can't help but keep staring at the ceiling with a silly grin spread across my face as I replay those moments in my mind.

I reach for my phone in my pocket. "Hey, you up?" A sense of nostalgia washes over me as I press the send button. Memories from the time when we used to talk all night seems to be alive all of a sudden. I check my phone for her message but sadly she hasn't read my message yet. So I place my phone on the side and pull up the pillow close to my chest, hugging it tightly. Am I too old to snuggle with a pillow? I hope not.

Sleep was miles away, but still, I take a deep breath and close my eyes. I hear my phone ping and I immediately pick it up. "Just entered my room." The text read.

"Wow, you walk slow."

"Haha, I was with Shruti."

"Oh, that explains."

"Why are you still awake? It's already late."

"I got home about half an hour ago, from a date." I text her, feigning innocence.

"Oh, I am so sorry for you."

"Why are you sorry?"

"Because she didn't stick around to come back to your place." I can feel her grinning.

"Ouch." Because that one hurt.

"Don't worry, maybe some other time."

"Yeah. Apartment's good but doing it in a car and that too on a public parking lot, not bad for a first date, huh." I was smiling before and now I'm grinning.

The typing dots blink on, then off, and then appears again. "Ah, but watch out for the cops. You can get fined." Her text appears, but she's still typing, so I wait. "And FYI, we didn't do anything."

"If you say so." I am grinning goofily and I can tell she's doing the same. "Jokes apart, you were looking really beautiful today. I wish we had more time."

"Thank you and you too. I wish that too. But I gotta go now and you should probably get some rest now—don't wanna be late for work!"

"Really."

"We have all our life ahead of us for late night talks. It's already past one."

"Okay. Good night."

"Good night. Take care."

"Take care." I wait a few seconds after sending it. "I love you."

"I thought you wouldn't say it. I love you too. Now don't text back. Good night." Her message appears and I smile, then put the phone aside. We have all our life together for late night talks. I hope so.

▷▷▷

It was a really hectic day at work, juggling between presentations and meeting, but thankfully it's over and now I have some free time with me.

"Can I borrow your phone for a minute? I need to call Anya and my phone's dead." Shruti asks.

"Yeah, hold on a sec." I retrieve my phone charger from the bag and hand it to her along with my phone, then shift my gaze back on the computer on which I was scrolling through websites to find some events happening in the city to go to.

"Oh thanks! You're a lifesaver. I'mma plug my phone here." She says and I nod as she leans over and plug her phone into the socket above my desk.

"Here." She says as she returns after a while and hand me back my phone.

"Everything okay?" I ask as she was about to leave.

"Yeah! I forgot to tell Anya that our maid won't be coming tonight."

"I see. So that means you're gonna boil water for dinner. Oh no, wait a sec, you guys can make maggie, right?" I tease.

"How *delightful* our misery is to you, huh? By the way, we'll be going out somewhere."

"Oh, it's totally amazing." I grin. "Anyway, do you wanna go to a food fest? There will be food." I say pointing at the computer screen. "Here have a look." I say and shift aside. She walks forward and leans towards the computer screen. "There will be loads of cuisines and drinks from the finest restaurants across the city and then there's music too.

"Looks good to me. This could be fun." She says, her eyes still locked on the screen. "Wait a minute, are you planning yourself a date? It's only been a month since you two started dating, so you're still very much in the honeymoon phase of your relationship. So if you both are going to ditch me, tell me now. I don't wanna be a third wheel on your date."

"Hey! I'm not that shallow and neither is she."

"Look at you defending her." She remarks with a smirk. "Give me your phone." I hand her the phone and she dials Anya's number. "By the way, I was meaning to ask—haven't you come up with any nicknames for her yet?" She teases, but as I was about to say something, Anya picks up the call.

"Hey, it's me. How does food fest sound to you for a dinner?" She asks Anya. "No, it's good, courtesies to the apple of your eye."

"Anya says you aren't the apple of her eye." She turns towards me before returning back to the call. "Okay, see you in twenty." She says on the phone.

ᐅᐅᐅ

I stop the car at the entrance of Excel Marketing Solutions. Anya hops in the back seat and settles in the middle.

"Hey." She says once she's settled. Shruti greets her back and I pull the car on the road.

"Anya, do you know?" I say and she shifts her gaze on me. "I heard from someone that you can only boil water and heat pre-made food and that too gets burnt at times. Don't you wanna know whose words these were?" I point towards Shruti and start to laugh, only to realise that I was the only one who was laughing. So I immediately shut my mouth.

"You're so dead now." Shruti says, her gaze sharp and intense. "And by the way, that whole thing about burning the food? Total over-exaggeration."

"It's okay Shruti. The next time our maid takes a leave, we will be crashing at his apartment." Anya says, her gaze fixed at Shruti.

And now both of them are looking at me. What am I supposed to say? "Well, that's an interesting way of inviting yourself to my home." I say very earnestly.

"Damn!" Shruti remarks and falls back on her seat. "That was smooth." I look up in the rear view mirror to find Anya gazing out of the window with a smile. I reach for Anya's hand and intertwine my fingers with her.

"You can do all your couples stuff. I'm closing my eyes." Shruti teases, covering her eyes, but at the same time peeking from the gap between her fingers.

"There's nothing to do." Anya says and pulls her hand back.

"Really? I don't even get a kiss?" I ask, putting on an innocent face as I glance at Anya.

"Eyes on the road."

13

Chapter Thirteen

I park in the designated space for parking. The music was loud. "After you guys." I had to shout to over the noise.

We walk inside the arena, making our way through the crowd towards the stage. The place is buzzed with energy and the lights are going wild—the lasers flashing in every direction, slicing through the haze in time with the music. There's a guy up there singing with his band. I don't recognize him, but he's got the crowd hooked. People are packed in close to the stage, practically on their toes, totally caught up in the moment.

"Want me to grab you something to drink? I'm going to get one for myself." I ask.

They look at each other. "Mint mojito?" Shruti asks Anya and she nods. "Two mint mojitos."

I walk towards the counter. "Three mint mojitos please." I say to the barista behind the counter and then turn around to look at them. I mean, Anya.

They were standing a little off to the side, talking, and I couldn't help but watch. Shruti says something to Anya, and I could tell it caught her attention right away. I swear I heard Anya laugh, "No way!" as she looked at Shruti, who just nods, like she knew exactly what's going on.

I'm not sure if Anya noticed me staring at her or if she just had a feeling, but she casually tucks a few loose strands of her hair behind her ear and dear god, she is beautiful. She didn't look my way, though. There's this thing about her I just can't figure out—how does she look so effortlessly beautiful? And that too after a whole day of work. And that smile—so easy, so natural. How does one pull that off?

"Sir! Your drinks." The barista says and hands me the glasses.

I walk as steadily as I can, trying not to spill any drink on my hand, or worse my clothes. "Hey! Your drinks."

"Thank you." They say in unison and take the drink from my hand.

"Let's get a little closer to the stage." Anya says and we start walking towards it.

The area around the stage was more crowded than the rest of the arena. People were grooving with the beats, a few people, supposedly couples, were dancing in each other's arms as the singer was singing a romantic melody. So instead of walking too close to the crowd, we stop at a distance which gave us a decent view of the stage and from where we can have our drinks without people bumping into us. Anya stood in the middle of our little trio with Shruti on her left.

She pulls my hand and I look at her. She leans in towards my shoulder and whispers in my ears. "I bet you can sing better than him." She says, eyeing the singer.

"No way." I say, shrugging it off. She doesn't say anything and shifts her gaze back to the stage, but her words got me thinking if I could really do it. I have done it once before, but that was back when we were in school. There were friends around, so it didn't feel too out of my comfort zone as I knew even if I really messed up, it would still be fine. But here, in front of complete strangers, I could totally make a fool of myself. And then there's my stage fright. What if I walk on the stage and it kicks in and I start shivering. I can't.

"Stay here. I'll bring something to eat." I say, then head towards the food stalls, but my mind keeps wavering, unsure whether I should go through with it or not. My eyes fall on a Chinese food stall. I walk over and glance at the menu, then order a plate of manchurian and paneer chilli.

Somehow, the mere thought of me being on the stage makes my palm sweaty and cold. So, I stuff it in my pockets and try not to think about it because I've already made up my mind. The plates were ready, so I pick them up from the counter, then make my way back to where they are waiting.

"Hey!" I say, as I approach them. They turn around to look at me. "Umm, here's cottage cheese with capsicums and I don't know any fancy name for manchurian." They smile and take the plates from my hand. "I'll find something else. You can start with these." I say and turn around.

"Wait!" Anya shouts. I turn around and look at her. She puts a fork into one of the manchurian balls and take a step closer to me. Holding it in front of her, she blows gently on it to cool it down, her eyes catching mine for a brief moment. Then with a playful smile, she brings the fork closer to my face, offering me to bite.

"You guys have your moments every now and then." Shruti teases.

"And you spare none of them." I smirk. "I'll be back soon. Don't go anywhere."

I pretend walking towards the food stalls but stop after covering some distance, then glance over my shoulder and look back at them—her. She is smiling as she takes a bite from the plate.

My heart is beating faster, but I tell myself that it's okay. "It's okay. I can do this." I mutter under my breath. Even if I stumble, even if things don't go perfectly, I know she'll get it. She'll understand. And moreover, I have been practicing this song for a while now—I won't mess it up. And with that reassurance, I take a different path from where they were standing to the stage.

On my way towards the stage, I pick up a water bottle to drink and calm my racing mind. As I got closer, my heart started pounding out of nervousness that I could feel it in spite of the loud noise around. The band has taken a break and I could see people from the crowd performing until the band is back.

"Hey, are you still letting people sing or is the band back from their break?" I ask to the volunteer on the backstage.

"Yeah! You can sing after him." He says, pointing towards the person who was already on the stage. "Do you have a track or something, or would you prefer an instrument?"

I nod towards his guitar. "Would it be cool if I used your guitar?" He gives a small nod, then turns away.

My hands are still trembling, and the air feels like it's been ripped from my lungs, as if a dementor were draining my soul, just like in Harry Potter. I thought I had overcome my fear of stage because usually I have grown comfortable speaking in front of people in office or clients but somehow it is kicking in again.

I drink the water left in the bottle in one go, then inhale a long breath and hold it for a few seconds before letting it go. "I can do this." I reassure myself. God, if I die of a heart attack, please tell my parents that I loved them and I only did this for their future daughter in law.

The volunteer gives me a quick nod, signalling that it's my turn as the singer before me finishes. I close my eyes and take a few deep breaths to shake off the nerves before walking towards the stage.

"Hello everyone." I say on the mic, but the blinding lights make it impossible to see anyone's face. It's kind off for the better—I mean, the lessor people I see, the less nervous I am. "This one's for my beautiful girl out there in the crowd—though I can't see you right now with these lights on my face, I know you're there. The song's called *Perfect by Ed Sheeran*."

ᗡᗡᗡ

I can feel my heart pounding in my chest, like it's trying to tear it's way out of it. There's an applause but it feels so distant. My body is too heavy for my shaking legs to handle. But at least I did it. "Thank you." I manage to say on the mic, then get off the stage.

"Yo bro! That was good." The volunteer shouts from the back.

"Thanks." I turn around and mumble at him.

I feel a hand on my shoulder. I turn around to look—it was Anya. Shruti was standing behind her. "Where were you? We've been looking for you." She questions, looking concern. *What?*

Before I could say anything else, she wraps her arms around me. "Hey," she says softly. "Aahil breathe with me. Breathe with me, okay? In... and out. Slowly. Like this."

I don't even know how to respond, so I breathe with her, slowly, until I finally start to feel I'm getting control of it. The tightness in my chest start to loosen and world comes back into focus.

"I'm here. With you. Always." She says, pulling back just enough to look me in the eyes. Her hands are warm on my face. "You were incredible out there." Her voice soft, trying to comfort me.

I shake my head, slightly embarrassed. She smiles, and brushes a strand of my hair from my forehead. "Everything about your performance was perfect, because you're perfect and I love you so much for doing that."

"You liked it?" I smile back at her.

"Liked it! I loved it. Really-really loved it." She says all smiling and hugs me again. Her words eased the anxiousness in my chest. I take a deep breath and hug her back.

"Hey, love birds. Do you mind going to some other place? People are watching us." Shruti calls out. A flushed smile appears across our faces as we look at her.

We start to walk. "You okay?" Shruti asks. I nod. "You know, this man has lied to me more than my ex ever did. I never knew he could sing. No one in the office does."

Anya looks at me and I still had that flushed smile from before. "He once sang in front of the whole school, for me." Anya says to Shruti. "In fact, his voice is one of the reasons I fell for him in the first place. You know, the first time I knew he could sing was when he uploaded a song on youtube and sent me the link. Back then we didn't knew each other in person—I mean, we used to talk on facebook but we hadn't seen each other. And when I heard his voice, I'm not sure why, but I couldn't stop crying." I keep looking at her as she narrates the whole story to Shruti.

"And she lied to me that her friend was the one who cried." I laugh.

"Look at you, back to your normal self. Now, how long should I wait before making fun of you?"

"You can start, right about now." I say.

"I will. Just waiting for a right moment. By the away, you're a rock star dude. And a mysterious man." Shruti says and I scratch the back of my head with a shy smile. "I mean, there were parties and functions, but no one had the slightest clue that he could sing."

"If it makes you feel any better, no one has heard me sing in years."

"No, it doesn't. How is that supposed to make me feel any better? You are supposed to be my friend—you should tell me things."

"Aww, he is sorry." Anya says, wrapping her arms around Shruti and playfully shaking her.

"No, I'm not." I snickered. "And I'm not gonna join in this." I shake my head at the girls who are laughing as they try to pull me in a hug. "So, anyway, what shall I bring for you guys?"

"Oh, you know what I would like? Too bad, they don't sell them on stalls." She says and winks. "And you are not going alone this time."

"First of all, I can't help you with that. Try tinder or something." I chuckle. "And I am out of all the tricks."

"Has he always been like this?" Shruti asks, looking at Anya.

"Like how? Self-obsessed?" Anya says.

"Yeah."

"You tell me. You've known him for almost two years now."

"Hmm, let me think. At first he was very shy—then we got to work together and since then he's like this. So for about year and half."

"I am standing right here." I interrupt.

"Shhh." Shruti shushes. "So how about before?"

"As far as I remember, he was always like this, even before our relationship, when we were friends. He calls it self-love." Anya says, making air quotes gesture with her fingers.

"And you're okay with it?" Shruti asks.

"Okay. First of all 'ouch', I'm not self-obsessed." I had to interrupt them or they would just go on. "And I am way too good looking for someone to not be okay with me." I wink with a smug look on my face.

"There he goes again." Shruti says in mock exasperation and Anya laughs.

"Naah! He says such things on purpose you know, to make things lighter—but only to people who are close to him." Anya says to Shruti.

"There's my cute little defender." I say with a grin and wrap my arm around Anya and pull her close. "Although—she totally fell in love with me for my charm." I nudge her playfully.

Anya rolls her eyes. "Wow, that's really presumptuous of you," she says, shaking her head. "I didn't fall for your *charm*. I just felt sorry for you."

"Hey! Now that's just rude." I say, pretending to be offended. "Are you trying to hurt my feelings?"

She leans a little towards me and whispers, "I love you."

"You better."

14

Chapter Fourteen

We were on our way back home. Anya was sitting on the front seat while Shruti sat in the back seat, her elbows resting on either side of the headrests. "So, how did you guys meet?" Shruti asks, her voice giving away her curiosity.

"We met on facebook." I shrug.

"That is so not the way to answer a question when someone is asking you some juicy details. Help me out here Anya." Shruti whines.

Anya laughs. "Ask him why we met on facebook."

"Yes Aahil, why did you?" Shruti nudges me.

"We were from the same school but we didn't knew each other. So facebook recommended her profile and I sent her the friend request."

"Nuh-uh. He's taking all the fun out of it." Anya exclaims, throwing her hands up in the air, then shifts in her seat to turn towards Shruti.

"Why are you sucking all the fun when you can—never mind. Go on Anya. I am all ears." Shruti says and I laugh, knowing what she was gonna say.

"He had a friend who used to show off how popular he was among girls in front of him and made him feel like-"

"-a loser." Shruti interrupts.

"Not the word I was gonna say, but more or less." Anya tries hard to keep a straight face.

"Really? Not you too." I groaned.

"I didn't say anything. She said it." She exclaims before holding my hand and runs her fingers around my knuckles. "Anyway,"

"No wait. How's his friend?" Shruti interrupts her.

"Eh. Don't wanna think about him at all." Anya says dismissively.

"That bad. Huh?" Shruti exclaims.

"Yup. His friend used to send hundreds of friend request to girls and I'm not even exaggerating. So he did end up talking to a lot of girls on facebook. So one day Aahil decided to do the same, you know, fear of missing out." She goes on.

"So you used facebook as your tinder." Shruti chuckles.

"Well, when you put it that way." I shrug.

"When you put it that way." Shruti imitates me and they both laugh.

"How come you don't know this stuff? Don't you guys talk?" I ask.

"She didn't tell me anything. She said it will be fun when I asked it when you both were together." Shruti says with a long face.

"I see. So, moving on, we started talking, but you know what, we never got to see each other for a long time, all thanks to this beautiful lady next to me."

"You didn't get to see me. I saw you way before you saw me. And how am I responsible for you not seeing me sooner?"

"She thought I was too handsome and she isn't beautiful so she hid herself." I chuckle and Shruti fell back laughing.

"That is so not true." Anya scowls.

"So you didn't find him handsome, then why the hell did you accept a stranger's friend request?" Shruti teases Anya.

Shruti nudges her. I feel her grip tighten on my hand. "Because he was really good looking." Anya finally admits and we burst into laughter.

"See I told ya." I say.

But Anya interrupts me immediately. "But that is not the reason at all. He was too chicken to come towards my class wing even after we have been talking for almost a month."

"No, I wasn't." I counter back.

"Okay, so tell her when did you actually ask to see me?"

"Two and half months later."

"Two and half months. Really, dude?" Shruti exclaims, her voice filled with astonishment.

"In my defence, it was summer and there was a break of a month and half, or I would have asked her sooner."

"Yeah, sure." They both roll their eyes at the same time and laugh.

"So, how did you see him?" Shruti asks Anya.

There was a special assembly on the last day before vacation and he was the lead in the choir group. So I saw him first." Anya says. "And he saw me after vacation."

"And you know what, when I asked if I could see her, mind you, after waiting for more than a month and half, she was like..." I look towards Anya, with the most pointed look I could give her, "...Nope." Shruti bursts into another fit of laughter.

ᗡᗡᗡ

June 14th, 2016

"So do I get to see you tomorrow?" I text her. It was already past midnight but I was nowhere close to sleeping. The thought of seeing her for the first time in person was too exciting for my brain to slow down and rest. Talking to someone on phone and in person are too different things, and to be honest, the latter is quite nerve wrecking.

"No, you won't." her text appears on my phone. It isn't fair. We have been talking for a while now, like genuinely talking, and not just casual hellos. The only reason I was looking forward to going back to school was to see her.

"C'mon, you've seen what I look like, only fair if I get to do the same." I text her back.

"Well you look proper handsome, so you've got nothing to worry about."

"Thank you for the compliment, but seriously you don't have to stress about anything. You could look like a potato and I wouldn't care. Also, I'm coming over to your class wing tomorrow."

"Okay, but don't be disappointed or make a bad face when you see me. Got it? If you did, I'll smack that disappointment right off your face."

"Wow, you really don't want me to see ya, do you? Just say the word and I won't come. You're really hurting me here." I text her and keep my phone down to take a breath. What if she actually says no? God, I shouldn't have been so stupid. But there has to be a reason, right? She can't think I'm that shallow to only focus on looks. What if I come across...

My thoughts are interrupted by the notification tone of my phone. "Okay fine. I'll be there in the lobby. See you tom."

"See ya, good night :)"

"Good night."

I keep my phone aside and take a deep breath to calm my racing heart. She said I looked handsome. And I know she's beautiful, but I don't see why she was making such a fuss about meeting in person. But anyway, I finally get to see her tomorrow.

The next morning, I take extra care as I get ready for the school. Hairs checked, uniform checked, shoes checked. It was no less than a first date for me. The thought of seeing her for the first time in person is making me smile like a fool. My mind, creating scenarios, as to how our first meeting will be and most of them coming straight out of movies, the ones I knew deep down wouldn't ever happen.

I jump out of the school bus as soon as the bus stops at the school compound, then pace towards my classroom. After keeping my bag on my seat, I take a mental note, double checking everything, my hairs, uniform, even rehearsing my smile to not appear a creep as I walk across the corridor in a hurry.

My steps slow down as I was about to reach her class wing since my heart was racing faster, and my hands were becoming sweaty. I haven't done it before, never. Not knowing what to do next, I lean against the *side of window on the corridor. She was nowhere to be seen and I know that she is hiding and she must be seeing me from a distance, so I try to appear casual and confident but then paranoia hits me and I check if I was standing correct. I was getting anxious with each passing second, but she was taking her sweet time to let me see her.*

Finally she decides to show up, ending my misery. Our eyes lock for a brief moment, my heart skips a beat, for the first time in my life and before I could even let out a breath which I was holding, she turns away and hide among the crowd. My face falls immediately.

I start to doubt myself. Why did she turn away? Was I too persuasive yesterday? And was it the reason she came to see me? My heart sank, my eyes wandering everywhere, trying to find her again but she was nowhere to be seen.

My eyes finally meet hers, again, as she was about to enter her classroom. She was looking over her shoulder at me, with a smile, a smile more beautiful than anything I have ever seen and then I saw her face. My eyes wandered all over her face, from her eyes to her lips and to her ears, then back to her eyes, the long eyelashes when she blinked, her cheeks and how they curve when she smiled. She wasn't just beautiful, but the most beautiful girl I've ever seen. Camera couldn't capture how perfect she was. I gasped for breath. I wasn't sure until this morning, whether it is love but now, she had stolen my heart away.

She enters her classroom, going out of my vision but the moment of her turning away towards her class, and how her hair flew in the air kept playing in front of my eyes as if it were a movie.

I walked back to my class but I longed to see her again. I felt jealous of her classmates that they get to see her whenever they want.

ϷϷϷ

"You are one hell of a tease." Shruti nudges Anya who simply blushes in response. "And you have this habit from the very beginning." She turns to me.

"What habit?" I ask.

"Habit of staring at her like she's your prey." Shruti chuckles.

"I do not stare at her like she's a prey. I look at her in awe, and who wouldn't? She's beautiful." I hold Anya's hand and squeeze it, then entangle my fingers in hers.

"Hey, you better grab that damn wheel properly. I don't wanna die two streets from my apartment." Shruti says.

"So where do you wanna die?" I ask with a hint of tease.

"She knows. And you'll never know." Shruti smirks. I look at Anya. She is hiding her laugh with the back of her hand. "Don't look at her, she isn't gonna tell you."

"So you're gonna keep secrets from me Ana. It's okay, I mean, I don't keep anything from you but that's fine I guess."

"Don't be so dramatic. I don't tell your secrets to her either." Anya says.

"Really?" Shruti whines, acting as if she was betrayed.

"Don't worry." Anya mouths, glancing towards Shruti.

"I saw that." I comment.

We reach at the entrance of their apartment. Shruti climbs out of the car. Anya was about to open the door when I hold her wrist. She stops and look at me. "Will it be okay if I made you breakfast this Sunday?" I ask her, unsure of how she would react, since it is the first time we would be doing something like this.

"I haven't seen your apartment, so you'd have to pick me up. It will be an unnecessary trouble for you to pick me up and also make breakfast. How about lunch?" She says with a straight face. Okay, are you dumb or pretending to be?

"How about, if I didn't have to pick you up in the morning." Still trying to say in indirectly, knowing well that if I asked her directly and she said no, then it would hurt no less. Although the chances of her saying no is very slim, but just in case.

"If you are planning to make breakfast and bring it here, then you would have to make for three because Shruti will be here too." She says, still no change in expression, as if she isn't even trying to understand what I am trying to say.

"Okay, I don't think you are getting what I am trying to say."

"So why don't you say it directly instead beating around the bush." She finally smirks.

"That was good." I pull her closer with her wrist and envelope her palm between mine. "Would you like to stay at my apartment this saturday? I'll make you dinner and then we can have breakfast in bed in the morning." I say.

"Okay. But only for dinner and breakfast." She says in a teasing tone. "And don't forget paneer tikka."

"Done." I smile at her. She was about to open the door when I pull her again. Gently I place my palm on her cheek and kiss on her forehead. "I love you so much."

She leans forward and whispers, "I love you too." She brings her lips closer, pressing them on mine very briefly, before climbing out of the car. "See you saturday."

ᚦᚦᚦ

"What time shall I pick you up?" I text Anya as I enter my apartment. The clock on the phone showed 7 PM. I left a little early from the work because I wanted everything to be perfect. After all, it isn't just any dinner, it is our first *at-home* date.

I usually keep my apartment tidy but tonight, I want it to be spotless. So I quickly change into pyjamas—it's time to get to work.

I start with changing the bed sheets, fluffing pillows and cleaning the slabs with a cloth for any residual dust. My phone pings. "Hey. Don't worry about picking me up. I'll just grab a cab. Text me the address."

"Oh c'mon, let me pick you up. After all I'll get to spend more time with you." I text her back.

"No. Just text me the address. I'll be there by nine." Her message appear. She isn't going to budge so I text her the address and resume cleaning.

I take the paneer cubes out of the fridge and set them on the counter to warm it up a bit. While they are resting, I grab a container and start mixing up the marinade. It's a simple blend of yogurt, spices and a little squeeze of lemon. Once it is ready, I coat the paneer cubes with the sauce, making sure each one is nicely covered, and then set them aside to soak in the flavours. Next, I grab another container and begin making the dough for the chapatti.

By the time I was done cooking, I was sweating and running out of time. I kept double checking everything, making sure it was perfect, and it kind of threw me off track. So I run into the bathroom to take a quick shower before running back to my bedroom to change into something appropriate.

I throw the sweaty clothes in the laundry so that they do not lie around on the floor and pull out a navy blue t-shirt and a black sweats.

She would be here any time now, so I light up some scented candles for a sweet fragrance, then walk around the apartment one last time making sure everything was just right.

I splash on some cologne and take a good final look of myself in the mirror, when I hear the doorbell ring.

15

Chapter Fifteen

There she is.

She's standing in front of me, looking effortlessly stunning. She's wearing a black dress that fits her like it was made for her. Her dress ends just above her knees, and I can't help but notice how the fabric of her dress moves when she shifts. She has layered it with a long beige overcoat that falls just below her thighs, adding a touch of sophistication to the outfit.

"Hi." She says with a teasing smile.

"Hey. Come on in." I say with a smile. "You look amazing."

"That I figured." She grins and I scratch the back of my head. She steps inside. "You have a nice place." She says, looking around the living room. "Actually, cosy."

"Thank you." I say. "Not exactly what we used to dream of when we were kids."

"It's better. That didn't have a sea view." She interrupts me.

"Hmm! Let me help you with the overcoat." I step a little closer to her and slide the overcoat off her shoulders.

"I see we're already drifting from the 'dinner-only' plan." She chuckles, her smile full of mischief.

"Well," I say with a sly smile, "I figured we could start with a little appetizer before the main course."

"Wow," she murmurs as her eyes fall on the plants near the balcony. To be honest, I'm a little nervous whether she'd like the way things are arranged in the apartment. I follow her as she walks towards the balcony.

Her fingers brush against the leaves of the plants there, each one potted in ceramic pots, there green shades standing out as the light from the living room fell on them.

"You have a thing for plants?" She leans in, gently touching a long, slender leaf. "This one's pretty."

"Yeah. I read somewhere that plants bring peace, and that's when I wanted one. Now I have a bunch of them."

She straightens up, turning her gaze to the view in front of her. "This view," she says softly. "I don't think anyone would ever get tired of it."

I shift closer to her, sliding my arm around her waist as I look out at the same stretch of ocean, although this time, it feels even more special. "You won't have plenty of space to run in here." I whisper.

"Better, hm." She says in a playful voice. "How long have you lived here?"

"A little over a year," I reply. "It wasn't always like this. Took me some time to get used to the place."

"I like it." She says, her voice soft. I pull her a little closer as we watch the view in front of us. She takes a deep breath as if she's trying to drink it. I don't remember being this happy in my life—I mean, I was really happy when she came back in my life, but this—it tops everything. "Oh, I forgot, I've got something for you."

"You didn't have to do that."

She opens up her purse, pulling out a little unicorn figurine, and hold it in her hands. "Remember this?"

"I think I do. Is that the," she shakes her head with a childlike grin on her face. "Oh my god, you got it like six years ago and you still have it. Does it work?"

"Yeah it works fine. I just had to replace its cells." She turns the switch on and the unicorn starts glowing.

"Thank you so much." I say as I hold the unicorn in my hand. She bought it for me six years ago but I couldn't keep it with me because I lived with my parents back then. "Wanna keep it inside?"

"Wait a second, let me take my heels off first." She leaves her purse on the couch and takes off her heels. "After you." She says.

"First hold this. I want you to choose a place for it." I say, then lead her towards the bedroom.

I watch her as she walks in the bedroom, slowly. Her eyes wandering everywhere. My bedroom's got more character than my living room, I think. But it's the bookshelf that catches her attention.

"Hey! You got a really pretty bookshelf." She leans in, running her fingers along the spines of the books. "I'm placing it here. Hope you don't mind."

"Nope! Anywhere you like." I say and she places it on an empty space on the bookshelf.

She sits on the edge of the bed. "You've read them all?" She asks as she scans the titles of the book on the shelf.

"Not all. Most I have read and some I mean to."

"I see. So, what's your favourite genre?"

I sit beside her and lean against a pillow. "Anything that lets me escape. Fiction's my go-to but I like anything that's sad."

She glances up at me, her gaze soft, like she's trying to read in between the lines. "Sounds like you like being sad."

"Umm, I'm not so sure. I like being with you and right now I think I'm the happiest man alive and I'm really liking it."

"U-huh!" her gaze shifts back to the shelf again. "Oh, you've got *Looking for Alaska*. I've heard a lot about this book."

"Yeah, I haven't read it completely."

"Why? Isn't it good?"

"Oh, it's really good, but in the story an incident happens that made me so sad that I couldn't read another word." I say. She grabs the book from the shelf and flips it open to read the back cover. "Come, let me show you the balcony I sent you the photo of."

"Oh yes! I forgot about that." She places the book back on the shelf. I hold out my hand for her and she intertwines her fingers with mine.

"I have some extra space here as it bigger than the one in the living room. So I've placed a carpet and some more plants here. And there I have some cushions. That spot kinda feels like the best place to bring a cup of coffee and curl up with a book for hours."

Anya walks over to the railing, her gaze on the sea in front of her. "This is beautiful. Ten times more beautiful than in the photo." Her voice seems relaxed. "It's so peaceful up here."

"Yeah. I love it here. I just wish I could share it more often with you."

She turns her gaze towards me and our eyes lock in the moment. "I wish that too." Her voice is low, and she shifts her gaze back to the sea. "Anyway, so tell me one thing. Is this how your apartment looks every day or is it just for today?" She asks with a mischievous grin, and somehow her voice isn't low anymore.

"Why don't you stay here and find out." I caress a strand of her hair on her face and tuck it behind her ear.

"Hmm, then there won't be any fun in it."

"I can live without it." I say. "Say, how about I bring our dinner here?"

"That would be amazing. I'll come with you." She says and we walk inside towards the kitchen. "I'll be very nit-picky—you made fun of me the other day."

"Oh, I'm scared."

"You should be."

I hold her by her waist from behind as we stop near the counter where dish's container were. She raises the lid of the container having paneer masala in it. "It smells delicious." She grabs the spoon next to it and takes a bite. "This is so good." She says, her voice filled with genuine surprise.

I grin, feeling proud of myself. "Glad you like it."

She turns around to face me, still holding the spoon. There's something in her eyes that makes my heart race, those beautiful chocolate brown eyes, which I've loved so much. Maybe it's the moment we are in but somehow they look even more beautiful.

I pull her a little closer by her waist. She closes her eyes as my fingers touch her cheeks, gently caressing them. I lean towards her and brush my nose against hers. I could feel her breath on my skin.

"Hey," I say, but before I could say anything else, she presses a quick, soft kiss to my lips and then open her eyes.

I rest my forehead on her and pull her closer. She leaves the spoon on the counter and wraps her arms around my neck, her fingers buried in my hairs as we kiss.

Her lips are soft against mine—our eyes are closed, and our kiss, slow, like we are savouring every moment of it. I tighten my hold around her waist as the kiss gets longer, and deeper, until everything around us fades.

"I love you so much." I say as we break apart to catch our breaths. "I don't wanna let you go ever." She rests her head on my shoulder.

"Me too." She mumbles. "I wanted this for so long but you're an idiot." She says, her voice on the verge of breaking.

I take a step back to watch her face, trying to read her face. "Idiot?" I ask, confused.

"Yes, a complete idiot. It took you this long to invite me here even when I out rightly asked you to show me your apartment."

"But that was even before we sorted things out." I say. "I thought you were just messing around with me."

"Why would I be messing with you and that too when we were talking after so long? I wanted to be with you. But no, you won't take hints, you won't message me—I was the one who messaged you! And now you're trying to distract me?"

I lean in with a playful grin, "I'm not trying to distract you... I just thought you might need a little kiss to lighten your mood."

"I'm mad at you. Stop it."

I still lean in further and kiss her cheeks softly. "I wish I could show you just how hot you're looking right now."

She takes a step back. "No, stop! I wanna be mad at you."

"Okay, okay. Tell me, how can I make it up to you?"

"Hmm... Apologize."

I smile at her. "I'm sorry."

"No, you're saying that just because I told you to, not because you actually mean it."

"Okay, that's not fair! What do you want me to do then?"

"I don't know." She isn't able to hold back her smile anymore, so she turns around.

I walk closer to her. "Can I hold you?" I whisper in her ear.

"U-huh."

I hold her, leaning towards her, I place a kiss on her shoulder, and then another, slowly moving up through her neck to the back of her ear. She tilts her head and lets out a deep breath. "I am sorry." I whisper in her ear. Then turn her around and cup her face in my palms and kiss her forehead. Her eyes are closed, so I gently kiss her eyes. A tear slide from the side of her eye and before it could fall from her cheek, I kiss the tear, and it's trail, then gently brush my nose against her. Finally, I kiss her lips.

She opens her eyes slowly, and her lips curve into a smile. "Apology accepted."

"There's your paneer tikka." I point towards another container. "How about we start with it?" I grab a plate. She takes the fork from my hand and sticks it in one of the paneer cube, tasting it as I continue to serve it on the plate.

"Okay, you've chose a wrong career dude. These are like one of the best I've ever had." She dips another cube in the dip I've poured into a small bowl. "Aren't you gonna eat?"

"I am."

"Where's yours?"

"I thought it would be cute if we ate from a single plate." I say.

"Oh, no-no. Maybe some other time. Tonight, this plate's all mine." She says and takes the plate from my hand. I grab another plate and then we walk back towards the balcony.

"Wait for me." I say and walk back to the kitchen to grab the cold drinks. On my way back, I grab two glasses and light a candle.

As I step back into the room, I switch off the main lights, letting the soft glow of the fairy lights take over. I adjust the dimmer to a soft, medium glow to give the place a cosy vibe, then walk over to her. I lean down a little and hand her the glasses and the bottle, then place the candle in front of us.

The soft glow from the candles fall on her face as she leans forward to pour the drink in the glasses. "You're looking really beautiful."

"Even more than your favourite actress?" She raises and eyebrow and smirks.

"Umm, how can I choose? I'll tell you when I get to go on a candle light dinner with her." She narrows her eyes. "Only to find out that you are way more beautiful than her. You should let me complete my sentence before giving that look." That was a close one.

I sit beside her and she hands me a glass. "To my first day here." She says, raising her glass.

"And many more to come." We clink our glasses.

A few moments pass, and we just sit there in silence, letting it sink in—like we were both trying to wrap our heads around the fact that this is actually happening. "So, how did you learn to cook? And that too, this good." She says after a while.

I look up pretending to think something. "Umm, there was this scene I used to think of in my head, that one day, you'll come barging through the door and say that you've come back in my life and will be there with me forever. I'll get so happy and make your favourite food."

"Okay, nice try." She scowls.

"No, seriously! I'm not joking. I even learned how to cook mushrooms—and you know I don't like them at all."

"Really? Aww, but too bad—I don't like them anymore." She nudges me with her shoulder. "It's really beautiful out here."

A light breeze blows through her hair, making it fall across her face. I reach over and tuck a few strands behind her ear. "I'll get the rest of the stuff," I say and she nods with a smile.

I grab the rest of the containers, along with some extra plates and cutlery, and head back to her. Dropping everything in front of us, I grin and say, "Dinner's served." Then, I sit down beside her.

"I'm beyond impressed with you today."

I joke. "Impressive is my middle name, baby."

"Ewww. You can do better than that."

"Never mind. It sounded way cooler in my head." I shake my head, then open the containers and start serving the food on the plate and pass it to her.

"So, how's everyone at home?" She asks, a little distracted as she digs into the food.

"Umm, good." I say. She shifts her gaze on me. "You know, my mom was asking me to come home tonight for dinner."

"What did you say?"

"I said, that, I'm going on a date with her future daughter in law but I'll come next weekend for sure."

"No way, you actually said that?"

"I wish. I said, I've dinner plans with friends and can't cancel on them."

"You shouldn't have lied to her. We could've met some other day."

"I didn't technically lie to her. You are my friend, right?"

"I am, but still." She glances at me in slight apprehension, her eyes softening, and for a moment, I feel like I could stay like this forever.

"How's uncle and aunty?" I ask her.

"Fine. Dad's usually busy and after I moved out, I think mom feels a little alone at times, but other than that, all good." She takes a bite.

We eat in silence for a while, the comfortable kind, the kind that doesn't need words.

"Do you remember the first time we kissed? You had your face on my lap and I couldn't resist, so I kissed you on the side of your lips." I say, eventually breaking the silence.

"Yeah, I do." She covers her mouth with the back of her hand and says.

"And then you started crying—thinking how are we gonna find our way together and I was like, is she crying because I kissed her." I say and she laughs. "I swear, I didn't know what to do at that time."

"But then we kissed like some hungry monsters. Can't blame us, no one taught us how to do it." She chuckles. "I still sometimes think of moments like those."

༆༆༆

I keep the plates in the sink, then walk back to her. "You kinda have to leave that spot to wash your hand. You know that, right?" I say to her.

"You know what? God should've made some sort of mechanism to unscrew the wrists. That way, you could just take it, then bring it back and I wouldn't have to get up."

I know she's isn't going to budge from that place any time soon, so I walk to the kitchen and bring her a bowl of water and a tissue along with it. "Here." I hand the bowl to her. She turn to look at me, sheepishly smiling. *Thank you*, she mouths.

I leave the bowl in the kitchen, then walk back and sit next to her. She rests her head on my shoulder, and I wrap my arm around her, giving her a gentle hug. She snuggles closer, and I press a kiss on the top of her head, then rest mine on hers. "Thank you so much for everything. It would've been exhausting, making everything and that too after a whole day of work." She says, her voice barely above a whisper.

"Umm, honestly, I actually enjoyed every bit of it because I was doing it for you. The excitement of you coming here was way bigger than anything else, and when I saw you happy, it made everything totally worth it."

The wind is blowing softly, carrying a hint of chill with it. The full moon is shining brightly, its light reflecting on the waves, creating a peaceful glow. She lifts her face, and plants a soft kiss on my cheek. I squeeze her waist and pull her closer, our gaze fixed on the serene view in front of us. "The moon looks beautiful tonight." I say.

"Mhm."

"I don't know how to dance, but I can try if it makes the moment more romantic." I extend my hand to her, and she places hers in mine. We step inside, and I pull the drapes shut. "Just a second," I say, reaching for the table lamp and flicking it on. I didn't want to turn the main lights on and the table lamp lights up the room just enough, while maintaining the intimacy of the moment.

"I hope you aren't gonna step on my toes." She smirks.

"I'm not that terrible." I snort, then twirl her in close, placing my arms on her waist. I dial down the volume and play the romantic hits playlist on spotify.

She places her hands on my shoulder and we sway to the music, slow and intimately close. Our eyes are locked, and her body fits mine perfectly. She then leans in and rests her face on my chest. She is warm, soft, and the way her cheeks brushes against my chest makes me smile. I can feel her breathing, steady and calm, like the world outside has just melted away.

I pull her even closer, one hand slowly moving down her back and the other still on her waist. Her breath hitches, and it feels like the world has paused just for a second. It's not about the music or steps anymore—it's just us, here, now.

I lean in a little, my lips close to her temple, and my voice soft, almost a whisper. "Stay close to me."

She doesn't say anything, but I feel her hand slide up to my neck, fingers lightly tracing the line of my jaw. She pulls back just enough to look at me, her eyes soft, her gaze lingering, and in that moment everything else fades away. The time was frozen or it was running at a pace higher than usual. It just didn't matter.

I lean in further such that our foreheads touch, our eyes closing instinctively for a second. My lips brush against hers. She slides her hand up to my hair, her fingers gently tugging, and we kiss.

Our kiss deepens with each passing moment, our lips briefly pulling apart to catch our breath before meeting again. Our eyes lock for a split second, and without thinking, I slide my hand down and lift her up in my arms. She instinctively wraps her legs around my waist. While my hands are wrapped around her, she pulls our faces closer with hers.

I pull back a little and she holds my gaze. Without breaking eye contact, I press my lips on her cheek, gently tracing down to her jawline, then back up, moving toward her ear. She lets out a moan as I lightly nip her earlobe, then moving down, gently kissing the soft skin of her neck and her shoulder.

I pull back again and watch her for a moment. Her eyes soft, and sparkling. So I lean in and kiss them, then place a kiss on her forehead and kiss her lips again. I was breathing hard, and so was she, so we rest our forehead against each other's as we breathed.

She leans in, wrapping her arms tightly around my neck and burying her face on my neck. I pull her closer as if there was any space left between us.

"I missed you so much." She mumbles on my neck.

16
Chapter Sixteen

We lay on the bed, with Anya lying on her back, looking at the ceiling and I'm lying beside her, popped up on my elbow, my head resting in my hand as I watch her. It has been quiet between us for a while—just the sound of us breathing.

I let my fingers trace the line of her jaw, brushing lightly against her soft skin, slowly moving towards her cheeks, and gently caressing them. She leans into it, just a little and closes her eyes. To be honest, I just can't get enough of this—her reaction to the simplest of things, her breath hitching when I do something as small as this.

"You know, I could stare at you all day," I say quietly, my voice barely above a whisper.

She chuckles. "You're ridiculous."

"I know." I reply with a grin.

She shifts slightly, her eyes fully on me. "You're lucky I like you."

I lean in to her and press a kiss on her forehead. "I'm lucky to have you." My hand still on her cheek. I gently slide it down, brushing over her lips with my thumb in slow, soft strokes. "Ouch! What was that for?" I exclaim, as she bites my finger.

"It was getting tickly."

"Uhuh! Let me show you what a real tickle looks like." And with that, I slide my hand to her waist and tickle her.

She starts to jump on the bed like a fish out of water. "No stop! Anything but this." She says in between her laughs, trying to hold my hand to stop. "Please stop."

"Okay. How about this?" I climb on top of her and lean in, planting soft kisses on her lips. She places one of her hands on my chest and the other around my neck. Her lips part as I gently nibble on the side of her lower lip and tug it slightly with my teeth.

She slides her palm inside my t-shirt and traces her fingers along my skin, leaving a trail of goosebumps with it. Her breath hitches as I kiss her neck, slowly tracing down to her shoulder. She tilts her face to her right, licking her lip at the spot where I bit her, then she slides her hand that was wrapped around my neck down, slipping it under my t-shirt, slowly pulling it higher, and exposing my torso. Our eyes meet for a moment and I remove my t-shirt, then gently slide my hand under her. Her hands glide over my chest as I lean down towards her and our lips meet in a passionate kiss.

I reach for the small metal zipper on the back of her dress and slowly pull it down, revealing more of her soft skin below her neck. I could feel her pulse quickening beneath my mouth as I slide my hand down to her thigh. She buries her fingers in my hair and tug them, letting out a deep breath as I plant kisses along her collarbone.

With a gentle tug, she pulls my face closer to hers and gives me a long, lingering kiss. She then pushes me back, her eyes never leaving mine as she slowly sit's up and gestures for me roll over. I follow her lead and watch as she climbs on me, straddling my waist.

I place my hands on her thighs to support her weight as she looks down on me with intense eyes. Then, with a slow movement, she runs her palm down my chest and abs, causing shivers to run through my body.

For a few moments, we hold each other's gaze before she slides her dress above her head and tosses it to the side of the bed. "*Fuck!*" I whisper under my breath. She then leans forward, planting kisses along my abs before moving up to my chest and then my neck.

She pulls back a little, bringing her face in front of mine. My mouth goes dry, looking in her eyes. Her hair falls around my face like a curtain, making sure my only focus is her face. She holds my gaze for a few brief moments, her eyes intense but kind of fragile, like there's something she wants to say but can't. Then, she leans in, and there's a subtle glimmer of tear in her eyes. I reach up, cupping her face in my palms, wanting to know what's going on. But she takes my hand and move it to her back. She brushes her nose against mine, and I can feel her breath, warm and shaky. "Not now," she says and then presses her lips on mine, but this time it's different. It's as if she's trying to soothe her pain out with this kiss. I wrap my arms around her, hugging her and kiss her back with equal intensity.

She straightens herself, her gaze fixed on my chest. I know something's bothering her. I place my palms on her waist, moving my thumb in soft strokes. "Hey," I say. "You okay?"

She holds my gaze but only for a moment, then looks away. "Yeah-yeah." She says, looking at the curtains.

I sit up and gently place my palm on her face, tilting it so she looks at me. "Tell me," I say, with a subtle nod. She shifts a little, avoiding my touch, and I can feel her body getting tense. She's pulling away, and it makes my chest tighten, even though I know I can't force her to open up. Her lips are pressed into a thin line and her eyes look like they're trying to hold back a lot of emotions.

I watch her for a moment, trying to make sense of the distance in her eyes. She looks so lost, and it bothers me more than I can admit. "Did I do something wrong?" I ask.

"No," she shakes her head. Then, without warning, she suddenly falls forward, burying her face into my chest. My breath catches in my throat, and I freeze for a second. I could feel her body trembling, her sobs coming in ragged bursts.

I don't know what's wrong. I don't know why she's crying, and as much as I want to know what's bothering her so much, I want her to feel at ease first. So I wrap my arms around her, and let her cry.

Her hands clutch at me, and I can feel her pain, but I don't say anything, instead I pull her closer. "I'm so sorry…" Her voice barely above a whisper. My heart tightens.

"Shh…hey, there's nothing to apologize for," I murmur, pressing my lips to her hair, and then I place my hand on the back of her head, slowly running my fingers through her hair, stroking it slowly. "I'm here for you. Just breathe."

"I'm not sorry about now," she says, her words catching me off guard, and I pull back a little, just enough to see her face clearly. She looks up at me, her eyes bloodshot, and her expressions raw and vulnerable. I could feel a lump form in my throat, so I stay silent, letting her continue.

"I'm sorry for that day—I saw you that day. I saw you in the morning, also before walking out of that gate." She says, her voice shaky. "And it's been eating me up ever since. I saw you catching your breath. I knew you were hurting but I just… couldn't do anything except for hurting you more."

She pulls back slightly, placing her palms on my chest, avoiding my gaze. Tears continue to fall from her eyes, as she takes a shaky breath, trying to gather herself before speaking again. "I wanted you to hate me, and that was the only way I thought I could protect you, so I did what I did but then I saw you fall on your knees and that was when I realises that I didn't do the right thing. Maya told me that you'd be okay and it is for the better, but I knew that what I did wasn't me protecting you—I was the one hurting you."

"I could never hate you." My voice barely above a whisper.

"Why?" she whimpers, then rest her forehead above my heart. "Why would you even wanna be with me when I've hurt you so much?"

"Cause, I love you." I press my lips on the top of her head.

She finally looks up into my eyes. "Why?"

"Cause, you're worth every pain in this world. You're like the sunshine in my otherwise gloomy life. You're the reason I look forward to waking up each day, and there's nothing in this world that makes me happier than seeing you happy. I love you so damn much."

"A part of me always wished you could hate me—maybe take revenge or something. At least then, I'd feel a little less guilty about what I did." Her voice low, but a little less shaky.

"I wanted you back in my life, and I thought the only way to make that happen was to work hard and do something good with my life, so your parents wouldn't have to worry about you being happy with me."

"Stop, you're making me cry more."

"Oh...sorry! *Soft kitty, warm kitty*"

"That's for when you're sick." She replies, immediately catching on the reference.

"How about I squeeze you in my arms?"

"Mhm."

She presses her face on my chest, letting out a deep, steady breath. "I really wanted you, you know? Every day, I tried to hold it together during the day, but every night, it all felt apart. I'd lie awake for hours, crying. I just needed to hear your voice again, even if it was for a minute. There were so many times I almost picked up my phone to call you, but I couldn't." She brushes her nose on my chest. "I couldn't say anything to my parents because well, you know. I couldn't say anything to you because I knew I was the one who hurt you. And with Maya, I stopped sharing after a while, because it started to feel like everything was always about me with her."

"I used to feel like I was the reason everyone close to me got hurt, and in a way, I guess I was. But I always wished someone would just come up to me and say, even if it was just to say it, 'it's not your fault.' " She says.

"It wasn't your fault." I say.

"You're ridiculous." She almost smiles.

"Oh I missed it." I say and she nods up. "Your smile." She presses her lips in a thin line. "I know what you're doing."

"Mhm!"

I place my hands on her waist, moving my fingers slowly, teasing her with light tickles. She bites her lip, trying not to smile, but eventually she couldn't hold it in any longer and with that, I roll her over on her back and lie on top of her. "It looks really beautiful on you, Ana." I say.

She grabs a few strands of my hair, twirling them in between her fingers. "Not fair," she says, her voice lighter now.

I gently caress the strands of her hair on her forehead, then after gently placing a soft kiss on her nose, I brush mine against hers. "I wish I could keep you in my arms and never let you go." I whisper in her ear. She snuggles her cheeks against my stubble.

"This looks like a nice spot." She says as she kisses my shoulder.

"For what... Ouch!" I wince as she bites me.

"You looked so biteable. Now love me." She says with a childlike grin.

"I am loving you." I look at her. She's squints her eyes, giving a mischievous look. "Oh you mean... I got it."

I lean against her, pressing my lips at the base of her neck. Then moving down, I plant kisses at her naval, taking in the sweet scent of her perfume mixed with her natural scent. She gasps as I move upwards, slowly trailing kisses along her stomach. Our eyes lock for a brief moment as I slide one of my hand under her and the other hand caressing the insides of her thigh.

Gently, I kiss the top of her breasts then slowly trace her cleavage. She runs her fingers through my hair, guiding me to where she wants me. I reach for the hook under her and unhook the clasp of her bra, then slide it away. She moans quietly, arching her back and pressing herself closer to me as I place kisses on her breasts.

A soft sigh escapes her lips as she tangles her fingers in my hair. Her heartbeat quickening beneath my lips, growing faster with each touch. I try to lift my head to kiss along her neck, but she grips my hair tightly, silently begging me to keep focusing on her breasts. And so I do, as if my life depended on it.

Our lips meet in a passionate, longing kiss—her hands gliding over my torso. Slowly, she moves her fingers down, tugging at the button of my jeans. I look into her eyes. Her gaze is intense, like it's pulling me in deeper, daring me to hold my ground. I can feel the weight of it as the silence stretches between us, thick and unspoken, yet somehow clear.

She nods to her right with a subtle shift of her head, like she's made up her mind. I lean down and place a kiss on her lips then reach into the drawer of the bedside table and grab a condom, then lie down on top of her.

The air is filled with the sound of heavy breathing. A tear slips down her cheek, and I gently kiss it away. Her nails dig into my back. I pull her close, and we just melt into each other.

ᗰᗰᗰ

The sunlight pierced through my eyes, turns out we didn't completely shut the drapes last night. So with half open eyes I try to get out of the bed to fix them, but I couldn't. There was something on my hand, stopping me from moving. I turn my head and it was Anya.

Anya was deep asleep, with her face resting on my shoulder. Her hands rested on my chest and her leg was entwined with mine. Well, this is a feeling I'm not really familiar with, but it kind of feel really incredible. There's this quiet calm, this sense of peace, and a kind of love that just feels like it's here to stay. I have dreamt about this moment for so long and now that I'm living in it, it's everything I imagined—and so much more than I expected.

So, instead of waking her up, I gently snuggle with her and pull up the blanket to cut off the light, then doze off to sleep.

My eyes open after a while as Anya softly mumbles something in her sleep. I reach for my phone on the bedside table to check the time. The screen showed nine fifteen—I haven't slept for so long in year and to be honest I haven't had such peaceful sleep in ages.

Anya's hand was still on my chest. So I slowly lift it, making sure I don't wake her up and also slide my hand out which was under her. As I do, she let's out a soft sigh and I quickly pat her head softly, hoping I don't wake her completely.

I roll out of the bed, but instead of walking out of the room, I stand there, watching her sleep. She looks like an angel from heaven, her features delicate and peaceful. I can't explain how much I want to kiss her right now, but I fear that would wake her up and I don't want her to wake up until everything's ready. So, I silently admire her for few more moments, then slowly pull up the blanket over her and tuck it in around her shoulders.

The breakfast was almost ready, so I walk back to the room to wake her up. But she was already awake, sitting on the bed wrapping the blanket around her. She smiles as I walk in, her smile soft and unguarded. Her eyes are still half-lidded with sleep, but there's warmth in them.

"Sleep well?" I ask as I place a kiss on her forehead. She nods.

"Give me your tee." She says, her voice still wrapped with the softness of sleep. I turn towards my closet, when she tugs my t-shirt with her fingers. "The one you're wearing." I look back at her. She has a playful grin on her face, not wide but peaceful, so I slide out my t-shirt over my head and pass it to her. "Well, someone's been working out. Now turn around."

"Glad you noticed or I was about to flex a bit. And by the way, I thought you liked it when I look at you."

She rolls her eyes. "You've used all your luck yesterday. Now turn around, I have to change."

"Okay-okay. Bathroom's on the right." I say and walk out of the room to check on the toast.

I've got in front of me scrambled eggs, avocado toast and a couple of pancakes stacked high, and a mug of coffee. I balance everything on the tray carefully, making sure nothing spills, then head back towards the bedroom.

As I push open the door, I pause for a second, an overwhelming feeling of happiness coursing through me as I see her walk in the room wearing my t-shirt. The t-shirt looked too big on her, falling below the top of her thigh. I have no idea how she does it, but she somehow she manages to make me gasp for my breath no matter what she's wearing.

"Breakfast, my lady." I lift the tray up a little, showing her. "There's avocado toast, some scrambled eggs and pan..." my voice trails off as I smell my body wash. "Did you just take a shower? How long have I been in the kitchen?"

"Yeah, just a quick one. Why?"

"Umm, I was hoping, you know, maybe—do it together."

She raises herself on to her toes and presses a kiss on my cheek, "maybe next time."

I walk to the bed and carefully place the tray at the centre, then sit on the edge of the bed. She walks close, standing between my legs, slowly caressing my hair. "Is this how our mornings are going to look when we live together or is it just for today?"

I grin, my palm softly gliding over her waist. "Well, it could be, but I wouldn't want to spoil you too much."

She snorts. "Huh! I'll be just fine. I just want to know whether you'll be this thoughtful every day or was this your one and only perfect boyfriend moment?"

I snuggle up my face in her stomach and wrap my arms around her. "Um...well, if I do this every day, I might run out of new ways to impress you."

"I guess so, but it's a good thing you're cute. I won't ever be bored of you."

I look up at her. "Really! I mean, that's all I have?"

"You're the one who ran out of ideas. Not me." She smirks.

"That's being mean."

"Aww!" She says, wrapping her hands around me. "I love you." She then gets out of my grasp and settles beside me, grabbing a fork and sticking it in one of the pancakes, she transfers it to a plate before handing it to me. Then, she serves herself a portion and takes a bite. "These are nice."

"Thanks." I say.

"Can I ask you something? If you're okay with it." She hesitates, taking a sip of coffee. "Umm, never mind."

"Don't be foolish. You don't need to overthink before speaking—not with me." I say, nudging her.

"Umm...okay." She pauses for a few second and I wait for her to say. "How do you manage all this? You have your own car, you live in this beautiful apartment, an apartment that has a sea view in not one but two balconies, that too all by yourself. I mean, Shruti and I share the rent, and it still takes a significant chunk of our salary, and then there are other expenses like food, maid, bills and stuff. You're just twenty four."

I look up, pretending to think, then say "Umm, first off, I don't have a maid or anything. I cook and take care of the chores myself. Secondly, living alone makes it easier to keep things tidy, and I rarely have anyone over—just my parents, sometimes. So I end up saving a bit of expenses. And being a management consultant is pretty decent paying job, plus there are bonuses."

"But still, this view must cost a lot and how do you manage your time, doing all the chores along with the job?" She interrupts.

"I'm telling you, wait."

"Oh-okay, sorry."

"Don't be. So the thing is—I manage my time by doing things as I go, like I would not leave the dishes in the sink, instead wash them right away... you get the picture. And then I've kinda assigned spot for everything in my head, and I make sure I put things back in the same place. That way, I don't waste extra time picking stuff up and cleaning up later." I pause and take a sip of coffee. "Next, management consultancy is my main job, but it isn't my only source of income. I've been investing my money for a while now, so that's another and then there's freelance work. Am I boring you too much?"

"No-no, I like it. So, you do freelance work too?"

"Yeah, you remember I was good with computers back in the day. It started as a hobby—developing websites for other people, and I haven't stopped it. Right now, I develop websites for small businesses, maintain them, you know doing some tweaks and handling back-end updates."

"That is a lot of things to do in a day, week, maybe a year."

"Umm, it kinda has become a habit now."

"How the fuck do you manage time?"

"The goal is to keep it simple. And plus I don't have many friends, or go to parties or clubs. I have a boring life."

"Are you kidding me?" She playfully shoves me, rolling her eyes. "You're really hard working, and smart."

"Thanks. I try to." I hold her palm between mine, gently rubbing it. "Can I say something?"

"Go ahead."

"I know things weren't good with us in the past, but I had this feeling, that everything will be alright in the end. I never gave up the hope of us living together."

She gets closer and hugs me. "And I love you a million times more for that." She whispers in my ear. "And for everything. I don't think I even deserve any of this."

"Hey!" I pull her face in front of mine. "Why would you say something like that?"

"I don't know. It's just..." She was saying but I interrupt her by placing my finger on her lips.

"You know, I never knew happiness like I know it with you. I was a completely different person before I met you and you know that, but you helped me be better, be considerate, and most of all, what it really means to love someone. I don't think I'd be half the man I am today if it wasn't for you. And you know, this beautiful, kind and caring heart of yours." I say, placing my palm over her heart.

"But that's no reason to touch my boobs." She chuckles, with a childlike innocence in her eyes.

"And also this sense of humour you have." And with that, I slide my hand inside her t-shirt and lightly tickle her. She jumps on my lap, laughing, while I keep tickling her. She presses her lips on mine to stop me from tickling, and it worked like a charm because soon, I forgot about everything but her soft lips.

She pulls back a little. "The plates," she says and frees herself from my arms, sliding out of my lap. I balance the plates and the mug on the tray and take them back to the kitchen, leaving them in the sink, then walk back to the room.

17

Chapter Seventeen

"I think, by tweaking our original strategy a bit, we can have an additional one percent savings in overall cost of the project. Here, have a look." I propose. I was in the conference room with other team members, discussing the strategy for reducing the cost of a product.

"That seems to be a reasonable estimate." The team lead says. "How about we call it a day and pitch it to the client in tomorrow's meeting?"

We nod then get up from our seats. The team lead walks up to me and places his hand on my shoulder. "Good job Aahil." He says and I smile.

I walk back to my desk and slump on my chair. It feels good to be appreciated in front of everyone but I think it would feel more rewarding when I get to see the actual result. But the way our company works is we tell the clients the strategy, and help them implement it, then move on to next client. We hardly know how well our strategy worked. And that is why I want to start something of my own.

ᗐᗐᗐ

"It appears that Aahil left you breathless that day." I was on the phone with Anya, lying on my bed, my gaze fixed at the ceiling above.

"Since when did you start talking about yourself in third person?" She replies.

"Ah! I thought I should try something new." I say pulling up the blanket and turning to my right. "I know you're smiling."

"No, I'm not."

"Liar."

"Okay, but it's not because of what you said."

"I'll still take that as because of me." I chuckle. "I wish you were here."

"Ah, I know, I'm irresistible—I'm like the drug that gets you hooked the first time."

"Look at you, being all me." I say and I know she's grinning. "Now don't tell me it wasn't fun."

"Yeah, it kinda was." She says. "Do you remember the time when we used to talk about our future—like living together stuff?"

"Yeah, like it was yesterday." I sigh, looking at our present situation, because we still kind of have no idea if our parents would approve of us. "That was the best part of my day."

"Yeah, mine too." She says. I could literally hear her sigh. "But you still fell asleep."

"Hey! That's not fair. It only happened five times... okay maybe six... definitely not more than seven."

"Yeah, sure."

"It was a good time, isn't it? Telling about our day, me cracking some lame jokes, you trying to muffle your laugh by biting your pillow, you not speaking much and hiding under the blanket, so no one hears..."

"Yet you still understood me." She completes my sentence. "Come to think of it, your jokes were lame, but back then, I had to bite my pillow really hard. You know, our maid used to think that I chew clothes in my sleep. Although, if you'd tell the same jokes now, I swear I'd leave you."

"Hey! Why would you even say anything about leaving?" The thought of her leaving just hits too hard.

"I didn't mean it that way."

"No, just don't."

"Okay-okay, sorry. I won't. Now happy?" She says.

"Yeah," I reply.

ᗡᗡᗡ

I ring the doorbell, my hands sweating slightly as I stand on the porch. My parents have always supported me in everything I do, and I couldn't feel more fortunate to have such incredible parents. But when it comes to relationships and love, they are a bit old-school.

My mom opens the door, her face practically glowing when she sees me. "Hey, sweetie," she says, throwing her arms around me like I'm still a kid. "How are you?"

"Hi mom." I say hugging her back. "Never been better."

She rushes back to the kitchen to stir the puree she was making and I follow her. The smell is making me hungrier than I already am, but I need to stay focused. I've something more important to talk about today.

She places down the spoon and looks at me. "What's going on? You look like you have something to say?"

I laugh, rubbing the back of my neck. "Well, yeah, there is something."

Her gaze now fixed at the container, slowly stirring the puree, then bring forward a spoonful of gravy. "Your dad will be here soon." She says.

"No, I kinda wanted to talk to you first."

She scoops up a tablespoon of gravy and holds it out to me. "Taste it," She says. "Is it about a girl?" She adds, her gaze back towards the container.

"It's good. And no... um, yeah. How do you know it?"

"Let's just say that I'm your mother and I can read it on your face." She puts the lid on the container and then turns off the flame. "And lately, you've been a little more busy than usual."

I don't know what to say. "Does dad know?"

"He chooses not to say, but yes."

I'm trying to read between the lines, but she stays so calm and composed, it's hard to tell if she agrees or not. "So, you guys against it?" I finally dare to ask.

"We are…" She is interrupted by the doorbell. "That must be your dad."

"I'll open the gate." I say, heading for the door, my mind screaming, *please don't be against us.* "Hey dad." I say and hug him.

He hugs me back with a smile. "Good to see you. When did you come?" He asks.

"A few minutes ago." I reply.

"Dinner's ready." Mom calls out from the kitchen.

We take our seats at the table, my mom serving us dinner. "So, how's everything?" Dad asks.

"Everything's good." I say stalling, trying to sound casual as I have to focus on finishing my food fast. The thing is that I eat my food slow, really slow and dad had pointed it out several times before, so today, I don't want anything to come up in between the actual conversation I'm about to have.

As I have eaten more than half of the food on my plate, I look at mom, hoping she would initiate the conversation with my dad. My dad usually is my go to person to talk to about anything and everything, but this, it's different. And knowing how they used to frown upon on relationships in the past, the thought of their disapproval scares me. And that is why I wanted to talk to my mother first because it is well known, that mothers have a relatively softer heart.

"Aahil wants to say something." My mom says. Clearly not how I was expecting her to start this conversation.

Mom and dad exchange a quick glance, then look at me. "Yeah, what is it?"

I try to gather myself up but somehow the more I try, the lessor strength I had. "There's this girl he's seeing and he want to marry her." Mom says while I was still nowhere close to speaking.

No-no! That's way too direct. She didn't even bother to sugar coat it at all. "I didn't say anything about marriage." I blurt out, and I know I'm making it worse but I just can't help it.

"So you don't want to marry her?" She raises an eyebrow.

"No! I want to. I just..."

"I just?"

"Thought you might have eased into it a bit more." I say, looking at her face which never did lose its composure as if she was already expecting this conversation. I look towards my father who haven't said a word and judging by his expression, he doesn't seem angry, which is a relief.

"Okay. I am seeing this girl. Her name is Anya. We've been seeing each other for a couple months and yes I wanna marry her."

"Few months?" Dad asks.

"Um, we dated before." I reply.

"Same girl from school?" Mom asks.

"Yeah, but how do you know that?" I ask puzzled. Looks like I'm not the one who was going to surprise them but they were.

"We've all been there." She says.

"But you didn't like the idea of dating, why didn't you say something?"

"We were gonna, but your studies were never affected by it."

"How long have you known?"

"I think it was about a month before your final exams, but we didn't want to mess with your focus, so we decided to hold off until they were done. You aced your exams, and by then, you were still with her. That's when we realised it wasn't just some fling—you were serious about her. So, we figured we'd just let things be." My mom tells the whole story, and suddenly, all the little lies I told to sneak around and see her come flooding back.

"I'm sorry, you know, for lying." I say, embarrassed.

"It's okay. We understand." She says.

"But how are you guys so cool about it? You use to tell me to stay away from it." I ask.

"We never wanted to tell you who you should or shouldn't marry," my dad says, his voice calm and firm. "It's your life, after all. But we always wanted to protect you, to make sure you're making choices that help you grow, not hold you back."

He pauses and leans back a little. "One should learn to take care of themselves first before they can really take care of someone else. Teenage years can be tricky, and relationships can sometimes pull your focus away from what matters. But with you... it's been different. And if she can help you do that, maybe it's something worth supporting."

"Look honey, it's always been your decision who to be with, but we'd like to get to know her too." Mom says.

I sit there, absorbing every word, processing it carefully, and doing my best to keep my heart from bursting with happiness. "She's great. You'll love her." I say.

"So, how about you invite her for dinner and introduce us." My mother says. She seems excited and I just don't have enough words to express how happy I am. Dad's phone rings and he excuses himself. "So can I see her?"

"Yeah!" I grin, then walk up to her and hug her. I couldn't wait to tell Anya—she too will be beyond happy. I hand her my phone with Anya's photo on the screen.

"She's really pretty." She says, her eyes still fixed on the screen. "Am I allowed to slide or I'd end up looking at something I don't wanna see."

"You can slide." I grin.

ᕱᕱᕱ

"How about you start paying me some rent. You've been living in my mind rent free for far too long." I text Anya, then put the phone next to me while I sit on my couch, working on a website that has already taken most of my day.

I pick my phone after an hour, but there was still no message from her. Why is she taking so long to reply? Since there was no text from her, I toss the phone aside and continue to work.

My phone pings after a while and I grab it. "I was gonna ask you the same. By the way, I miss you too," Her message appears on the screen, making me smile.

"So, how about I come and pick you up and we can spend rest of the day together." I couldn't control my excitement any more, I have to tell her the good news. It would be a sight to watch her when I break it to her.

I was so lost in my thoughts that I didn't notice her message and as my eyes fall on the screen, my face falls with it. "I'm so sorry, but I am out with Shruti. She had to buy something. How about tomorrow?"

I don't think I can wait that long. Each passing second is a test to my patience, but I don't want to tell her over the phone. I was so sure that I'd meet her but I guess, that's not happening anymore. "Fine, but don't duck me tomorrow."

I cross my arm behind my head, my gaze on the wall in front of me. "How should I tell her?" I ask myself. It's big, it's important, and it needs to be perfect. After all this time, it feels like we finally have something more than hope. After all we are half way there.

How about I take her to the hills? I mean, all this time we have been to beaches, because... Mumbai. But we could try hills for a change. I have to get her something. Flowers or chocolates won't do this time. I have to get her something meaningful, which she could keep with her for a long time.

I grab the keys and slip my phone in my pocket, then head out of my apartment.

The streets are a little busier than usual due to evening traffic—everything seems to move faster. Maybe they are, or maybe it's just because of my excitement. I can't give her a ring because we're not getting married yet, so that's out of option. I could get her a necklace.

I step inside the jewellery shop, and the door automatically closes behind me. The place is calm, with not much rush. I spot a salesperson near the counter, adjusting some display cases.

"Good evening." She greets with a polite smile. I nod back, trying to shake off the nervous energy that's buzzing inside me. I haven't done it before but there's always firsts.

"I'm looking for something special. A necklace." I say, my voice steadier than I feel.

"Looking for a gift, I take it?"

"Yeah," I reply. "Something elegant. Simple but... beautiful."

She nods, leading me towards a display case near the back. The soft light above cast a warm glow on the pieces, making everything look beautiful.

She opens the case, showing several options. I glance at each of the necklace, but none of them feels... like her. I want to get Anya something which she would want. And that is when I spot it.

It's delicate-simple, but with a quiet elegance that makes it stand out. There are three unblemished diamonds in the pendent, and the chain is thin and sleek—just the right balance. It's beautiful. It's perfect.

I hold the necklace in my palm, trying to imagine how it would look on her. "How much for this one?" I ask the salesperson.

ᗡᗡᗡ

It has already been too late as I enter my apartment and I want to just fall flat on the bed and sleep, but my mind is way too excited for tomorrow. I take out the box from my pocket and place it on the bedside table, then gently opening it, I take out the necklace on my palm. The diamonds on the necklace shimmers as the lights reflects through them. A rush of emotions sweeps through me as I look at them, trying to believe that this is actually happening. All those years of waiting and longing has led us to this moment. "This time we'll be together Anya." I whisper under my breath.

I place the necklace safely, back in the box then reach for my phone in the pocket. She hasn't seen my last message yet. How long are they going to shop? It's already late, and I am getting too impatient.

She has always been fond of shopping, a lot. The last time I remember going with her, we ended up staying for four hours at the mall, walking from one outlet to another.

"Hey, please take second half of the day off from work. I'll pick you up at two." I text her, but the message doesn't deliver. So, I leave the phone on the bed and then walk towards my closet to change into some comfortable sleepwear.

The phone buzzes and I grab it right away. "Looks like someone's really missing me." Anya message pops up.

"I am. Can you take off from work tomorrow? And also sleep here at night?" I text back.

My phone rings and I pick up the call. "Hey, you okay?" She asks, her voice soft.

"Yeah, I just miss you so much." My voice low.

"Don't hang up. Give me a sec, let me change," She says quickly.

"Okay."

She comes back on the phone a few moments later. "You there?"

"Yeah, I'm here."

"Are you in bed?"

"Uh-huh."

"Alright, now pull over the blanket and grab a pillow. I'll see you at two tomorrow. Now let's sleep together, okay?"

"I love you Anya." I say.

"I love you too Aahil. Now... shh, Sleep."

ᐳᐳᐳ

"Shruti, I've got to show you something." I lean against her desk, glancing around casually to make sure no one's watching, then pull out the box from my jacket and place it in front of her on her desk.

"Yes!" She exclaims, then grins. "But hey, at least get down on one knee, will you?"

"Why?" I ask, but then it clicks and I can't help but laugh at myself. "This isn't for you."

"Oh, you are breaking my heart." She says, being dramatic. "So, what's this?"

"Open it. I got it for Anya. Do you think she'll like it?" The excitement I have is clearly reflecting in my voice.

She opens the box and take out the necklace, holding the pendent in her palm. "It's really beautiful. So beautiful that I'm kinda jealous of her right now." She says, her gaze shifting back and forth on pendent and me.

"Do you think she'll like it?" I ask her again.

"She'll love it." She says and places it back in the box. "So, what's the occasion?"

"My parents agreed." I grin.

"That's great news. I'm so happy for you." She says, her voice full of excitement. "When did this happen?"

"This weekend, I talked to my parents about her and they agreed. They've even invited her on dinner."

"Look at you, taking a girl to your home. I'm so happy for you guys." She nudges me playfully. "Does she know?"

"No, and that's on you. You have an awful timing."

"That I know. You'll have to be a little more specific."

"I was thinking of picking her up from your apartment but you took her shopping. But that gave me..."

"What shopping?" She interrupts, looking a little confused.

"You guys went shopping yesterday, right?"

"She told you?" She exclaims. "That's so not cool. You don't get to keep track of my life. Is there anything else she told you?" She says, raising an eyebrow.

"Should she have told me something?" I furrow my brows. "Now I'm kinda intrigued."

"You can try but she won't tell."

"Oh, we'll see." I say with a mischievous smile on my face. "Anyway, I couldn't pick her up last night, so I started thinking about how to tell her. I'm taking second half of the day off and then I'll take her to tiger point. A little road trip, some hills and sunset."

"That sound like a plan."

"Yeah!" I say. "I'm gonna ask her about your secret, you know that right?"

"Yeah-yeah"

ᗞᗞᗞ

I pull up to the gate of Anya's office, then reach for my phone in my pocket to let her know I'm here. "Waiting for you at the gate." I text her.

"Be there in a minute." She texts back. I can already feel the excitement buzzing in my chest, my gaze fixed at the entrance.

A few minutes pass. I tap on the steering wheel absentmindedly, then look up when I see her stepping out of the building. There she is, looking effortlessly stunning again, wearing a burgundy dress paired with black stocking and heels. She's holding her handbag in one hand, the other adjusting her sunglasses as she scans the parking lot.

I smile to myself, then climb out of the car, walking towards her. "No, not here." She says as I take a step closer. So I take a step back towards the car and open the door for her. She slides in the front seat.

"So," she begins, turning her body towards me, "are you going to tell me where we're going, or do I have to keep guessing?"

I chuckle, pulling the car on the road, driving safely amidst traffic. "You'll see soon enough. Patience, babe."

I sneak a few glances of her from the corner of my eye, unable to resist the urge to admire her. She hides her infectious smile behind her fingers, her elbow propped on the hand resting across her waist. "Okay, stop it now or let me drive. I want both of us in one piece."

"Stop what now? And if I let you drive, we surely won't reach in one piece."

"You think women can't drive safe?"

"Women can. You, can't." I chuckle.

"Uh-huh! So stop staring at me and focus on the road." She says.

"Is it my fault that you look absolutely phenomenal?" I gently reach for her hand and entwine my fingers with her, slowly pulling it closer and kissing it.

She blushes and leans towards me, wrapping her arms around my left hand, she then rests her temple on my shoulder. "Is something special?" She says, her voice soft.

"I missed you so much and I wanted to spend time with you." I confess, my voice filled with longing and sincerity. She smiles and places a kiss on my shoulder before shifting her gaze on the road ahead.

18
Chapter Eighteen

"You should have at least given me a heads up that we are coming here. I am wearing heels." She complains climbing out of the car.

"What's the fun in that?" I hold her wrist and pull her towards me, sliding my arms around her waist. "It was overdue at the time when you said 'not here'." She looks up with a smile, her cheeks turning pink. I press my lips against hers, and kiss her slowly. "And this is its interest."

"Why do you work in a consulting firm? You would've been a mighty fine banker." She says.

I place my thumb on her lips softly. "I could do this all day but we gotta go see the view, so let's go before the sun sets."

"Hey, do you wanna keep your bag in the car?" I ask her, to which she nods in agreement.

"Let me take out my phone first." She searches for her phone in the bag before handing it to me. I take the bag from her and keep it inside the car.

While I was still looking towards the car, I subtly put my hand in the pocket, just to reassure that I haven't lost the box, and it was. So I turn around towards her and hold her hand. She swiftly moves her fingers and entangle them between mine.

It wasn't too windy, but you could still feel the cool air brushing against your face. We walked on the pathway towards the Tiger's point to watch the sun set behind the hills. Well, it wasn't actually watching the sun set because of the clouds blocking the view but we could still see the lights shimmering behind the hill and the clouds on the top of the hill looked like their golden crown.

"You wanna eat something?" I ask her as I see a few stalls on the aisle of the road.

"I am already drooling over that pink cotton candy. They don't sell it in the city." She says, her gaze still fixed on the cotton candy. "Never mind, it's a lot of sugar." She closes her eyes, then look the other way.

"Why? Let's take it. Promise, I won't tell anyone."

"No. Please don't... I am trying to control myself. I don't wanna gain weight." She turns towards me to avoid getting tempted by the cotton candy.

"Oh, c'mon. Wait here, I'll be back." I walk towards the stall and buy the cotton candy, then walk back to her. "Here. You can gain as much weight as you want, just promise me you won't look like a beach ball." I chuckle and she pushes me back. She takes the cotton candy from my hand and hands me her phone. I keep her phone in my pocket, while she tears up the packet and takes a bite with a childlike grin. Moving to the next counter, I grab a parcel of cheese and corn Maggie.

I turn around and look at her eating the cotton candy. Her eyes sparkled with innocence, and her face glow in golden as the rays from the sun fell on her face. It is moments like this, when I see her happy, carefree, seeing the innocent child she is, makes me feel very happy. It feels like my heart gets so excited that it beats a few extra times, making me fall for her even more. I walk towards her and slide my hand around her waist and we started walking on the pathway.

"I can't walk anymore. Let's sit here." She says pointing towards an empty spot on a big rock.

I hold her hand and steady her, then sit next to her. The rays were turning into a shade of deep orange. "Hold my hand." I say as I open the container of maggie with my hands and I don't want her to fall off the cliff.

"I'm not gonna fall."

"Just in case if you do, take me with you." I half joke. She rolls her eyes but shifts a little towards me and wraps her arms around my bicep, then lay her face on my shoulder.

"Is this better?" She asks.

"So much better." I say as I lay my head gently on hers. We look at the hills in front of us. "Look, there's a waterfall."

She lifts her head a little and then lay it back. "Hmm." She says. I dig a fork in the container and bring it in front of her face. She takes a bite. I take another forkful and eat in silence as we both admire the beautiful green hills in front of us.

"It's beautiful." She murmurs on my neck.

"I am handsome. Not beautiful." I chuckle.

"Haha. These lame jokes will be the reason of our breakup."

"Hey! No breakup talks." I didn't even want to think of a possibility of us not being together, especially today when I'm going to give her such a great news.

"I am not gonna breakup with you ever." She tightens her arms and then place a kiss on my cheek. I dig another forkful and hold it in front of her. She takes a bite.

With her head on my shoulder, I couldn't see her face properly, so I kiss the top of her head. "You okay?" She lifts her face. I nod, touching the loose strand of hair on her, caressing it, then slowly I tuck it behind her ear. I didn't realise I was holding my breath, because the beauty my eyes were seeing, my heart wasn't able to process. Maybe I didn't notice not breathing because she was breathing air for both of us. In this moment, if I fall back, I breathe with her and if I fall forward, I die with her. In either case, my heart will be at peace.

"Where are you lost?" She snaps her fingers in front of me.

"Um, nothing." I smile, then put aside the container in my hand. "I've got something for you. Close your eyes. And no peeking. And for few moments, you kinda have to let go of my hand."

"You aren't gonna push me, right?"

"What is the matter with you?" I throw back at her.

"I'm kidding. What happened to you? Why are you annoyed?"

"I'm not annoyed. Just don't say anything about breakup or anything of that sort."

"Okay. I won't."

"Thank you. Now close your eyes." I say and she closes her eyes. I take out the box from my pocket, opening it carefully, then take out the pendent from it. "Can you turn around? Please." I extend my empty hand to her. She holds my hand and turns around. Moving closer to her, I gently move her hair aside and secure the necklace around her neck. I lean further towards her and then place a kiss on the nape of her neck.

"Can I open my eyes?" She asks, her voice low.

"One sec. Let me help you turn back towards me and then you can open my eyes." I hold her securely around her waist and she turns towards me. "Open your eyes."

She opens her eyes and her gaze falls at the pendent. She holds the pendent in her palm. Her eyes looked like they were trying to hold a storm of emotions. "Hey." I whisper softly, as her eyes start to well up with tears.

"Nothing." She says, then leaning forwards, she wraps her arms around my neck. I tighten my arms around her. "It's beautiful. Really beautiful." She whispers on the back of my neck.

"Please tell me you're not crying." I ask her to lighten her mood, but I knew she was.

"Only a little. Happy ones." She laughs. She leans back and hold the pendent again, then shifting her gaze so that her eyes meet mine, she asks "What's the occasion? Tell me now, you've built up enough suspense."

"I'll tell you but first you have to promise that you'll not jump up and down, or you'll take us both down the cliff."

"Okay, don't milk it anymore. Just tell me already."

"Okay." I pull her close and hug her tightly. "I..." I place a kiss at the corner of her mouth. "...met my parents, the day before yesterday." I kiss the same spot again. I could feel her heart starting to race faster against my chest.

"And?" Her voice breathy, full of anticipation.

"And they like you a lot." I kissed her again. "And they have asked me to bring you over for dinner." I look at her face, trying to gauge her reaction.

She frees herself and leans back. "What? Are you kidding me? Like really? Oh my god. Tell me you are not kidding. Oh my god." She keeps her palm on her mouth, not knowing how to react. I hold her tightly and try to keep us as steady as I can but I can't stop smiling, watching her reaction. "Stop smiling and tell me it's true and not some elaborate joke."

"Okay Anya look, I said take me with you if you fall, but now is really not the time to die. And this is not some joke. This is true. Can we now go to the other side and then you can jump all you want?"

"I don't wanna..." She leans forward and buries her face on my chest. I pull her closer as she starts sobbing. "I am sorry. I am so happy. I need a moment." She says in between her sobs.

"It's okay Ana. I am here." I comfort and she wraps her hands around me. Slowly, I caress her back as we sit there for a while.

The sun has set and it is only a while before the sky turns dark. Clouds have gathered too and it could rain anytime soon. "Let's go to the other side of the pathway."

She looks up at me and nods. "Pull me up. My legs are numb."

I wrap one of my hand around her back and place the other hand below her knees, trying to pick her up. "Okay, you can at least pretend to help." I say. A small smile appears on her face and she wraps her arms around my neck.

Gently, I place her down as we reach the other side of the pathway. "Now you can jump as much as you want."

"Jump? I think I'd rather kiss you." She throws her hand around my neck and stands on her tip toes. I wrap my hands around her waist, pulling her closer and as our lips were about to touch, our eyes lock in the moment. She smiles and leans in. "I love you so much. You've made me the happiest girl in the planet." She mumbles in my mouth as our kiss intensifies. It was worth waiting after all, or else I would have missed it forever.

The drops of rain falling on our cheeks bring us back from the moment we were lost in. It has started to drizzle. I pull out my jacket and hold it over our heads to prevent us from getting drenched in rain while we ran towards the car. She slows down briefly, eyeing at the cotton candy stall again, but then we sprint towards the car.

I keep the jacket above us as she opens the door and enter in the front seat of the car. "I'll be back. Lock the door." I say and immediately run towards the stall and buy another cotton candy, then run back to the car.

The jacket was completely soaked by the time I got in the car. She removes her sandals and I throw it on the back seat. "Here." I hand her the cotton candy. She is grinning ear to ear holding it, but places the packet on the dashboard. She then place her hand on my shoulder as she rises from her seat, slowly leaning towards me, while I press the button on the side of my seat to recline it, to get some extra space.

She climbs over on my seat and I push the seat back as she sits on my lap. She places her palms on my chest while I hold her thighs and pull her closer. For a few moments, we look into each other's eyes in silence.

She slowly slides her palms from my chest to my face, entangling her fingers with my hairs and leaning down, until our foreheads meet. We breathe in each other's air with our eyes closed. I pull her closer, as if there was any space left and our lips meet. "You are intoxicating." I say.

"Hmm." She breathes, and shifts on my lap, trying to get closer as our tongues meet. It started to rain heavily, but we were unbothered as we were too engrossed in ourselves.

Our lips part as we gasp for breath. Her fingers clutch my hairs as I kiss her neck, tenderly pulling the strap of her dress from her shoulder and placing kisses on her shoulders and below her neck. Lost in the moment, she leans back to unbutton the top of my shirt and the car honks. I abruptly pull her towards me such that our heads collide. I place my fingers on her forehead and caress it while we both laugh at the same time, then press our foreheads against each other.

She gives a peck on my lips and unbuttons the top of my shirt. "I wanna bite you." She slides her palm inside my shirt, then place kisses on my chest followed with a bite. "I love you. This is the best day of my life." She whispers and we kiss again.

"I can think of something that can make the day better, but for that, you'll have to sleep over at our apartment." I wink at her. She laughs and makes her way back to her seat.

"Not that it hasn't crossed my mind." She grins as I start the engine. "And by the way, why is it okay for you to talk about us breaking up and not me?"

"When did I say something like that?"

"Falling forward, death. Ring a bell?"

"I was implying that even if we fall we will be together in our last moments and one doesn't have to live without the other... Never mind, I am sorry and let's not say things like this. Today we have to celebrate."

"Yeah." She beams as I drive out of the parking.

ᗰᗰᗰ

The rain had stopped leaving a refreshing and chilly air. Once the rain stopped, Anya immediately rolled down her window and leaned towards it, resting her head on the edge and her feet rested on my lap. The chilly air flew through her hair making them sway in its direction but she seemed unbothered. Her feet were cold, and it didn't matter how much I tried to warm them by rubbing my palm on them, they were still cold.

"Ana, bring your head back inside and roll up the window. You'll catch a cold." I say, because I know if she stays like this, she'll get sick before we get back home.

"You sound like my mom." She says.

I park the car at the side of the road and take out the first aid kit from the dashboard. From the kit, I tear out some cotton and roll it into small balls, then put the box back in the cabinet. Playfully, I hold her wrist and pull her inside but she pulls me back towards her window. "Okay, you win. But if you wanna do it, take these and put them in your ears. I don't want you to catch a cold."

She smiles as she take the cotton balls from my hand, putting them in her ears. "These are the reasons I wanna marry you." She says, her words felt like they were pumping a new life in my heart. I smile, then continue to drive.

We were about to reach the city. "Tea? It will warm you up." I ask her, knowing how childishly she's been peeking out of the window the whole way here. She nods.

I park the car at a distance from the stall as there was no parking space near it. "I'll be back soon. Keep the doors locked." I say as I climb out of the car and walk towards the tea stall.

The phone in my pocket starts to vibrate as I reach the stall. "Two cups." I say as I take out the phone from my pocket. It wasn't mine, but Anya's. The dial screen showed a call from Akash. I silence the call and put the phone back in my pocket. Ignoring it, I wait for the tea when it vibrates again and then again.

I know that it's morally so wrong to invade someone's privacy, especially when it's the person whom you love the most but in that moment I couldn't help but wonder what it is about, especially this late at night. I know there were two texts because the phone vibrated twice. Suppressing my guilt, I take out her phone from my pocket once again.

Akash: "Hey. It was nice meeting you yesterday.

"Can we meet again, say tomorrow evening?"

I immediately place the phone back in my pocket before it falls of my hand or worse, I throw it away. It felt like someone pulled a rug out from under my feet. I turn and look at her sitting with her hands on the edge of the window, looking outside. My brain stopped processing things. I place my hand on the stall, gripping it tightly as I try to calm myself, reassuring that it's nothing. Maybe it's something about work and Shruti was there with her yesterday too. If something was wrong, she would have said something. Nothing's wrong, I tell myself again, but somehow my grip on the stall only tightens further. But why the fuck would she lie to me yesterday? I take the cups of tea and head back to the car.

Anya smiles as I enter the car and takes a cup from my hand. "Oh, it feels so good to hold it." She says.

I don't say anything. I knew that if I said something now, she wouldn't drink it.

She takes a sip. "I needed this so much. I'm starting to feel cold." She says, holding the cup with both her palms.

"Yeah." It was all I could manage to say. I chose to drink in silence. It was so good, rather perfect until now and one thing just ruined everything. I wish I had given back her phone, at least I wouldn't have known. I try to calm my mind until she finishes her tea. I don't know how to feel right now, but there's one thing I know and it is that I don't want her to get sick.

She finishes her tea. I take the cup from her and throw the cup in the trash can along with mine, then walk back and get in the driving seat. I reach for her phone in my pocket and hand it to her. "Hey, Akash called you." I watch her as her expression changes from happiness to concern, and then settling on guilt.

She looks at the screen which shows a missed call and the notification of two other messages from him. I start to drive the car with a lump in my throat, preventing me from saying anything. Neither of us speak for a while as I silently drive towards her apartment.

"Who is Akash?" I ask, as we reach near her apartment, even though I already knew the answer. I hated how my voice was giving away the anger that I was trying to keep at bay.

"Dad's friend's son. My parents asked-" Her voice was trembling but I interrupt her.

"Okay." I park the car at the entrance of her building. She was about to say something but I cut her off again. "Good night, Anya." I say curtly, without looking at her. Looking at her would just make things worse.

She climbs out of the car but stands there, maybe waiting for me to say something, but I don't. Neither do I want to say anything to her, nor listen to what she has to say. I turn to look at her but then look away the same instant, because I was angry, angrier than I've ever been before, so instead I press the ignition and drive away.

I turn the car and park it at a distance from her apartment once I was sure that she wouldn't see me. "Can you check on Anya? She's at the entrance of your apartment." I text Shruti. I see her standing at the same exact place she got out of the car. I see Shruti walking out of the building and meeting Anya at the entrance. She takes her inside and I instantly turn towards my apartment.

19

Chapter Nineteen

I lay awake in my bed, staring at the ceiling, my hands crossed behind my head, watching the fan go round and round. I don't feel like getting out of the bed either. The demons of the past came crawling back to haunt me again. Everything was perfect until that cursed phone call. But I need to get up from the bed, because the longer I am here, the more I am going to wallow in my misery.

I didn't feel eating anything, so I just make myself a cup of coffee, then get dressed for office. I grab my phone from the table beside the bed. There were missed calls from Anya, but I swipe the notification away and ignore.

Shruti comes to my desk but I keep my gaze glued at the computer screen, pretending to work. "Hey, you okay?" She asks, her voice soft.

"Yeah! What could possibly go wrong?" I reply sarcastically without looking at her.

She slumps on my desk, "I'm sorry." She apologizes.

"For what?" I turn and look at her as I say, then shift my gaze back to the screen.

"I should've told you yesterday. I just thought it would be better if you heard it from her."

"Tell me what Shruti? That she's going on a dinner date with some guy who her family want to be her future husband."

"I know you're hurt, but it's not what it looks like."

"Yeah...right!" I scoff. "How long has this been going on?"

"Only once." She says.

"Huh!" I look away for a moment then look back at her. "You know I was really happy yesterday—like beyond happy... my parents agreed to us and all I could think was that we're half way there. You saw how happy I was—everything was perfect, until I saw that call and it ruined everything." I sigh.

She listens to me without saying a word. "I'm sorry you feel that way." She trails off.

"No, why are you sorry?" I interrupt her. "You did nothing wrong. You were protecting your friend, but you know what, I am your friend too, or at least I thought I was." I pause for a moment to maintain my composure. "You and I are not friends because of her. We were friends before I met her again. You shouldn't have kept it from me."

"I wasn't protecting her. It was just, she was about to tell you everything and I thought it'd be better if you knew it from her and not from someone else."

"Yeah, right. I am so grateful for that." I say in a sarcastic voice.

"I know you're angry, and I'm letting that go, but remember how you felt when you were not given a chance to explain yourself. You're doing the exact same thing to her. All I am saying is that it's not what it looks like and nothing is ruined. She still loves you and only you. Please pick up her call." She says, then straightens herself and walks back to her desk.

ᐖᐖᐖ

I am running in the rain, my heart pounding louder than the storm. My shoes are soaked, covered in mud, but I don't care. Shruti's word echoed in my mind but I just can't shake off the feeling of being betrayed.

I sit on an empty park bench. The rain's coming down harder now, as if it's trying to wash away my pain with it. I close my eyes and look above, letting the drops fall directly on my face, when my phone rings in my pocket.

I know whose call it is. I don't want to pick it up but I am also longing to hear her voice. "Why'd you have to lie to me Anya?" I whisper to myself. I pull out my phone from my pocket, holding it in my hand and my gaze locked at the screen. I was about to hang up the phone but then Shruti's words echoed loud in my head, "Remember how you felt when you were not given a chance to explain yourself?" So I swipe and answer the phone.

"Aahil," her voice soft, and nervous. "Open the gate. I can explain. Please." She says.

"I'm not home. Can't you say it over phone?"

"No, I'll wait."

"Okay." I hang up, my voice cold. With a sigh, I wipe the water from my face, then shove the phone back in my pocket and run, as fast as I can. I wanted to see her again. I wanted her to tell me that everything I'm thinking of is not true. I wanted her to tell me that we'll be together, and she'll never leave me.

As I reach my apartment, I saw Anya standing at the door waiting. She sees me coming and walks towards me. "Where were you? You're all drenched." Her voice filled with concern.

I shake my head as I open the door and step inside, holding it open for her to come inside. Then I take off my muddy shoes and leave them in a corner. I watch her as she tosses her purse on the couch without saying anything and runs inside towards the bedroom. I see her walk back to me with a towel in her hand.

She stands in front of me, rising on her toes, she wraps the towel around my head and starts to dry my hair. I flinch, trying to take a step back, but she holds her grip. "Aahil you're angry with me. Don't take it out on yourself." She says in a firm voice.

I break away from her hold. "No, Anya. How could you do this to me? I thought we were in this together. I thought we'd fight for our love this time and that is why I talked to my parents about us. After all we've been through, how can you still agree to go out with someone whom your parents want you to marry?"

"It's not that simple Aahil."

"Yeah...right!" I scoffed.

"At least let me explain myself. I didn't have a choice." She says, her voice feeble.

"The hell you didn't have a choice. I don't even wanna talk to you right now." I start walking away from her. "I thought you loved me and I thought you were gonna fight for us this time, and not just give up again like this."

"Why do you think I'm not fighting for us? You don't trust me, do you?"

"Like you are making it so easy to trust you?" I walk in the bathroom to avoid her and lock it from inside.

"Please listen to me Aahil. I can explain." She says banging the door. I rest my forehead on the door and close my eyes, wondering who's hurting me more at the moment, me or her. She's right here, trying to explain herself but all I'm doing is trying to avoid her and it's not because I don't want to be with her, it's just I don't want to go through it again and if she has to leave, she can leave now.

I know it'll be hard now, but it'll be harder tomorrow and if we are not meant to be together, maybe it's for the better that we stay away from each other. I don't want to live holding on to a hope which isn't there in the first place. I cannot go through it all again. I just can't.

"My mother knows about us Aahil, way before you told about your parents. She knows we're dating again. I just didn't tell you because she's still not ready to accept us." She pauses for a few seconds, maybe trying to compose herself because her voice felt like she's on the verge of breaking. "I know you don't trust me Aahil, but here—come outside, take my phone and call her." Her voice finally breaks into sobs.

I open the door, expecting her to be standing, but instead, she's sitting on the floor, her knees pulled up to her chest, tears streaming down her face. My heart sinks. What did I do?

I fall on my knees in front of me but she doesn't look at me. The look on her face is making my heart ache. I reach for her hand but she pulls away, her body tense. Instead of taking my hand, she curls up tighter, pulling her legs closer.

I place my palm on her wrist. "Anya, I'm sorry. I'm really-really sorry. I should've acted better." My voice low and full of guilt.

"No Aahil, you acted like that cause you don't trust me. All you had to do was to give me a chance to explain."

"I know-I know. I was being stupid."

She wipes her nose with the back of her hand. "Last time I was here, you made me feel like it was our apartment and I wanted to come here so bad but you dropped me back to my place without saying a word to me. How do I make you trust me Aahil?" She takes a breath. "I'm sorry for what I did years ago, but you didn't have to do the same to me. You knew very well how much it hurts, and still you did it. I hate you Aahil. I hate you." She says sobbing.

"I know Anya. I'm stupid. I didn't give you a chance to explain. I was scared that I'd lose you again just like all those years ago." I say and gently pull on her wrist and I pull her towards me. She slides in my lap and I hold her in my arms very tightly.

"You're not losing me Aahil. I'm not gonna leave you. Not again." She mumbles on my chest.

"I know. I know now, and I'm sorry. I won't act like that again." I rest my cheek on the top of her head.

We sit there in silence for a while, our heartbeats slowly starting to calm down, sinking with each other. "I'm not running away Aahil." She snuggles her face in my chest, her voice low. "You never asked why it took me a week to reply. It wasn't because I needed that much time to think, in fact, if it were to me, I would've said yes then and there, and I did say it. But I didn't want to hurt you again, so I talked to mom first. When she didn't tell me no, I decided to say yes to you."

"Why didn't you tell me this before?"

"And say what? She didn't say no, but she hasn't said yes either. And then there's my dad—he doesn't know about us, yet. He told me to meet Akash, and when I asked mom about it, she said the same, that I should go meet him until I was ready to talk to my dad about us." She pauses and leans back a little, then start to unbutton my shirt. "You'll catch a cold." She says. I take out the shirt and throw it in a corner in the bathroom floor.

"I wanted to tell you about Akash the moment they mentioned him to me, but not over phone. And you've been out of town for work for the past month, so I never got the chance to meet you. And when we met yesterday, you told me that your parents agreed and I didn't wanna spoil that day, but before I could tell you, you saw the message and this happened."

"I'm sorry." I say.

"No, I am sorry. I should've told you sooner." She pauses. "But can you promise me something?"

"Yeah! Anything."

"When you left me at my apartment, I looked at your face. It looked like you don't even wanna look at me anymore. I could see the hurt on your face, and your eyes." A tear slides from the side of her eye. "Please never ever look at me that way. I'd rather die than see you looking at me like that."

I wipe her tear with my thumb and hug her tighter. "Never. I promise you. I won't do that again." I place a kiss at the top of her head.

"You know, I was hoping you'd come back. But then Shruti came to me—apparently you texted her, but I really wished you to come back and take me with you. But it's okay, I understand, it must have hurt a lot—knowing it from a text and that too when everything was perfect."

"I did come back." I confess. "Just not the way you wanted. I just didn't want you to see me."

"Really! So you didn't trust me there either?"

"No! No-no, it's not like that."

"It's exactly like that." Her lips curve into a small smile.

"Even though it feels stupid coming from me, but it's just that I don't want to see you get hurt, and that's why I stayed there to see you." I brush my nose in her hair. She pulls back a little, just enough for me to see her face. "At least I got to see that beautiful smile of yours."

"You know, when you make me smile, I feel like I really made the right choice about you." She places her palm on my chest. "Mom also says, lately I've been more... *me.*"

"You deserve every happiness in the world." I slowly caress her cheek with my thumb.

I gently try to lift her up but she immediately holds my hand. "I don't want you leave me today. Not even for a second. I want to stay like this and I don't care." She says, her voice barely above a whisper.

"I'm not leaving you. It's just that I am covered in mud, and since you're sitting in my lap, now you've got some on your dress too. So I was thinking maybe we should clean ourselves first, and I am feeling kinda cold too."

"Okay, but I wanted to ask—how the hell did you get mud on your shirt? I get it on your pants, sure, but your shirt?" She says as we stand up.

I scratch the back of my head. "I kinda tripped."

"And they say I am clumsy."

"They say you're cute."

20

Chapter Twenty

She says sitting on the edge of the bed with a towel wrapped around her. I walk back to her with a baby pink t shirt and light grey pyjamas.

"Why do you have a pink t-shirt in your closet?" She says as I stand in front of her.

"First of all, that's sexist, and second—I love pink." I wink at her. She rolls her eyes.

I lean towards her, helping her slide the t-shirt over her head, but her hair gets caught in the collar. "Hold still." I say, but she wiggles her head out of the t-shirt's neck like a cat. She's laughing and I smile back at her, then gently pull her hair free, brushing it off her shoulders.

I cup her face in my palms and plant a short kiss on her lips, then extend my hand to help her stand. I pull the pyjamas up her legs, and as I tie the drawstring around her waist, I can't help but chuckle. The clothes look too big on her.

"Don't I look like the kid who just raided his dad's closet?" Her eyes roll as she looks in the mirror but she's grinning.

"You look cute." I say as I walk back to her with a blow dryer. She sits back down on the bed, looking at me expectantly, and I turn it on, gently running the warm air through her hair. She closes her eyes and wraps her arms around my waist.

I gently run my fingers in her hair when I'm done. She looks up, and I take a step back, placing back the dryer in the drawer. "Lift me up." She says and raises her arms like a little baby.

I walk closer to her and lift her up in my arms, while she wraps her hands around my neck and her legs around my waist. She snuggles her face on my neck then rest it on my shoulder. "I'm hungry." She mumbles.

"I'll order something." I say, caressing her back with my palm.

"No! I want you to make something."

"Like this?" I ask.

"Yeah, like this. That's your punishment for making me cry." She tightens her arms around me, not ready to let go. I turn around and walk towards the kitchen.

"Dammit." I say to myself as I open the fridge because all the vegetables were at the bottom shelf. "Hey, you gotta help me out here. I lean and you'll have to take out capsicum and cauliflower from the bottom shelf."

"Nope. Dude, you have like eight packs and you can't manage a squat with me?"

"I could, but my legs are sore from all the running before."

"Fine," she says, making a playful, yet childlike angry face. I lean down holding her, maintaining my balance while she reaches out and grabs the vegetables.

I walk towards the counter and reach out for the pasta from the shelf above and place it in a container to boil and on the other container I start preparing the sauce.

"What are you making?" She asks, clearly enjoying the moment.

"Pasta." I say as I stir the sauce.

"It smells good." She brushes her nose against my neck, tickling it lightly. "So, chef Aahil, What's the secret ingredient?"

I chuckle, giving her a sideway glance. "I could tell you, but then... you know, you might have to sign an NDA."

She snorts. "Yeah, right. Just tell me, I won't tell anyone." She mimes ceiling her lips and throwing the key.

I smirk, scooping some sauce on a tablespoon. "How about you taste it and find out."

She leans in. "It's hot, but it's good." She says. "I wanna do something."

"Uh-huh!"

"You are not allowed to kiss back or drop me." She whispers in my ear.

"Wait, what are you... oh" I find myself with a loss of words as she gently sucks my earlobe, slowly leaning down, kissing my neck. I hug her tighter, my eyes closing—not just to keep her from falling, but because it feels so damn good.

It took everything in me to open my eyes, but I do to mix the pasta with the sauce and the vegetables. I then lower the flame and cover the container with a lid, then walk out of the kitchen to the living room and sit on the couch.

She's sitting on my lap with her face in front of me. "Your lips look dry." She says and leans towards me and start kissing my lips. My hands grip her thigh and I pull her close. She leans back a little, just enough to see my face, then nod up with a grin on her face.

"You're not playing it fair." I say.

"Aww! Okay, I'll get off." She says but I hold her and shake my head.

"No... Don't." I whisper because I don't want her to stop. "I just need some water first."

"I can get that." She slides off of my lap and pours a glass of water from the jar on the table. Then, she sits back down on my lap, holding the glass up to my mouth, helping me drink. Then she leans back, and leave the glass on the floor, then press her lips on mine. "Kiss me." She mumbles on my lips and I pull her closer by her waist, her palms cup my cheeks, our eyes closed and we kiss.

I pull back, "pasta" I say. She slides off my lap, and we head back to the kitchen. I lift the lid of the container, letting the steam rise, then stir it a bit before plating it up.

"Just one plate," she says, her voice light, teasing. I look at her and she nods, grinning.

I laugh, shaking my head, then holding the plate in my hand, we walk together to the bedroom. Anya climbs onto the bed first, sitting cross-legged and making space next to her. I place the plate in front of her, then lie down next to her, resting my head on her lap. My eyes close for a moment as she runs her fingers through my hair, playfully stroking and caressing my scalp.

"Comfortable?" She asks, her voice soft, almost like a whisper.

"Yeah. Perfect."

She lifts up the fork, twirling it around in the pasta, then sliding her hand, she helps me lift my head up to take a bite. A shiver runs through my body as I take a bite, my eyes close on its own. Instead of feeling calm, my heart is pounding harder, racing out of control as if it has a mind of its own. "*Shit*," she says, and I look up, but before I can say anything, she gently places her palm on my face, closing my eyes.

We don't say much as we eat. My head is still on her lap and there is so comforting about it—food, quiet room and her hand gently caressing my face. I look up at her and she holds my gaze. She is leaning down slowly, but she's still holding my gaze—her eyes look beautiful, hypnotizing, and then she closes her eyes as she licks the sauce from the side of my lips.

She pull back, just enough that all my focus is on her face, her fingers running through my hair again. "Stay here. I'll take the plates to the kitchen." She places a kiss on my forehead and says, her voice barely above a whisper.

I watch her as she walks back in the room, the soft glow of the hallway light casting shadows across her as she flicks the switch to turn ours off. She then climbs on the bed beside me, and pull up the blanket around us.

"Come closer." She says, her voice low and warm.

Without a second thought, I move towards her. She wraps her arms around me, pulling me in until my face rests on her chest. I wrap my arms around her, feeling the warmth of her body. "Let it out." She whispers.

I look up at her, and she leans down, pressing a kiss on the top of my head. "You don't have to keep bottling things up anymore," she says. "Let it out."

Her words hit differently, like a quiet permission to breathe. And without saying anything, I pull her closer, burying my face against her chest and I let go everything. I hug her for every moment when I wanted a hug but I had to be alone. I hold her tight for every moment I longed for her. I love her for every moment I wanted to feel loved.

༺༻

I squeeze my eyes tight as the sunrays pierced through the curtain. With my eyes half open, I fumble for my phone to check the time. The screen showed eight o' clock, so I leave the phone on the table, then glance to my left, at Anya. She's sleeping like a baby—a cute and peaceful one.

The morning definitely looks beautiful waking up next to her. Trying to not disturb her, I carefully slide my arm out, then pull up the blankets on her. I step out of the bed, but before walking out of the room, I look at her, imagining how my life would look when we actually live together.

Once I finish with my morning routine, I walk back to her and softly place my palm on the top of her head. "Anya, baby wake up." She winces and squeezes her eyes. I tuck the strands of her hair behind her ear and then lean down and place a kiss oh her forehead. "Ana wake up. It's getting late."

She slowly opens her eyes, and her eyes meet mine. A soft smile spreads across her face as she raises her arms towards me. I pull her into a hug, kissing her forehead again, then lean down and kiss her lips, just a quick, soft kiss.

"You gotta hurry, cause we have to go to your place to pick up your clothes." I say and playfully pull her as she was reluctant to get up.

I place two slices of bread in the toaster, then grab a bowl and crack the eggs into it. While the eggs and toast were getting ready, I move over to the other side of the counter grind the coffee beans to make some coffee. I set the kettle to boil, then move back to check on eggs. The toast pops up, so I places another set of slices in it, then flip the omelette.

Anya walks in the kitchen, standing next to me. "Let me do something."

"Everything's already done." I say with a grin, grabbing her waist and lifting her up to sit on the counter.

She has a playful smirk on her lips. "Am I also a dish on the menu?" She teases, her voice light and mischievous.

I laugh, standing in front of her, leaning in just a bit. "Trust me, you're the best part of the meal." She wraps her legs around me as I pull the plate closer. "Here's your omelette toast and your coffee."

She grabs a toast and takes a bite while I take a sip of my coffee. "There is something I have to give to you, but you kinda have to let me free."

"Uh-huh!" She lets her legs fall from my waist. I take a step back then walk towards the living room.

"Here," I tell her, handing her the key. "I don't want you to wait for me to come and open the door for you. Here's a spare key." Her cheeks turn crimson as she takes the key from my hand.

"Thank you." She mouths.

ᐅᐅᐅ

Shruti opens the door and Anya rushes inside to change her clothes, while I wait for her at the door, my hands nonchalantly tucked in my pocket. Shruti was holding the door open and to be honest I was kind of embarrassed to look at her because of the way I talked to her yesterday. "You coming in?" She asks. I nod and walk inside. "So, everything okay between you two?"

"Yeah," I say. "Look, I'm really sorry for yesterday. I shouldn't have talked to you like that, and you were right."

"Ah, it's okay as long as you don't waste time staring at her when she comes out. And by the way, when am I ever wrong?"

"What about the time you said you knew the way Khushi's place?"

She laughs. "I missed it yesterday." She says and takes a step towards and briefly embraces me. "By the way, that was an honest mistake. I only missed one left."

"Yeah, sure." I laugh.

21

Chapter Twenty One

They say that a shower calms you down but what about when you are too excited, and happy. Can it still do it? I highly doubt it.

I walk out taking a quick shower, but rush is still coursing through my veins. Today I am taking Anya to my parent's for dinner, and judging by the tone of my mother's voice, she seemed equally excited to meet her too. My father, on the other hand, doesn't express much. But, he has his own unique ways of showing his happiness.

I know this will kind off piss off my mother a little but I am wearing a black t-shirt and navy blue denims and I've layered the outfit with a navy blue denim jacket. I have selected a black metallic watch as an accessory. My mother thinks I am colour blind, but not in the way most people think. It's not that I can't see colours at all—she just swears I can only see the darker shades when we're shopping. Anything bright or light, according to her, is a mystery to me.

I was wearing my white sneakers when my phone rings. It was a facetime call from Anya. I pick up but Shruti was holding her phone. "You're not Anya. Who are you?"

"Shut up, and tell her she looks good. She has turned her room upside down." She says and apparently Anya gave her a look judging by her expression. She then clicks on the rear camera toggle and I see Anya. She was wearing a full sleeved black coloured floral long dress. She twirls hesitantly, showing her dress, and I stare at her in awe. She has made her hair in a beautiful hairstyle, her hair crashing on her left shoulder. She wore the necklace I gave her, pairing it with silver earrings.

Every time I thought this is it, this is the pinnacle of how beautiful someone could look, and the next time I see her, somehow she manages to look even more beautiful than before. "Say something. She's getting anxious." Shruti's words bring me back. *But what do I say?*

"Can you give her the phone?" I say and she hands the phone to Anya. She looks at me, her face anxious. I couldn't say anything, instead I keep looking at her then tilt my head right with a smile. "They'll love you." She smiles.

ᐅᐅᐅ

I knock on the door, then take a step back, holding a bouquet of red roses in my hand. Anya opens the door. "What took you so long?"

"I stopped for flowers." I say and hand it to her. She doesn't smile, instead she turns around and waves at Shruti, then walks out of the apartment.

I reach for her hand and intertwine my fingers with hers. But her hand was cold, so I envelope it between my palm, rubbing it gently to warm it up a bit.

"I think I'll screw up everything. What if they don't like me? Or what if they ask me something I don't know or I say something stupid?" She keeps shifting her weight from one leg to another out of nervousness.

"Anya, breathe. Take a few deep breaths." I say as we walk towards the car. As we reach near the car, I take a step ahead and open the door for her and she gracefully slides in. I walk to the other side and get in the driver seat.

She is shaking her legs out of nervousness. I place my palm on her knee, silently reassuring her, then reach out for her hands, clasping them in mine. "Anya, my love, you know why I believe angels are real? Because right now, there's one sitting beside me.

And trust me when I say this—they will not just like you, they'll love you. You have nothing to worry." I start to drive.

"It's easy for you to say." She clutches the bouquet in her hand, her gaze shifting between the bouquet and the road. "This is huge Aahil. And I know I act dumb at times—I just cannot stop thinking."

"That's simply not true, and even if it was, I get to pamper you more." I say, my eyes fixed on the road. I know this is huge, even for me, because it is the first time I'm taking a girl to meet my parents. But they are my parents. I've spent my whole life with them, but for her, it's an entirely new experience. I mean for her they are just strangers who she had only heard about from me. Maybe I'll really understand what she's going through when I get to meet hers.

22

Chapter Twenty Two

Anya

I hold my breath as Aahil presses the doorbell. I am standing behind him, trying to keep my nerves in check as the anxiety I had a while ago, is slowly starting to kick in again. This is it, the moment I meet his parents.

I gaze down, looking at my dress and mentally double checking if I looked fine. He catches me and reassures me, "You look beautiful. Don't worry." But how can I not? I silently look at him. He's acting like he can guarantee that everything will be fine. If only I could feel the same. Maybe I should just trust him, but what if it doesn't go well? I immediately shrug the thought and shift my gaze on the bouquet in my hand—not the one he gave me. He apparently had bought two of them.

His mother open the door. She looks beautiful, her eyes kind. "Hey mom." Aahil greets as he hugs her. She hugs him back. He has her eyes, I notice. He then introduces me. "Mom, Anya."

"Hi, aunty." I say, hating the feebleness in my voice.

"Anya, it's so lovely to finally meet you!" She says, her voice full of warmth. I take a step forward and hand her the bouquet. "Thank you." She says, then holds my hand, taking me inside. Aahil follows us.

As we step inside, the atmosphere immediately feels different—calming yet full of life. The house smelled like home, with a faint scent of fresh cooking coming from the kitchen.

The living room is cosy, yet elegant, with dark wooden furniture, beautiful abstract paintings on the walls and some antique pieces on the shelves. It's like every piece was carefully chosen to complement the overall décor.

I watch her as she places the flowers in a vase, then walks back to us. "You have a lovely place. Now I see where Aahil gets it from." I compliment her.

"Thank you dear." She says, smiling. "So, Aahil showed you his place. He sure doesn't want me anywhere near it."

And there I go. This is what I was worried about. The first thing I say to his mother is I'm sleeping with her son. I instantly look at Aahil hoping for a rescue.

"Yeah, she has seen my apartment, you know get together and stuff." He says covering for me.

"Oh." She says, smiling, then shifts her gaze on Aahil. "Aahil, why don't you show Anya around. I'll serve the dinner in a bit." He nods and I watch her walking towards me. "I am so happy to see you dear." She takes my hands in hers and hugs me. I practically melt in her arms. It felt familiar, like she wasn't his mother, but mine.

I hug her back, my racing heart calming down. "I am glad to meet you too." I say as we part our hug. She walk back to the kitchen, and somehow after that hug, it doesn't feel as awkward to talk as it felt a while ago. Yet, I haven't met his father and from what I've heard from Aahil is that he isn't one to talk a lot. I take a deep breath. Everything is going to be fine.

"Come, I'll show you around." Aahil says, with a reassuring smile.

"Would it be okay if I went to the kitchen and help your mom or would that seem off?" I ask him, but that is when it occurs to me. "I wanna see your room too. Can you show me before we leave?"

"Yeah sure. If you want to be with mum, its fine. I'll show you after dinner." He says and I could literally feel my cheeks turning red, just by the thought of seeing the place where he used to talk to me at night. He shows me the way and I follow him to the kitchen.

I walk up to her. "Aunty, can I help you with something?" I ask. She was busy peeling the cucumber for salad.

"Everything's already done honey, thank you. Is Aahil not showing you around?"

"No, I asked him if I could be with you." I say and she smiles.

"That's so sweet of you, but don't worry, everything's ready here, uh," She says pointing at a container on the stove. "Would you mind turning the knob off?"

"Yeah sure." I say and turn the knob off.

"So, how are you dear?" She asks looking at me.

"I'm good. Actually happy, blessed." I lean against the counter and smile at her. "Where's uncle?"

"Um, he should be back by now." She says and the doorbell rings. I see Aahil walking up to the door to open. "He's back." I watch Aahil hugging uncle and taking a bag from his hand, then walking towards us.

"Ice-cream? In this weather?" he looks at his mother, smiling.

She simply smiles back at him. "So what were you guys talking about?" Aahil asks as he puts the ice cream in the freezer.

"Mother-daughter talks." Aunty says and I bite my lip to suppress my smile. Did she just call me daughter already? "Take these plates and set it on the table." She points at the shelf and he goes to grab them.

"Not fair, huh. You're already taking her side." He huffs and walks out.

"He talks a lot about you." I pause, finding the right words. "You knew about us from the beginning?"

"Not from the start, but yeah, pretty much. He was terrible at hiding it. Like, he'd put his phone in the middle of the book, acting like he's studying, but he could barely hide the grin on his face. And we also heard him talking at night when we walked past his room. So, we kind of knew."

"And you didn't stop him?"

"We would've, if we saw he's getting distracted but he was doing better, so we let him believe that nothing was amiss and pretended like we didn't knew."

I wish my parents were as understanding as his. I've been here only for a while and I could already see the difference in thoughts between his parents and mine. I wish talking to them was as easy as it is to talk to his parents.

"Can I ask you something? You can choose not to answer if you want." She hesitates and I nod. "What happened between you two for a while? Did he do something?"

My stomach turns into knots. I cannot tell her the actual reason. "We kind of stopped seeing each other, but not because he did something. He has always been good to me. It's just that we thought if our parents won't approve of us then what's the point of it all?"

"Honey, you kids were too young to take such decisions. But I am glad you are together again. He is happy with you." She places her hand on my shoulder.

"So does this mean you approve of us?" I could feel warmth spreading on my cheeks.

"Of course we do. We just wanted to meet you." She says, her words making me want to hug her again, but I hold myself back. "Come, let's have dinner."

I step out of the kitchen following her into the dining room. I'm about to sit with his family for the first time and for the first time today, I'm more excited than anxious. Maybe it is because how her mother made me feel or maybe it's because she already said that they approve of us, but it feels so damn good.

As we walk in the room, I spot Aahil coming in from the other side with his father. "Dad, this is Anya. Anya, my dad." He introduces us.

"Hello uncle." I say, with a smile.

"Hello Anya. It's nice to finally meet you." He says with a warm smile. He then pulls out a chair, so I walk around and slip into one next to Aahil.

"Tell me something about yourself." Aahil's mother asks as we start to eat.

ҏҏҏ

The dinner flows smoothly with light chatter, and aunty sharing some funny stories about Aahil from when he was younger and Aahil would jump in with his own commentary, and I'm laughing along with them, the nerves I had when I walked in were long gone. The whole thing feels easy, like I've been a part of their family for longer than I have. I don't even remember the last time we sat together to eat in my home. But here, I feel happy and lucky to be part of.

I kick Aahil's foot under the table to remind him that he has to show me his room before we leave. He looks at me and nods. We are definitely getting good at mind reading.

"Mom, I'll show Anya my room." He says and she nods. We get up from our seats and I follow him through the corridor. "This is my parent's room." I take a quick glance as I pass through the door. "And this one's mine."

He stands, holding the door open for me. I enter first, my eyes scanning everywhere. I always wished to be in his room.

He walks in, standing beside me, and slowly slides his hand around my waist. My heart skips a beat at his touch. I look at him "Stop, they're gonna see us." and try to take a step away from him.

"No, they'll not." He says and pulls me closer. I clutch his jacket with my fingers and look at his face. Ever since he picked me up today, I've been so nervous that I barely noticed how good he look. His beard, those beautiful brown eyes, and the way his arms are wrapped around me—I think I could stay here forever.

He leans down a little and I hold my breath as an instinct. His lips inch closer and I close my eyes on their own as if I don't have any control over my body. His lips briefly meets mine, and then he pulls away. After all these years, he still has this effect on me. "We can't do this here, maybe." I exhale.

I take a step back from him and look around at his room. There were some abstract frames on the wall behind his bed and then there are plants around the corner. I slowly walk towards his desk. "So, this is where you studied?"

"Um...no. Dad bought it for me to study but I kinda preferred to study on bed, so I used to leave clothes and stuff on it."

"Oh." My eyes shift to the shelf above the desk. It was full of trophies and there were lots of them. I can't help but smile, because it's kind of impressive. "All yours?" I ask looking at him. He scratches the back of his head and nods.

I wrap my arms around his neck, hugging him tightly. "Are you happy?" He asks, as he rests his chin on my head.

"Yeah. Very." I mumble on his shoulder.

I pull away from him and walk towards the mirror to have a final look of myself before walking out of the room. My cheeks were all red and I can only hope for them to return to normal by the time I see his parents again.

I look back at him. He's still standing at the same spot. "What?"

"Nothing." He shakes his head with a smile. "I just love watching you."

"Stop now!" I playfully hit him on his arm. "I love your parents, and this place. I want to be here more."

"Soon." He says and places a kiss on the top of my head.

We head back to the living room and bid goodbye to his parents. I walk towards his mom and hug her goodbye. She hugs me back with equal warmth. They walk us out to our car.

"At least you could've been a gentleman and opened the door for her Aahil." His mom says and he shrugs. I laugh, then wave them goodbye.

23
Chapter Twenty Three

I turn to my side, facing her and she does the same from the other side of the bed. "Are you sure you're ready? Your mom said to give it some time. You sure you're not rushing things?"

"I don't know. But after I met your parents, I couldn't stop thinking about it." She sighs, a little frustrated. "Honestly, I've had enough of this. I want to be with you now. I want this for me, for us."

I run my fingers through her hair gently. "Then you should go talk to them."

ppp

The cool evening breeze of late november sweeps through the apartment. Taking a break from my work, I decided to brew a cup of coffee. Holding the mug in my hand, I take a deep breath, then settle at the corner of the balcony.

I wish things had been different for us—simpler, to be honest. If they had been, we wouldn't have lost five years. The things she said, I want it too, more than anything. I too wish to come back home to her instead of this empty apartment. I really want to live one of those moments we used to talk about.

I stare at the waves crashing along the shore, but I'm not really focused on them. My mind has been elsewhere since she mentioned talking to her parents, wondering whether they'll agree or not. I have a feeling that it isn't going to be as easy as it was with mine.

Though her parents didn't agree back then either, she still dated me for three years. Would she do the same now? We are not teenagers anymore. We are adults with a lot of responsibilities on our shoulders. Even if her mother agrees to it, her father... I don't think so.

My phone pings and I reach for my phone in my pocket. "On my way. Wish me luck." Anya's text pops up on the screen.

I stare at it for a second, feeling the weight of it all. Tonight's the night we find out what's next—whether things will finally fall into place or get even more complicated. There's another possibility, but I really don't want to go there. I quickly type back, "Good luck, and I love you." My hands feels stiff as I type the text. I could only imagine what she must be going through.

ᐵᐵᐵ

I lay on my bed, anxiously waiting for her text and with each moment passing, my mind is racing through a gazillion different possible outcomes of their conversation. Maybe they told her that they were fine with it, or maybe she didn't talk to them because they were in a bad mood. Maybe she talked to her mother but she asked her to wait or maybe she talked to both of them and they didn't agree. I shrug the last thought immediately, but deep down I know that the chances of this happening is far more than all the other possibilities combined.

I kept the phone in my hand, clutching it tightly. My eyes are closed but my brain is wide awake, praying, rather begging god to turn this in our favour.

My phone pings and I immediately look at the screen. "Can you pick me up tomorrow?" Anya's message read. What does that mean? Did her parents agree or?

"Sure." I text back, then wait for her to say something. But she doesn't, so I text her again. "Everything alright?"

"No."

My heart drops in an instant. I immediately call her but it goes unanswered. A single *No*.

"Don't worry, we'll figure it out. We'll find a way. Don't worry. What time shall I pick you up?" I try to comfort her, even though I knew it was futile.

"Seven." Her text appears.

"I'll be there. I love you."

I leave my phone on the bedside table. She didn't text back, nor did I expect her to.

ᗡᗡᗡ

The sun's starting to rise slowly in the clear sky. There's a chill in the surrounding. I park my car at a distance from Anya's house and wait for her in the car. I still have no clue as to what am I going to say to her that might ease off her pain.

I look outside, laying back on the seat with my hands crossed behind my head. Her house definitely looks... expensive, and such big house at such a posh location—I can only imagine the money that goes into it. I look around at the other houses around me, they are definitely doing a great job at humbling me.

I let out a heavy sigh, and close my eyes. Is it really fair to ask her to leave all these, for me? People wearing expensive suits for work, their chauffeurs opening the doors for them, not to mention these really expensive cars parked on the streets. I don't have a big house or car, neither can I afford them. I don't even wear those stupid fancy suits for work. She could live like a princess here. She could be very happy here.

I open my eyes and glance over at her house. I see their driver standing a bit far away from their car, talking to someone. He's holding a suitcase, which he hands off to the guy. I hope he doesn't see me and go back to tell her parents. Thankfully, he doesn't stick around for long and walks inside.

My eyes are locked at the entrance, waiting for her. The door slides open and I see Anya walk out. It was just her, no one to see her off at the gate. I watch her as she slides the gate shut by herself, then turn towards the street trying to find me. I don't walk out of the car and receive her, because I would just be messing things more than they already are, but she spots my car.

She is looking around as she walks towards me, being careful that her parents don't see her. I look for the driver to check whether he came back but he hasn't. Once she reach near the car, I open the door for her from inside. She climbs in, "get me out of here, right now," she says hastily slams the door shut. Without wasting another second, I press the accelerator and drive us out of there.

After driving a little further from her parent's place, I pull into an empty spot and turn to look at her. She is staring down her lap, her fingers knotted together, clearly trying to hold it together. She has been quiet ever since she got in the car. "Are you okay?" I ask, taking her hand in mine.

She shakes her head and a tear falls from her eyes to her lap. "Hey, look at me Ana." I say, my voice soft and she turns her face towards me. I feel an ache in my heart, just by looking at her face. Her eyes are puffy and red, like she has been crying all night. I lean towards her, "come here." I say and pull her close.

I don't know what else to do. I am not sure what to say, I'm not even sure that anything I say would ease off her pain. Her fingers are clutching my shirt and she is crying uncontrollably. "Ana," I say caressing her back.

"I don't want you to leave me today." She mumbles on my chest.

"I'm not leaving you Ana. Let's go home." I say, my voice determined. She takes a few moments to compose herself, then she shifts back to her seat. I reach for my phone and without leaving her hand, I text the office that I won't be able to make it today, before driving us home.

ᐯᐯᐯ

I help her get on the bed, then turn to walk towards the kitchen but she holds my wrist, shaking her head. I gently place my palm on her cheek, "I'm not going anywhere Ana. I know you haven't eaten anything. Just give me a minute." I say and kiss her forehead, then walk out of the room.

I grab a glass of orange juice and some apples and a knife on a plate. I then walk back to the room and sit next to her. "I don't wanna eat anything." She says, her voice barely above a whisper.

"I know you don't and that's why I brought apples. I know you like them. I'll cut them for you." I sit next to her and she leans in, her face resting on my bicep and her arms are wrapped around mine.

There's silence between us as I cut a slice and take it near her mouth, "Here," I say, and her lips part as she takes a bite. She then shifts her face a little, her nose brushing against my bicep. I cut another piece for her as she eats the first one. I grab the glass of juice from the table as she finishes the apples.

I walk back to the room, walking straight to the balcony to shut the drapes off. I haven't said anything since our conversation earlier—about her not eating and neither has she. Honestly, I don't know what to say, I don't have any words that could soothe her. I just feel like I'm not enough for her. I mean, she can have everything she wants there, but instead, she came here with me, in my small car, to my small apartment. I just feel like I'm making her sacrifice a lot for me. She doesn't deserve this life—she doesn't deserve this pain. She could've lived happily but she's going through so much of pain, all because of me.

Her gaze is already on me as I turn back towards her. She doesn't have to say anything; I can see it in her eyes, the raw vulnerability. I take slow steps towards her. Her fingers tug at the corner of the blanket and raises her hands. So, I slide in and lie next to her.

With a gentle tug, she pulls my t-shirt up, and I know exactly what she is asking. I remove my t-shirt and leave it on the floor. She closes her eyes and presses her forehead on my lips, then snuggle her face on my chest. She then slides her arms around me, shifting closer and lock her leg between mine.

I gently place my palm on her head, caressing her hair and the other on her back. "I couldn't sleep there." She mumbles on my chest. "I wanted to be with you. I hate them so much."

"Hey," I say, my voice soft. "Don't say that. They are your parents."

"I don't wanna go back there." She says, her voice barely above a whisper.

I swallow the lump in my throat. "What did they say?"

"Same old crap." Her voice bitter. "We're high-class people. We sit with equals and not with... I know it's pathetic. I'm hopeless—we're hopeless." She takes a pause. So, I wait for her to continue but she doesn't.

"If you look the other way round, your parents want you to have a good life, and provide you with all the luxuries so that you're safe and happy." Am I really convincing her to consider her parent's decision?

"You don't think I can work hard and get those for myself?"

"Without a doubt. But if they could help and make things easier for you—they're just trying to do that." My emotions clearly taking over. She shifts back a little, just enough to see my face, looking me in the eye. "What?" I ask, raising my shoulders a little.

"Nothing." She says, then sits up, her gaze on me. "Guess they forgot the most important thing. Love."

"What do you mean?" I ask puzzled, sitting up and leaning against the back of the bed.

"They want me to have an easy life... sure. But are they sure that I'll be happy and loved?" Her voice getting louder with each word, like she's trying to let it all out. "You know, they let you believe that they are doing it for your good but it's nothing more than a mere business transaction. They have business partners and when they want to strengthen their business relations, they get their kids to marry each other. The boy, eventually starts handling business of his father and mostly hangs out with his friends. His wife is merely a trophy to him—a prized possession you show off on functions and occasions." She pauses for a moment, clearly frustrated. I look at her in silence, waiting for her to continue. "I've seen my mom Aahil, it's not the life I want."

"I wanna do something of my own Aahil. I don't wanna live in the shadow of my parents. I wanna make a name for myself." She says, her voice getting lower.

I reach for her hand. "So, like, girls aren't allowed to have a career?"

"They are… sometimes. But it's only up to a certain point, like when they decide it's time to have kids. And when the girl wants to work… after whatever period, they'd be like why, because everyone there has money and she can have everything she wants at home. And since husband is the one who's earning and pretty much everything is taken care by the maid, her only job is just to look good, so when her husband gets home after late night meetings or parties or whatever, she must make him feel good."

"What year is this, huh?" I ask, shocked, unable to believe people still think like that.

"I honestly don't know if that's right or wrong. All I know is that I don't wanna end up like this… alone. And that's why I want to marry someone I love. At least, I won't be forced to have a child to have a person in my life." Her voice low.

I pull her by her wrist, wrapping my arms around her. Then we slide back inside the blanket, her face resting on my chest. "Is that why you're closer to your mother?"

"She was all I had." She snuggles closer. "Mom and nana used to talk a lot. When I was little, nana would tell me stories every day. I wouldn't let nana sleep until she told me a new one. I was too stubborn as a child." She moves her head a little on my chest. "Mom used to scold me to let nana sleep but nana would stop her and tell me another story. And when she ran out of new ones, she'd just tell me the same stories again, but with different names. I was too little to figure out." Her voice soft. I could feel her tears on my chest, but I didn't move, waiting for her to continue.

"But after nana, mom had no one to talk to except me. Dad always came home late, and mom would be there with me, either helping me with my homework or we'd just look stuff up on the internet. Sometimes, she'd fall asleep next to me because dad was so late. But when I used to wake up, she'd already be gone—cause dad came home." Her voice was on the verge of breaking. I slide my hand to her waist and pull her closer, gently caressing her hair with my other hand. She brushes her nose against my neck and take a deep breath. "But then I moved out, for this job and she's still there... alone. Dad still come home late, and she waits for him, serves him dinner and then they sleep. And it's not just my dad—it's the same with all of them over there."

"So does your mom not see this?" I whisper over her head.

"Mom knows it, in fact every lady knows it. But, they kinda have accepted it the way it is. Ladies would form groups and meet, organise kitty parties, small talk, laugh and then come back to their empty homes." She stays quiet for a while, then lifts her head from my shoulder and kisses me.

It's the first kiss after spending all night and this morning wrestling with the thought that I'm not enough for her. But for her, I guess, it's the first kiss after realizing just how much she's willing to fight for us. Honestly, after everything she's said, I can't help but feel that, if I truly put in the effort, I could make her happy without asking her to sacrifice so much.

She pulls away and hides her face on my shoulder. She places a kiss on my chest, then gently bite the skin before placing her cheek on it. "That's why I wanna marry you." She says, her voice soft. "I don't want the same life as my mom. I want to be with the person I love... with you. I wanna share about my day with you, even if it is the same as yesterday and the day before that. And when I have to go somewhere, I wanna go with you—with you there with me, and not some driver who'll drop me off and leave. And when I'm sick, I want you to take care of me, pamper me, not some stupid maid who'd give me my medicines. I want to wake you up in the middle of the night and make you dance with me."

"I love you so much Ana, and I'm never gonna give you up."

She place her palm on my cheek, slowly moving it to my hair. "Were you gonna?" Her voice barely above a whisper.

I shake my head, but I could almost feel my eyes welling up. So, I lean down, peppering little kisses.

24
Chapter Twenty Four

I open the door of our apartment, then shift aside for her to enter first. She walks in, placing her palm on the wall as a support as she leans to take out her sandals. I stop her saying, "let me help." There's a puzzled look on her face but she straightens up. I kick out my shoes, then lean down, and without any warning, I slide my arm under her knees, lifting her up onto my shoulder.

"Aahil!" she yelps, her hands flying to the back of my neck, and I can feel her laughing as she tries to get steady. "At least warn me before doing it."

I laugh, but I can feel her starting to relax. "Nah, what's the fun in that?"

She rolls her eyes, but she can't hide the smile creeping on to her face. "You're ridiculous."

I slide my fingers to her heels and take them off. She shifts her weight on my shoulder, trying to get comfortable, placing her palm over my eyes. "Let's see if you could take me to the bedroom with your eyes closed."

"But if you fall, it's on you." I chuckle, trying to steadily walk towards the bedroom.

"Oh, you've made it to the bedroom. Now put me down on the bed." She says, her voice with a hint of mischief. "Slightly right," she says and I turn right. "No! My right—no left—right, right—your right."

With so much of confusion and my eyes closed, I accidently bump my legs on the corner of the bed, losing my balance. We fall on the bed, with her falling on her back and my face hits her stomach. We burst into laughter.

I slide next to her, laughing. She shifts her gaze on me and I look at her. "I'm so happy today." She says, her voice barely above a whisper.

"And I'm so freaking tired that I don't even have strength to change my clothes." I say closing my eyes.

She sits up, climbing on top of me, bringing her face above mine. She gently caresses my lips with her thumb then presses a soft peck on it. She then shift back, laying her face on my chest. "So, what was so special today?"

"Umm, can I be really honest with you?" I ask, my voice low.

"Of course!"

I wrap my arms around her and place a kiss on the top of her head before saying, "when you were talking about you and your family, and how our lives would be if we do not end up together, I felt how much more I want you in my life, and I wanted to celebrate that. And I also kinda had a feeling that if I did everything right, I might just help you divert your mind from everything and cheer you up." I say and she climbs up a little snuggling her face against mine.

I could feel her breath on my cheeks. "Thank you," she says.

"You know, while I was thinking about all of this, I remembered your seven wishes you wrote in that card for me back when we were in school. Do you remember them?" I ask.

"I remember I wrote it, but not vividly." She murmurs.

"I'll tell you." I give her a gentle squeeze. "First one was to love you unconditionally. Second, to always pamper and spoil you. Third, to take you to shopping always, and fourth was to let eat street food. Fifth was to plan surprises for you, and sixth... to always forgive you." I place my palm on her cheek, her eyes meeting mine, and I kiss her forehead, then her eyes, nose, and her lips. "Seventh was to kiss you to sleep every day." And with that, I hug her tightly. "I thought I could do some of them today."

She slides her hand under my neck and place her forehead on mine. "I don't know what to say." Her voice soft.

"You don't have to say anything." I reply, running my fingers in her hair, gently massaging her scalp.

"I don't ever wanna lose you." She says, pressing her lips on mine.

"You won't." I mumble on her lips in between our breaths. "And we'll figure it out."

She pulls back, sitting on my waist. "Come, change your clothes. I wanna sit with you in the balcony." She says, getting off the bed, and pulling me with her.

We quickly change into something comfortable. I watch her as she walks towards the bedside table and pick up the guitar in her hand then turn around towards me. "I hope you've learnt a few, in these months."

"Maybe," I say, settling on the edge of the balcony. She slides in my lap, with her back pressed against my chest and her head resting on my shoulder. She held the guitar in her lap. I lean forward and rub my cheek against hers and take a deep breath, holding the guitar in her lap, and softly strum the string once. "Can I ask you something before? But I want you to be honest with me."

"Yeah, anything." She says entangling her fingers with mine.

"Why me? I mean, keeping everything you said aside, you could still find a lot of guys who'd die to be with you and they would be very successful too."

She lets out a deep breath. "But none of them would be you. And you're successful too."

"No, that's not what I'm asking. I meant, you can have everything. So, why risk it on just a probability that I might do something great? I kind of feel like I making you sacrifice a lot for me." My voice low.

"I have everything with you."

"No..."

"Let me finish." She cuts me off. "You wanna know why you—because, I can be me when I'm with you. I don't have to pretend, I don't fear judgement, I don't have to overthink... it's just, I feel free when I'm with you. And I know you love me... a lot. Cause, I don't think I'd find a man who'd do a quarter of things you've done for me. You worked hard for me. You kept loving me, even when I wasn't with you and when I came back in your life, you made sure I was the happiest person in the world. Although, I don't thank you much for everything, but know that I appreciate everything a lot."

"Yeah, I get you but I don't have a big house or a fancy car."

"Yet. I don't like you undermining what you've achieved, you are so young and you can achieve so much more. I'll be right by you, and we'll build it together. And those big houses you talk about—they are full of empty rooms just like the people in it. And the cars, yeah, those fancy cars are good, but after a certain point, they stop adding any value." She says, her voice firm and composed.

"So you're saying that having a big house or a fancy car isn't worth it?"

"No, that's not what I mean at all. What I'm saying is, after a certain point, you are paying more for the name or the brand than what it actually does for you. Whether it's a car, clothes or even for a house... the value shifts. It's not just about the thing, but the status it represents."

"Then why is the whole world after those things?" I grumbled.

She sighs softly. "It's true that it doesn't provide any real value in terms of comfort, but there are other things. If you have money, it's okay to buy things you wish for. But the bigger reason most people buy these things is because it gives them access to more money. For example—you have a business meeting with a potential client, and you show up in a fancy car, it signals that you're successful, that you've got your life together. It gives them confidence in your ability to get the job done—more like a packaging of a product. The packaging doesn't change the product, but it sure as hell influences whether someone buys it or not."

She pauses, her eyes meeting mine. "Now about the house—think about it like this—if you don't live in a nice house in a good neighbourhood, you could miss out on opportunities. These neighbourhood often have help you grow your own networks, and if you're not a part of it, you might never get access to the right people, to those partnerships that can bring in the big deals. And that's why people pay extra, cause that money isn't for the house or the car themselves, it's about the doors they can open."

"I see." I say, her words slowly sinking in.

Her face looks a little hesitant as I look at her, as if she's trying to choose her words carefully. "Okay, so... please don't take it the wrong way, but I need to ask. And I'm just asking because we're on this topic, and I want to make sure that you never feel it that way."

She shifts a bit on my lap such that she's looking at me a little more directly. "So, I have a pretty good idea of how much Shruti makes, and since you guys work together, I kinda have a rough idea of how much you make. You said you bought the car with full payment, and with your rent, and just your overall lifestyle, I've kinda put it all together in my head. And it may be more but I'm assuming your freelance income is equal to all your expenses, I think I have a decent figure in my mind. But here's my question, how far off am I from the actual number?"

I think for a while, before saying "umm, you're at about forty percent of the actual value."

Her lips curve into a warm smile, the one reflecting how she's genuinely happy for me. "Fuck dude, you're rich. I knew I was making a right bet on you."

"Oh, so now I am a bet you made." I scowl.

"Of course. See my father has had a generational wealth. So he is definitely a lot more times richer but look at you being twenty four and being so incredible." She chuckles.

"And here I thought you were with me for love."

"I am, but it doesn't hurt to be rich and have a loving husband." She leans towards my face and kiss my cheeks. "Now think about the moment when you said I was at about forty percent of actual. How did it feel?"

"Fulfilling."

"That's the point I was trying to make. You are special Aahil. You have a beautiful heart, which loves, everyone and you have an incredible brain that could literally do wonders. I have heard from Shruti, about how good you are at what you do, especially how humble you are. It's rare, and you know—I feel like I'm the one who don't deserve you."

"Hey! After all this pep talk, you're the one saying it."

She wraps her arms around me. "It's not like I'm gonna leave you ever." She mutters, and I hug her back. "Don't you ever feel like you're making me sacrifice anything. I have everything I ever wanted, with you. But I want you to promise me something."

"Yeah, anything."

"Don't just say 'yeah, anything', because it's easier to say and tough to do." She pauses to look at me, and I nod. "Don't, ever become my father. Don't get me wrong—he is a good man. He took care of everything we need, but it's just he never had time for us."

She gently runs her fingers on my face, her eyes soft. "I don't wanna be an anchor to you Aahil. I'd rather wanna be like the roots—no matter how high you grow, we should still be connected. I want you to take out time for me. I want you to always love me, like you love me now."

"I promise. I'll love you the same and more."

"I trust you." She mumbles on my neck, then press a kiss on my lips. She then turns around in my lap, pulling the guitar close to her. "Now sing."

"How about *Thinking out Loud by Ed Sheeran*."

25
Chapter Twenty Five

Why do parents have to be parents? Why can't they be friends? I mean, it would've been a lot simpler to talk to them. With my parents, it was kind of went easy, even though I initially felt they would need a lot of convincing too. But with her parents, it seems like a tough road. Every step we take should be like walking on eggshells—one wrong step, and everything could break apart.

Even though the thought of her father accepting us seems impossible at the moment, I feel like her mother would try to understand us. I remember her father once told me, back when we used to date in school that, it is against their principles and stuff.

Her mother was the one who asked her to end things up the last time but from what Anya has told me, this time, her mother didn't just reject us—so that's kind of positive. Only if I could convince her that I can keep Anya happy, then maybe she'd agree to us, because I think there's nothing a mother wants more than her child's happiness.

I think we should just talk to her first, but not in her home, you know, outside, in some café or hotel and try to convince her. I think it's worth trying. So I grab my phone from my pocket. "Call me when you're free. Need to talk." I text Anya.

My phone rings almost immediately. "Hey," I say, picking up the call.

"Hi." She says cheerfully.

"Where are you? I ask as I hear a vehicle pass by.

"Went to a park after work. Wanted some fresh air. Walking back home right now."

"Oh, we'll talk when you get home." I say.

"Don't worry its empty."

"I just heard a vehicle. Call me when you get to your apartment."

"It's fine. I can talk. Anyway, I'm almost there. Now don't hang up." She says.

"Okay." I give in. "I was thinking if your mother would agree to meet us both in a restaurant or something? Maybe if we both tried to convince her, she might just agree. After all, she knows that we aren't just messing around with each other."

"Maybe. I don't know but we can try." She pauses. "I'll talk to h…" There's a scream from the other end—a loud scream.

"Anya! Anya." I scream on my phone, but there is no reply. There's dead silence and my hands are starting to tremble as the situation is sinking in. "Anya," I shout, but there's still no reply. So I immediately hang up the phone and call Shruti.

Why the fuck she isn't picking up? Dammit! "Shruti, Anya has had an accident… she was walking back from the park." Saying these words out loud, I could almost feel my legs giving up. She doesn't say anything instead just hangs up the phone. I hold the wall in front me and take a few breaths, and at the same time calling an ambulance.

I dash out of my apartment, running towards my car, to get to her as fast as I can. When you're in a hurry, nothing works as you want them to—like this stupid key won't just go in.

I try not to break any traffic lights on the way, as it would only get things worse. I try to reassure myself, telling she is okay to keep my heart from breaking down from the constant assault of thousands of emotions. My phone rings and I immediately pick it up, hoping it would be Anya and she'd say that she's okay.

"Aahil… Anya—we're in the ambulance, on the way to AIIMS. Anya… doesn't look good." It was Shruti, her words in broken sentences.

"I'm coming." I say, trying to hold my emotions, then hang up. This wasn't what I was hoping to hear. So, at the next intersection, I take a sharp U-turn and press the accelerator hard to reach to the hospital as fast as I can.

Only if she'd listen to me for fuck sake. I told her to go home and then call me back. I should've forced her to reach home first, at least then she would've been a little more aware of her surroundings. It's all my fault. "Dammit." I hit the steering.

I rush through the hospital doors, my heart pounding in my chest. I pull out my phone and call Shruti. "Where are you?"

"Outside the operation theatre." She replies, her voice shaking. I hang up the phone and run towards her. I'm not sure how many people I've bumped into, but all I know is I have to reach near her as fast as I can.

As I approach near the operation theatre, I spot Shruti sitting on a chair just outside the door. Her face is hidden in her palms, her elbows propped up on her knees, crying. "Shruti," My voice barely leaves my mouth, but she straightens up and looks at me.

My steps start to slow down as she stands up and my eyes fall on her dress which was covered in blood. Anya's blood. I could literally feel my heart choking in the moment but I still continue walking, even though the steps got heavier with each breath.

She has been trying to hold herself together but I think when she saw me, it all came crumbling down. She runs to me and bury her face on my chest, her fingers clutching my shirt, crying uncontrollably. I lightly place my arms around her, hugging her and let her cry.

"Anya... was lying on the street, covered in blood. I saw ambulance—brought her here. I didn't know what else to do. I don't... I'm sorry." She mumbles on my chest in broken sentences. I don't say anything, instead I hug her tight. She wraps her arms around me as she cries to soothe her heart from everything she's seen in past hour, while I feel numb, just cursing myself and praying she's okay.

Shruti pulls back as a nurse comes up to us. "Are any of you her family member?"

I shake my head. "No," oh, how I wish I was. "Friends."

"Her mom will be here soon."

"We cannot wait any longer. She's in a critical state. We'll have to perform surgery fast. Ask her parents and we'll need you to sign here and here." She says, pointing at the papers. I glance at them, not really taking in the details, just following her finger. My hands are trembling so much that it's hard to hold the pen steady, but I somehow manage.

"She's gonna be okay?" I ask her, my voice barely above a whisper.

The nurse hesitates before speaking. "The patient has lost a lot of blood. We're doing everything we can." She says and walks back inside. The papers are signed now, and I feel like I'm drowning in helplessness. It's all because of me.

ⰔⰔⰔ

I sit there in front of the door, my chest tight with panic, watching doctors and nurses move in a blur, fighting to save her. My whole world is in there, and all I can do is wait... wait outside with this feeling of helplessness, and knowing nothing about what was going on inside with her.

We were so happy yesterday. She was happy, laughing and jumping with me, and today I am sitting here and she's fighting inside. It's like fate doesn't even want us to be happy. The happier we are, the greater the sorrow comes to crumple us.

Shruti sat next to me with her arms crossed, her gaze fixed at the floor. I hear footsteps approaching us, and in hopes that it will be of a doctor I look up, hoping for some answers. But it wasn't of any doctor, rather it was Anya's mom, running towards us.

I place my palm on Shruti's shoulder. She looks up and then at Anya's mother. We rise from the chair and I instinctively take a step aside allowing Shruti to meet her. Shruti walks up to her, and they hug each other tightly, crying. I stay silent in a corner, watching them as Shruti explains her everything. Anya's mother looks at me, but only for a moment, then shift her gaze back to Shruti. She makes her sit on the chair, settling next to her, while I slump on the nearby wall, my arms crossed and my gaze fixed on the door.

The door swings open and a doctor walks out from the operation theatre, and I immediately stand straight. Shruti and Anya's mother also rise from their seats, taking a step closer to the doctor.

He stops in front us. "The patient is stable for now, but her condition is still critical. She's suffered significant internal bleeding, which we've stopped, and there are fractures in her legs and ribs which the doctors are tending to right now." The doctor says, his words hanging in the air, heavy with worry. "We'll shift her to the ICU in the morning."

"Can we see her?" Anya's mother asks him, her voice on the verge of breaking.

"No, not yet." He says and walks away. Anya's mother falls on the chair. Shruti immediately places her arm on her shoulders, trying to console her, but instead starts to cry herself.

I look at them and then at the door. She said she'll stay with me, and I know she will. But my heart just doesn't listen and my eyes are just too tired to hold back any more emotions. She's been in there for more than five hours. It has already been past midnight, but even a slight movement in surrounding would bring all of us to attention. We'd look up expectantly only to be disappointed. We really wished for someone to come and tell us if she's okay, even if we don't get to see her. I sit down on the floor and scratch the back of my head, trying to shift my focus to anything other than crying. Don't you worry Anya, I'm here, with you and I'm not leaving you. You don't leave me either, you have to fight hard, for us.

26

Chapter Twenty Six

My forehead drops to my knee as sleep starts to take over. The sky has started to change its colour. I take a deep breath and look at the chair where Shruti and Anya's mother were. Shruti had propped up her elbow on the handle of the chair and her head rested on her hands as she dozed off. Anya's mother, on the other hand, had her arms crossed. With light footsteps, I walk towards the restroom to wash my face.

Shruti and Anya's mother were both awake now, sitting quietly, waiting. I walk back to them and slump against the wall, my eyes fixed on the door, not really saying anything.

The door swings open, bringing all of us to full attention. The doctor steps out, closing it gently behind him, and I straighten myself as he walks towards us.

"She's stable... for now," his voice was calm but heavy. "We'll be moving her to the ICU and running post- op tests. You can collect the pre-op reports from the Trauma Care department in about an hour. Make sure you get all the scans and X-rays reports."

"I'll get that." I say, my voice filled with an obvious stutter. The doctor turns and walks off, and I glance around. My eyes meet Anya's mom's, but I quickly look away and start walking in the other direction. I'm not sure how to even start a conversation with her and honestly, this doesn't feel like the right moment—she's already dealing with so much. So, instead I walk toward the hospital cafeteria to get them something to eat.

I carefully hold the coffees in my hand and stuff the packet of biscuits in my jacket, then walk back to them. Shruti looks up, and I hand her both the coffees. She passes one to Anya's mother. I then grab the packet of biscuits from my jacket and hand it to her, then take a step back, walking towards my spot and slump against the wall.

The dead silence in the hallway only added to my anxiety, intensifying it with each passing second. But I need to keep myself together. I have to be strong for her. And with these thoughts running in my mind, I take a glance at my watch. It was almost an hour. "I'll go get the reports." I say, not particularly saying to someone.

ᘘᘘᘘ

I am walking back to the operation theatre, looking at the reports in my hand, trying to make some sense of them and figure out if she'd be okay. But despite how hard I try, I am clueless as fuck.

As I look up towards the place where the others were, my feet abruptly stop on their own. Anya's dad was standing in front of his wife, and they were talking. She is the one doing most of the talking, probably just filling him on everything.

I hadn't noticed that he wasn't here until now, and judging by the looks of his suit, he must have been coming here directly from work. There are a lot of things that could happen right now, and I know very well that none of them are going to be in my favour, but I still walk towards them.

He turns around and his gaze falls on me. If he could kill people with his eyes, I would have been long dead by now. His eyes were red with anger as he walked towards me. I stop, my heart starting to beat faster.

He stops right in front of me, and snatches the folder from my hand and tosses on the ground. The loose reports in the folder scatter on the floor. I could see Shruti watching us in horror out of the corner of my eye, while Anya's mom tries to take a step

192

towards us, but he snaps at her. Instantly, she freezes at the same spot. He then takes a step towards me, grabbing my collar, "You bastard," he growls. "I warned you to stay the fuck away from my daughter, and here you are. I know people like you and all your motives—pretending to be someone else to trap girls from rich families to steal their money." His voice gets louder with each word.

"Sir... please, this is not the time." I place my hands on his wrists to remove them from my collar but he jerks them away, gripping my collar tighter.

"Sir? You made my daughter rebel against me. You're the reason my daughter is in this hospital and you want me to believe you have no other motive. I won't let it happen, you lying piece of shit. She thinks you love her, but I'll show her that you are nothing more than a liar and a fraud."

"Okay, enough is enough." I raise my voice. "You stand here yelling at me and throwing her reports on the ground—if you loved her so much then, where were you last night when she was fighting for her life? This suit tells a lot about your priorities." For a few moments, he is stunned. I think he wasn't expecting me to talk back, but he didn't leave me any choice. I grab his wrists again and yanks it from my collar.

I take a step back and then walk toward where the reports lie scattered. Leaning down, I pick up the pages and place them back in the folder, then walk towards Anya's mom and give her the folder. We have a brief eye contact as she takes the folder from my hand, and then I turn around, walking towards I don't know where—just away from this place.

ᑭᑭᑭ

I am sitting in a chair out in the corridor, far enough from Anya's parents, but not too far from her, when I suddenly feel a hand on my shoulder. I look up, and it's Shruti, standing there with sad and tired eyes. "You okay?" She asks, her voice soft.

Without waiting for an answer, she moves around, sitting beside me. She slips her arm through mine, leaning her head gently on my shoulder. Her voice is barely above a whisper. "She's gonna be okay."

"I know." I say, trying to hide the pain inside. "You okay?"

She nods against my shoulder. "Yeah."

A few minutes pass and neither of us says anything. I can feel the weight of the situation hanging in the air, but I try to keep my voice steady. "You should be with aunty. They're gonna shift her to the ICU soon. She might need you."

Shruti shifts slightly, "I know," she replies, her tone softer now. "But I needed some space from her dad. And... I wanted to check on you, too." She pauses, then adds quietly, "I don't like him at all."

"Yeah," I mutter. "Me neither. But it's fine. We just... deal with it."

She straightens up then, pulling away slightly and looking at me more seriously. "Will you be okay?" She asks.

I give her a small, reassuring smile, though I'm not sure I believe it myself. "Yeah I am."

She doesn't seem convinced. She looks at me for a second longer, like she's trying to find the words she could say to make it better. Then, with a quiet sigh, stands up and walks back toward where Anya's parents were.

The doors of the operation theatre opens, and a stretcher rolls out, carrying Anya. My heart stops. She's lying there, barely recognizable—her body covered in bruises, bandages, and plaster. An IV drip hangs from the pole beside her, and a fresh bandage is wrapped tightly around her forehead. Seeing her like this makes my chest ache in a way I've never felt before.

The nurses carefully move the stretcher sown the hall, her parents and Shruti walking close behind. As they pass me, I instinctively take a step forward, wanting to be near her, to make sure she's okay. But her father's voice cuts through the air, cold and sharp.

"Stay away from her."

I freeze. The words hit me like a punch, and I stood there, rooted to the spot, watching them take her further down the hall. My chest feels tight, like it's being crushed under the weight of everything. I turn slowly, my eyes blurry as I blink rapidly, trying to stop the tears from falling.

ᗡᗡᗡ

It has been an hour since Anya has been shifted to the ICU. I stand at a distance from the ward where she is. Her father left for work as soon as she was shifted to the room. To be honest, I'm not sure whether I should be grateful that he's gone or resent him for abandoning his daughter.

"Hey, can you come here?" I text Shruti, then put my phone back in my pocket. I watch her glance at the message, then look over at me. She raises her eyebrows, and I nod. Without a word, she gets up and walks over towards me.

"If you want, you can go home and get some rest. You haven't slept last night. I'm here and aunty is here too, and there is nothing we are doing except sitting and waiting." I say.

"I don't wanna leave her." She replies.

"It's okay. Take rest and come back. Take my car." I reach for the keys in my pocket and hold it out to her.

"Okay, but call me if anything comes up." She says, taking the keys from my hand.

"Sure." I say and she turns around. "Hey, wait. Can you give aunty, my number? You know... just in case." She looks at me over her shoulder and nod.

She walks back to her. I watch her talking to Anya's mom from the corner of my eye as I don't want her to catch me looking at them. I see her take her phone and type something on it. They hug each other before she turns around and walks toward me. She hugs me and then leaves.

27
Chapter Twenty Seven

It has been three days since Anya was moved to the ICU. There's only a set time to visit her—or rather, to see her, since she has been in a coma the entire time. Not once has she moved, just lying there with tubes attached to help her breathe and drip to give her the nutrients she needs.

As if knowing that she is in such pain wasn't miserable enough, I don't get to see her when everyone else does. Her father doesn't stay at the hospital, except for the scheduled meeting times, and even then, he just stands there. It's aunty and Shruti who go and hold her, talk to her hoping that she would listen and wake up, but she doesn't. Maybe I am overthinking it, but it feels like he only comes to the hospital to stop me from seeing her.

Shruti would often make videos of Anya and send them to me, and I am incredibly grateful to her for doing that, but it's not the same as seeing her with my own eyes, holding her hand and talking to her. But thankfully, the door has a glass window in the upper half. So, when no one's around, I take a peek and look at her.

Rohan and Khushi visited us, and I know they meant well when they asked not to worry, and to be honest things look a little dire right now, but I know it in my heart that she's going to come back. She isn't leaving me this time.

My parents also visited yesterday, and I met them outside, because you know... if they met her then they would inevitably meet her parents too, and that is the last thing I want right now. And moreover, I don't want anyone talk rudely to my parents. I know her mother wouldn't, but her father has been nothing but a jerk. So, I sat with them outside the hospital, in the campus park. Mom hugged me, trying to console me but instead ended up crying. I hugged her back, but I didn't cry. I haven't cried since she was shifted to the ICU.

Shruti has joined the office, actually, I asked her to. But she still comes by in the morning and then again in the evening after work. So most of the time, it's just me and Anya's mom here. We have started to talk, even if it's only a little. It started with me bringing meals for her. She was reluctant to eat at first, but I told her that Anya wouldn't want to see her like this, so she agreed. Good old trick, and now we eat together. I mean, we don't talk much, but we do have our meals together.

ᔕᔕᔕ

I stand at the door of the ICU, looking at her through the glass since no one was around. It was around ten at night. My hands stuffed in my pockets, shifting weight from one leg to another.

She looked pale amidst all those machines. I place my palm on the glass. "What happened to us, Anya? Did we do something wrong? Then why do these things happen to us? I know it's too much to ask for—I know you're in too much pain, but please fight harder. You said you would stay with me. You promised." I say, my voice barely above a whisper.

"Aahil." I hear my name and I turn around to look. Anya's mom was sitting there. My heart starts to race faster, and I instantly pull away my palm from the window, stuffing it back in my pocket.

"I... I was—nothing." I stutter, taking a few steps away from the door, my gaze anywhere but her. I really didn't know when she came back, or how much has she heard.

"Aahil, come here." She says, her voice low and soft. I take slow steps towards her and sit on the chair beside her. A silence settles between us. Maybe she was thinking about how to start the conversation, so I kept my mouth shut and sat there quietly. "Your parents know about this?" She finally asks.

"Yes." I nod my head. "They actually met her a few days ago."

"Oh, that explains why she was in such a hurry to tell her father." She sighs. "You know she and her father are like each other. Stubborn. If they have made their mind, they want it to happen at any cost." Her voice low.

"Yeah, I've seen it." I agree. "Once she has made up her mind, there's no turning back."

"Yeah, but sometimes being so stubborn gets her in trouble, and she just doesn't understands." She leans back a little. "But I see why she is ready to fight for you."

I force a smile. "You know, we were gonna meet you in a café or something so we could convince you. We were talking about it on the phone when this..." my voice trails off. "I told her to go home and then call me back, but she wouldn't listen saying that it's an empty street and nothing would happen, and I left it at that. Maybe if I didn't give in, she would've been a little more aware of her surroundings and maybe we would be having a conversation in a café, instead of a hospital bench." I hold myself back, I don't want to look weak. I close my eyes and take a deep breath, to hold back the tears. Lately these tears have been too eager to come at any instance. "I still feel guilty for not pushing her harder to go back home and... I just never thought that I'd have to talk to you here."

She lets out a deep sigh. We have been doing it a lot lately. "Maybe it's was for the better that you were on the phone with her, or if something would've happened to her, we would've... lost her. At least now we have a hope." She forces a smile. I cannot imagine the amount of strength she had to gather to say this amidst everything that's been going on.

"Can I ask you something?"

"Yeah,"

"What do I have to do to deserve her? I promise I'll always keep her happy." I say, my gaze low but towards her.

She thinks for a moment. "Convince, a lot." She says.

"I don't understand." I ask, puzzled by her words.

"You'll need to do a lot of convincing before you can ask for our daughter's hand."

"Okay." I nod and turn away from her.

There is a silence between us for a while. "You know," she says, and I look at her. "Anya has never been an easy child. She has always been mischievous, always looking for opportunities to turn the house upside down. But that's what made her so special. She made our lives special. She's always smiling and she would talk so much that you'll get a headache. But the moment she isn't around, I start missing her voice. But when… you know, you guys had to break up, everything changed. I thought I was protecting my family, and I did, but in the process, I lost her."

She pauses for a moment before speaking again. "She wouldn't laugh, she wouldn't speak much—always in her room. You know, when she used to tell me about her day, or when she threw tantrums on me—I felt like I was a part of her life, and that felt good. But it all stopped after that day. She wasn't the Anya I knew. It was like she was right there in front of me, yet she wasn't."

Her voice started to break, so I quickly grab the water bottle and offer her, but she politely declines and continues. "When she came to me to talk about you a couple of months ago, it was as if I saw my Anya after a really long time. And when I didn't stop her, she smiled like she used to, she hugged me like she used to. I know you'll keep her happy, because I've seen her happy with you, and I know you truly love her. I have seen you these past couple of days and maybe it's my emotions talking but I'm proud of her that she chose you." She puts her palm on my wrist, giving it a reassuring squeeze. "But despite everything, you still have to convince her father, and you just loving her won't do it."

"I don't know what to say. I wish I could tell her what you just said. She would've been really happy." I trace my palm with my thumb, a shiver running through my body.

"Then tell her tomorrow. Maybe then she'll wake up. I'll make an excuse and get you some time with her, but make it quick."

Her words felt like a gallon of water to a person who's been walking in a desert for days. And as much as I want to look strong, a tear slides from the side of my eye, and instead of wiping it away—I just let it fall.

ᗞᗞᗞ

The meeting time starts at nine. I stand there outside, gazing at her through the window while the doctors performed routine checks. I look at my watch again and again, growing impatient. There are still fifteen long minutes before I could finally meet her, touch her and talk to her.

I keep shifting my weight from one leg to the other, just can't afford to stand still. Anya's mom and Shruti are sitting behind me, having breakfast. I'm not joining them though—I'm way too excited to even think about food right now. I'm just not in the mood to eat.

Honestly, I'm kind of thankful to Shruti. She could be making this a little awkward, but she's not. It's like she's letting me do it without giving me a hard time, and I really appreciate that.

The door swings open, and the doctor steps out, holding the file. Without waiting to hear what he has to say, I rush past him into the room. My heart, which had been racing so fast, suddenly stops. All this time, I imagined what it would be like to finally be inside, to see her. But now that I'm here, seeing her—her beautiful face in such a fragile, miserable state—it's almost too much to bear.

A shiver runs down my spine as I sit on the chair next to the bed. Slowly, I run my fingers on her hand, caressing it, then gently running my fingers on her palm. I close my eyes as I feel an unbearable ache in my heart. The hands she used to wrap around my neck lacked its usual warmth. The legs she used to wrap around my waist are covered in bandages. Although, the bandage wrapped around her forehead is now removed and instead a dressing is done on the left side of her forehead.

I gently run my finger on her forehead, running down to her cheeks and her lips—those soft lips now had stitches on it. I look at her, and I know she is in a lot of pain, but I can't do anything for her.

In all my life, I haven't felt so helpless before.

Gathering all my strength, I envelope her left palm in mine as I start to talk to her. "Anya, baby I know you can hear me. I am right here, with you." My voice is barely above a whisper. "I'm sorry I couldn't come earlier but I was looking at you, always. You know, there's a window on the gate and I look at you through that window. You already know I like staring at you while you sleep, and it's your fault that you look so adorable when you sleep."

I take a deep breath. "You know, I have learnt a new song on guitar and I wanna play it to you but you've been sleeping for so long. Now c'mon, wake up already. I know you wanna hear it too. We can play it the same way, like when you sat on my lap, with guitar in front of you, in our apartment, or if you want, we can go somewhere beautiful, maybe a place where we can sit on grass and above us would be a beautiful sky filled with twinkling stars, Anywhere—you name it, and we'll go. I'll keep my chin on your shoulder and tickle you with my beard. It has grown a bit. Maybe we could style it together."

She still doesn't move, and the longer she is taking to wake up, the harder it is getting for me to hold myself up together. Dammit Anya, wake up already. "You know there's a hot girl at the reception, and she is making passes at me. I swear I didn't talk to her, but you know how insistent girls can be when they see a pretty face. Oh wait! I forgot to tell you. Remember when we were talking that we should meet your mother and convince her? Well, guess what? I talked to her and you already know how charming I am—I convinced her. And you know the best part is, that we've become buddies, and we eat all our meals together. She even has my number." Still nothing. I gently place my forehead on her hand, making sure I don't hurt her. I am not really sure how long I have or worse how much longer I can hold myself together.

"Anya, baby c'mon, I gave you such good news. Wake up now honey... please. You promised me that you'll stay with me forever. Now might really be a good time to wake up because it is really getting hard. Anya, plea..." I feel her grip tighten around me a little.

I repeatedly press the button to call the doctor, along with me screaming, "Doctor!" Anya's mom and Shruti barge into the room almost immediately. "She's responding." I say.

28
Chapter Twenty Eight

A ray of happiness has finally pierced the dense clouds of sorrow that hovered above us during these few days. For the first time in a while, we have a smile on our face, our eyes filled with tears—happy ones. These past few days have been incredibly difficult for all of us, especially for Anya, and I know that the coming days are going to be harder as she comes to terms with the reality, but we have taken our first step towards it.

All of us were standing outside the ICU gate, watching the doctors perform some tests. Her father arrives and the slight smile that I had, almost instantly fades away. Now, he'll try to push me away and not let me see her. So, before he could say anything, I take a step back and sit on the chair. Anya's mom tells him that Anya has come out of coma, while Shruti comes and sits beside me.

"She'll be okay." She assures.

"She has to." I say, momentarily looking at her, then shifting my gaze to my palm on my lap.

"She will be. By the way, what the fuck did you say to her?"

Her question makes me smile. I look at her. "Nothing. I guess, she loves me more than you."

She smiles back, then crosses her legs, looking at the door in front of us. I keep shaking my legs impatiently, until a nurse calls us inside. The doctor was still standing alongside the bed.

But as I was about to enter the room, Anya's dad signals me to stop, but her mother touches his hand, and says something to him.

I am not sure what she said, but he allows me enter the room. I step inside quietly, and stand against the wall behind everyone. To be honest, I wanted to be ahead of everyone and see her, but the way things are, I should be grateful that I am in the room.

Anya has opened her eyes, and she is slowly observing her surroundings, looking at the bandages and equipment around her. Her gaze slowly shift on us, her face with a blank expression. Her mother walks towards her and takes the seat next to her, gently running her palm over her pale face. Anya blinks but remains silent. Her mother leans and place a motherly kiss on her forehead, tears streaming down her face. "I missed you so much Ana," she says, her voice barely above a whisper. "Look all of us are here. We were waiting for you to wake up."

Anya's gaze shifts from her mother to her father, then Shruti and then at me. Our eyes hold each other's gaze for a brief moment when she says, "What is he doing here?" No trace of any sarcasm, just plain blank expression. *What?*

"She doesn't want you here." Her father almost instantaneously jump in as if he had been waiting for the slightest opportunity to kick me out of the room. But what choice do I have? If she doesn't want me here, then I better walk out of the room.

What is he doing here? Like really dude? I look at the sky through the window in front of me, silently complaining to God as I take a deep breath and exhale. "Maybe…" I try to think of a reason but come up with nothing.

I walk back to the door of the ICU and peek at her through the glass window. To be honest, I was hoping that if she sees me again, maybe she'll want me back in there.

I keep looking at her until her eyes meet mine, only to part the next second. She looked away. A thousand deaths wouldn't have hurt so badly. Her mother kept talking to her. She would say something, a few times, but mostly nod. I walk back to the chair as I cannot bear her looking away from me again.

I rise from the chair as I see everyone walking out of the room. The doctor was still in there with Anya. Her dad walks directly towards me. "I've been very patient with you all this time because of my daughter. But it's clear that she doesn't want you here, so get the hell out of here and don't you ever show her your face again." His voice loud. Anya's mom tries to stop him but he points a finger at her. "I let him inside because you told Anya would want to see him, but now that she doesn't want him here, I'll do what I think is right." He says looking at her, then shift his gaze on me. "Now get the fuck out of here."

ᗡᗡᗡ

I was sitting with my hands crossed behind my head, leaning back on a bench in the hospital lawn, wondering what could've been the reason behind those words. Was she trying to say something? I don't know. I look above, shifting my gaze from one branch to another, and take a deep breath and sigh.

"Hey." I look at my left and find Shruti standing. "I've been looking for you. Why aren't you answering your phone?" She says.

I reach for my phone in my pocket. There were three missed calls from Shruti. "Ah, I didn't notice it was on silent." I say.

"Mind if I sit?" She asks.

"You already know, you don't have to ask anything."

"I was only being polite." She says and sits next to me. "My god, your aura is suffocating. How do you sit here with such negativity?" She starts swaying her hand over my head.

"What are you doing?"

"I am shooing away the negativity around you and I'm sorry in advance if I accidently hit your head. But of course that wouldn't be an accident." She says with a smile on her face. I know she's trying to cheer me up, but how can I smile—after everything? But I still force a smile to honour her effort. "See, this really works and I haven't even hit you, yet."

"You can stop now." I say. We sit there for a while in silence. "Thank you."

She rests her elbow on my shoulder. "You know what your problem is Aahil? You keep bottling up things inside, even if it keeps on eating you. You try to take burden of everything on yourself, like everything's your fault. You take stand for everyone but never for yourself. Look at how uncle has been treating you ever since we've been here, and yet you let him do it over and over again."

"What am I supposed to say? I don't want him to hate me any more than he hates me now and ruin my chances with Anya." I exhale. "I wish things had been different. It's clear that he hates me to the extent that he is ready to leave his precious business, just to stop me from meeting Anya. I shouldn't say it but really, if it were for me, I would've shoved his smug face on the wall and punched some sense in it."

"See that's what I'm trying to say. Standing up for yourself doesn't mean being disrespectful. You're smart. Try to find a line, and stop being an emotional fool and think with your head. You should've taken stand for yourself when he gave you shit, or think what are you conveying? That you're weak. When you can't even take stand for yourself, how the hell do you think that they would trust you with their daughter? I really don't understand what's gotten into you. Do you honestly think that you'll be an emotional fool and somehow they'll see that you love her and give their daughter to you, huh?" she shifts a little towards me.

"Stop being so naïve. Do you really want them to let you marry Anya out of pity? And even if they do, can you live with that? Knowing that it wasn't your love that brought you guys together, but their pity. And if you think he's here because he hates you, then I don't know since when you've become so delusional. Not everything is about you. You being sad won't change a thing. If it could, then let's do it together and cry all day."

I sigh, and sit there silently. "Maybe instead of being sad and miserable, you should get up and gather yourself. Make a fist and make it count, so that the one who caused this havoc in your life knows that he messed up with wrong person." She says.

"Yeah, you're right. This isn't gonna help." I run my hands through my face and hair.

"I don't have to tell you this Aahil. You already know these things."

"You're right. By the way, when did you become all smart and wise?" I finally smile.

"I was born smart." She smiles back. "And in case you're wondering why Anya said 'what is he doing here?', that's because she doesn't have any recent memory. So, for her, you guys never got together. The doctor said that it appears to be a case of retrograde amnesia, maybe because of the injuries, but they need to do some tests to confirm it. He also said that if we talked to her and tries to help her remember, she'd recover soon."

29
Chapter Twenty Nine

I was sitting outside Anya's room in the chair, gazing at the dark sky through the window. It was around ten o'clock at night, and Anya was sleeping inside. It was for the first time since the accident that Anya's mom had gone home at night. On other days, she would briefly leave and then come back to the hospital.

Although it is too reckless of me but I still sneak in her room. The room is dimly lit. I take slow steps towards her bed, then sit on the chair beside her. The tubes were no longer connected to her nostrils, and she was breathing on her own. A strand of her hair fell on her cheek, which I gently brush aside.

"Anya," I whisper. I know it is very selfish of me but this is the only time I can talk to her without any restrictions. Her eyes half open. She then turns to look at me, and was about to say something but I put my finger on her lips gently to shush her.

"Anya, please listen to me first, then if you want, I'll go." I whisper.

"Where's mom and dad?" She asks.

"Home. Just hear me once." I say and she nods. "Anya, I know this is clearly not the right time to say all this and I know that you need rest, so, I won't waste much of your time." I envelope her palm in mine. "I love you Anya. I've always loved you and I know you love me. It's just that the doctor here told that you've forgotten everything from the past two years. But deep down, I know you still feel that love for me."

I give a gentle, reassuring squeeze on her palm. "Anya, we've been back together for almost six months now. I know you think we've broken up few years ago, but our paths crossed again and we got back together. And you know, I don't make the same lame jokes I used to."

She doesn't say anything, her eyes locked on me. "You know, during these six months, we've had breakfast and dinners together in bed, and you especially liked your favourite paneer kebabs we had, at our apartment in the balcony, gazing at the sea." Her face is blank, as if she has no clue as to what I was saying, but I still continue. "Anya, we went on many dates—we walked on beaches. We saw the sun setting down in the sea and also on the hills. Please tell me you remember them Anya." An involuntary tear slide from the side of my eye, which I immediately wipe with my thumb. I don't have time for this. I have to make her remember.

"Anya, do you remember meeting my mom and dad, and how you were scared and worried that you'd do something stupid in front of them, but then when you met them, you were so happy. We were happy. You know, we decided to talk to your mother too, but you know what? I talked to her... while you were sleeping, and she kinda loves me. You know, we ate all our meals together too." I blink my eyes, because it started to get a little blurry.

"I love you so much Anya. I can't live without you." I take a deep breath. "I... I've died a thousand deaths while you were sleeping, but I knew it in my heart that you won't leave me alone because you promised, that you'll stay with me, forever. Will you?"

She nods her head, gesturing me to come closer. "You didn't tell me that we also did it a couple of times during sleepovers." Her voice was breathy as if she had just ran a marathon.

"Yeah, I know we thought back then that we'll do after we get married... what?" I look at her face, her eyes moist, but I saw the widest smile I had seen on her face in the last few days. I could barely control my happiness. "Am I awesome or what? I meet you the first time and you wake up from your sleep and I meet you the next time and bring your memory back. I think it's high time I should think of changing my profession."

"Don't get too full of yourself. I never lost my memory, stupid."

"Huh? Then why did the doctor say that. Anyway, I just can't tell you how happy I am to see you smiling." I lean towards her to kiss.

"Stop!" She says and I stop in the middle. "It'll taste like medicine."

I lean in, getting closer to her lips and whisper, "I don't care." I kiss her. Not a long kiss as she would run out of breath but enough to fill up the void that had been building up during these days. I then move up and press a kiss on her forehead.

"No you didn't. You were busy checking out that reception bitch. Is she beautiful?"

"Compared to you, not even a little bit." I say. She narrows her eyes. "You still look beautiful, I mean a little pale, but beautiful."

"Better, or I would've kicked her. As you can see that I have a solid armour on my legs." She couldn't laugh as it would lead to her coughing but she grins instead.

"Oh, you mean this." I place my hand on the plaster on her legs. "Rock solid." I laugh. "I missed you."

"You've said it already."

"I cannot say it enough."

"How's mom?" she asks.

"She's good. She has gone home at night for the first time at night."

She sighs. "And dad?" I didn't reply to her. I mean, what can I say? She looks at me and let's out another sigh. "How did you talk to my mom?"

"Umm, it kinda just happened. In the beginning, it was mostly like talking about necessary things like reports and stuff. But then we got to eat our meals together, because it was mostly the two of us sitting on the chair outside. Then one day, I was looking at you from that glass window, and she saw me. And that's when it happened."

"Why window? I don't remember you coming to me until today." She interrupts me.

I don't say anything for a while. "I like staring at you while you sleep." I say, but my voice kind of gave her the reason. She nods and I continue. "She called me and we sat and talked about you. She even said that she is proud of you because you chose me. In fact, she's the one who helped me meet you in the morning. She's a lovely lady."

She takes a deep breath. "I'm sorry for what I said in the morning."

"Ah, don't worry about it. You should focus on getting better as fast as you can, and leave everything on me. I'll take care of you, and I'll convince your father too. You have to worry about nothing." I say, then lean forward and press a kiss on her forehead.

"No, listen to me. There's a reason I said what I said in the morning, and it wasn't because I didn't want you here, but I wanted them to believe my lie that I've lost my two years of memory." She takes a pause as she gets out of breath.

"What! Why?" I look at her face, trying to read in between the lines, but her face didn't give anything.

"It wasn't an accident. Someone tried to kill me."

"What? Why? How do you know? I mean, why would anyone try to kill you?" I ask, clearly shocked to my very being.

"The driver who hit me, reversed his car to check if I was dead, but then people started gathering and he ran away. I wasn't unconscious at that time. My eyes were half open. So I know."

Instinctively, my grip tightens around her hand before I realise and let go of it. I don't want to add to her misery right now. "Who do you think would try to kill you?" I start pacing around the room. Kill her? Who in the world would want to do that?

She stares at me, as if waiting for me to put the puzzle together. "You've got to be kidding me." I refuse to believe what she said could be true. "How can you be so sure?"

She looks away. "I've seen him do shitty things for business. Here, his reputation was at stake. I don't see why not." Tears start to fall from her eyes.

"But why you? And not me? Killing me would have been so much easier than killing you. I would've been out of your life and they would've got what they wanted." I ask, confused, and frankly enraged.

"Killing you would've lead to an investigation. Your parents would've called the police and I wouldn't have kept my mouth shut either. And I would've gone against him too which would ruin his image and it would cost him too much. If I died in an accident, and my dad never got the police involved, the suspicion would've never fallen on him."

I hold her face in my palm and wipe her tears. "Crying isn't good for you. Please, don't. No one's gonna lay a finger on you now. I'll make sure of it, and I'm really sorry for what you had to go through, you deserve so much better than this."

"That's why I said that in the morning after I told everything to the doctor, just hiding the fact that it was my father who tried to... so, he helped." She says.

"Shit dude. Is he fucked in his head or what? But now that you mention it, I never saw anyone from the police come here too. I just didn't notice it before."

She shakes her head. "I was scared Aahil. I thought if he saw that I still wanna be with you, god knows what he'd do next and maybe I won't..." I put my finger on her lips.

"I'm right here next to you. I won't let anything happen to you. You focus on getting well and leave everything else on me. Now sleep tight." I kiss her forehead, then sit next to her.

We sit in silence for a few minutes before I get up to walk out of the room. But as I was about to turn around, she tries to lift her hand and I immediately hold it, supporting her. "Mom should never know." She says, and I nod. I then gently caress her head, then walk out of the room.

ᗞᗞᗞ

I slump back in the chair outside the room, my eyes locked on the door. I can't even begin to imagine what she must be feeling—realizing that the man she's called father her entire life, the one who's been there since the moment she was born, tried to take her life. And for what reason?

In times when the world feels like it's against you, you know that your mom would be there to support you but it is your dad who will shield you, protect you. A child learns to take his first steps holding his dad's hands. And when he runs, he knows that his dad is with him and he would not let him fall or let anything happen to him. He trusts him.

I remember how I used to wait for my dad to come home when I was a child, at the door and when he would open the gate and come inside, I'd jump on him screaming 'dad'. He would pick me up and take me for a quick round nearby. I remember sitting on his bike facing backwards as I couldn't see anything in front, singing and enjoying the ride. Whenever I screwed up, he was the first person I would go to, because I knew it in my heart that he'll always have my back.

With all the thoughts running in my head, I grab my phone from my pocket. I know it's late at night but I needed to make this call. "Hey, dad."

30

Chapter Thirty

"Is he fucked in his head or what?" Shruti says, her voice loud. We were sitting at a corner table in the hospital cafeteria as I tell her everything. Anya was with her mom, and I was a little relived that she is safe, even if I couldn't be there for a while.

"I said exactly the same thing, but you gotta stop shouting."

"Yeah, sorry. But I want to punch him so bad. I feel like going to Anya's room and punching his smug face so hard that his teeth fall off. I mean, look at the nerve he has—he's still there in that room after what he's done."

"Yeah. Last night when Anya told me everything, I felt like if I see him I'd kill him then and there. But that would be like letting him off too easy. I wanna hit where it will hurt him the most." I take a sip of my coffee.

"So, you have something on your mind? You seem pretty calm like you've everything figured."

"Oh, I'm not calm. I am anything but calm right now. But someone advised me not to let my emotions take over or I won't be able to think clearly."

"It's such a good advice. She must be really wise." She says nonchalantly.

"Nah, she stole that advice from someone else." I say and she playfully punches on my knuckles. "Anyway, here's the trail. Anya went to her father to talk about us and when I picked her up she was in a really bad mood. And knowing her and her father, they must have been heated argument. Her father doesn't back off and he couldn't risk losing his reputation in the market, especially when he tried to set her up with Akash to strengthen his partnership with fellow businessman—it would cost him a big hit in business. So he found an easy way out to save his business and his reputation by getting her killed, because he knew Anya wouldn't back off either. He gave his driver money which I saw him give to some shady man. Although it's a theory but it fits in perfectly."

I take another sip before continuing. "With the grace of god, Anya survived. All this time, I thought that he came at meeting times to stop me from seeing her. While that was one of the reason but he also wanted to keep a close watch on Anya, making sure that didn't know anything that could expose his monstrous actions." I say, and slump back with my hand crossed behind my head. "But you gotta give credit to Anya for thinking cleverly amidst all the suffering—thinking of amnesia, lost two years of memory, and not wanting me around. This way, it's a win for her dad that he can get her to marry anyone he wants."

Shruti kept listening intently. I lean forward and say, keeping my voice low. "Last night I was so angry that I didn't even know what to do, and after hearing what Anya's dad did to her, I kinda missed my dad. So, I called him and told him everything. He asked me to check if there are any CCTV cameras nearby. That way we could file an RTI and he has some connection through which we can get the footage as early as possible. So, as soon as Anya's mom came back, I went to the street where the accident happened and luckily there was a CCTV camera on a nearby street light. So, I've filed the RTI and have given the copy to my dad. Soon we'll have the video of the accident, and then we can make our next move. Until then, I'm gonna pretend that I still want to meet her, waiting outside and she'll pretend that she has not yet recovered her memories back—you know, so as to not arouse suspicion."

"Whoa! I just hope everything goes according to your plan and that bastard gets a taste of his own medicine." She lifts her mug and finishes her coffee in one go, then put the container on the table with a force as if she was doing shots. "And god, she's clever."

"After all she's her father's daughter, except for the evil part." I chuckle.

"And the conceited face." She agrees.

"Thank god, not his face. Unlike him, she's beautiful inside out." I smile.

ৰৰৰ

I sneak in her room again, thanks to Shruti, as she took Anya's mom with her to her apartment for the night. These five days since our last talk have felt far too long. With light feet, I walk towards her bed and sit on the chair beside it, gently poking her on her waist.

"You do realize that I'm trying to sleep right now." She says with a familiar smile but without opening her eyes. Her voice sounder so much stronger now.

"Oh I'm here to sing you a lullaby. Or would you prefer a good night kiss over it."

"Kiss would be better." She opens her eyes and says. I lean down towards her and place a kiss on her forehead and then her lips. "Now sing me a lullaby."

"Honestly, I haven't made one for you." I scratch the back of my head. "But I can tell you a story."

"Will it be better than the ones you used to tell at night?"

I hold her hand and caress her hair with the other hand. "I'll try."

"Kiss me again. Then I'll keep mum." I lean towards her again, but stop before kissing her, her face inches away from mine, and I look at her lips, then lean slowly and brush my nose against hers, and then kiss her.

Our stories were nothing fancy, but more or less, they were like imagining a day together in the future. I look at her eagerly waiting face, and how she innocently blinks her eyes like a child waiting for a story. I lean a little, intertwining my fingers with hers before I begin. "Okay, so the premise is that, it was a weekend and I had to go to work because something urgent came up." I say and she nods, with a beautiful smile. "I knock at the door of our home, then wait for you to open the door. You take your own sweet time to open the door, as if you were making me wait intentionally. And then, when you finally open the door, you were holding a knife in your hand. 'Take whatever you want, but please leave me.' I chuckle. You roll your eyes and then turn around, making your way back to the kitchen. You were wearing my t-shirt which looked way oversized on you and comfy pyjamas. I shut the door behind me, then place my bag on the couch and take out a carry bag from it, taking it to our bedroom and placing it on the bed. Without changing my clothes, I walk towards the kitchen and stand right behind you, so close, that I breathed in your scent. But you don't look back and continue to chop the vegetables on the board in front of you. All pieces uneven." She punches me playfully on my arm and I laugh, then place a kiss on her knuckles with which she punched me.

"Okay, it's a story. We can say imaginary things. All pieces even. Happy now?" I look at her and she smiles. I continue. "So, with a swift movement, I slide my hands under your t-shirt, wrapping them around your waist. I then slowly lean forward, and rest my chin on your right shoulder, and softly place a kiss on your neck."

I look at her biting her lip, her eyes closed. I place my thumb on her lip, slowly caressing it. Instinctively she releases it, and I lean towards her face and place a kiss on her lips on the exact spot where she was biting. "Don't bite it now. Let it heal first." She nods.

"So where were we?"

"Chin on my neck."

"I lean down and pick you up with one hand sliding under your knee and the other supporting your back. I carefully walk out of the kitchen towards our bed room. As we reach near our bed, I gesture for you to look towards the bed. You turn your head and look at the carry bag lying on the bed. I take a step forward and you stretch your arm and grab the bag while still being in my arms. You open the bag and there's a dress. 'What's the occasion?' you ask, taking out the dress from the bag. 'Noooo!' you say in a super dramatic way as you recall that it's the same dress you were looking at, the last time we went shopping. A black gown with a slit on the left."

"I lower you carefully on the bed, while you were too focused on the dress, grinning ear to ear. 'Tell me, what's special today?' you ask again. 'It was a weekend and I wasn't there with you. So I had to make up to you.' I say. You put the dress aside and stretching both your arms, you hug me. Your face rested on my chest. 'Thank you,' you say, and I hug you back tightly."

She pulls my hand again, and I open my eyes. I didn't realize closing my eyes—I mean, it all feels more real with closed eyes. I look at her, and she stares right back at me. This time, I didn't need her to tell me what she wanted. I lean towards her. Gently placing my palm on her face, I kiss her slowly—trying to tell her how much I longed for her, savouring every moment of it.

"Continue." She says as our lips part, her voice breathy.

"Just a sec." I say, and look at her for a moment. "You are really adorable, you know that right?"

She blushes profusely. I continue. "So, I pull you close and you grab the dress along with you. 'Here's a thought. How about we go out for dinner, some place nice? I ask. 'What about the vegetables?' You reply. Clearly you're too concerned about the vegetables and I understand because you cut them even for the first time." I chuckle and she pinches the skin of my hand in which I was holding hers.

I smile at her and pinch her cheeks lightly. "So, I caress the strand of your hair. 'We'll leave them in the fridge.' I say, resting my chin on your shoulder. You blush like you're blushing right now and nod. You walk inside the bathroom and I make my way to the kitchen to put the vegetables in the fridge."

"You wear the grown gracefully, then stand with your back in front of me, 'zip me up.' You say. I stand, shifting all your hair on to your left, but before I zip up the dress, I place kisses along the exposed skin of your back. Once I zip up the dress, you gracefully walk towards the mirror and wear silver earring that beautifully compliment the dress. You turn around to show me, and I swear to god—that dress looked like it was made just for you, the way it fits you—dude, you should look at yourself through my eyes." I pause and look at her. Her eyes are closed and her breathing even. "Ana," I say gently, but she doesn't respond. Her fingers still intertwined with mine. I carefully untangle my fingers, then lightly caress her hair and leave the room.

31
Chapter Thirty One

It has been a couple of hours since the discharge formalities have all been duly completed and now Anya is been discharged from the hospital. She was sitting on a wheelchair with her parents accompanying her. I walk a few steps behind her, you know, to make sure she safely reaches to her car.

It was a struggle for her to get in the car, but she is resilient. Once she is properly settled in the car, her mother came to me to bid me goodbye. She also placed her hand on my shoulder—that's reassuring, and comforting to know that she cared enough to come and goodbye, despite her husband and her daughter in her view, didn't want me around.

In the past few days, I kept on pretending to try to meet her, you know, peeking through window and she kept ignoring me in front of her parents—letting them believe on the lie that she still hasn't recovered her memory and then on nights when Shruti would take Anya's mom to her apartment, I'd sneak in and meet her.

A part of me is happy for her, she's going back to her home, leaving these grey and empty walls of these hospital behind. And another part of me is sad because I won't be able to see her every day, but a bigger part of me is scared for her. Throughout all the years I've known her, I never had to worry about her safety in her own home. However, with everything that has happened in the last few days, the idea of her returning to her home doesn't feel right to me. But what can I do about it? They say that if things are meant to be, they'll find a way, but that doesn't stop me from worrying about her. Although I've asked her to request her mother to sleep with her, and be there for her at all times, but this anxiety and concern isn't going away anytime soon.

There's a part of me which fears that I'll lose her again, and I don't even want to think about it. We have to be very careful with each step or else she would be in a big trouble. And to add the cherry on top in a negative way, she lost her phone in the accident and that worries me more. There is no way she could contact me in case of an emergency. I can only hope that it doesn't come to that, because the only way left for us to communicate is through texts from her iPad.

To be honest, I'm also not sure of how much time do we have before her father discovers about our secret and tries to pull another stunt. I hope we have enough time to gather substantial evidence, so even if he wishes to harm her, he can't.

ᛒᛒᛒ

I lie on my bed, finally able to experience how comfortable it feels to sleep on a mattress after fifteen days of sleeping on a chair. The sensation of my back sinking into the mattress feel so good, and I feel my muscles relaxing as I stretch my body. With my hands placed beneath my head, I wonder how Anya is, and whether she's okay. I reach out for my phone to check for any text from her, but there was none, instead there was a message from my dad, telling me to check my mail for the RTI.

There was an unread mail from the municipal authority, and there was a video attached to it. I tap on the video and it begins to play. I see Anya walking along the edge of the road, and a black car approaching towards her from behind. The driver hasn't turned on the headlights. "Bastard." I mutter to myself in anger. Due to the darkness, I couldn't make out the license plates. The car accelerates, and I watch in fury as it strike... Anya.

My blood boils at the sight, but I try to keep my emotions in check and continue to watch the video. As the car strike her and drives ahead, the light from the nearby street light fell on the car, making the license plate visible. I quickly pause the video and jot down the number, then resume it. "I couldn't protect you Anya but I will definitely avenge you." I mutter, my grip on the phone tightening as anger consume my mind. Slowly tears well up in my eyes as I watch her writhing in pain, but the video continues to play and I see the car coming back. No one comes out of the car and it drives away as people start to gather around.

I get up from the bed, my palm twitching, and turning it into a fist, I punch the wall and then again. Falling down on my knees, I then lie on the floor, cursing myself that I even thought of relaxing when she's in pain and the one who caused it is out there... free.

My phone pings and I grab it from the bed. "Sleep well. I am okay. Goodnight." The text read.

"Take care of yourself. I love you." I text her back.

Her father thinks that he can get away after committing such a heinous crime but I will gather as much evidence as possible to expose him. He shouldn't even be called a father. He doesn't deserve it.

I pick up the note in which I wrote the licence plate number and search the number on the vehicle registration website.

The website doesn't show any result. "Of course they would use fake number plates." I say to myself in disgust, then toss the phone on the bed and lie on the floor, looking outside at the moonlit sea. "Please show me a way." I close my eyes, thinking, and trying to keep my mind calm.

I have to wake up early for work after a fifteen days break, but my mind is too restless to sleep. I keep switching sides, but my mind refused to settle as it kept thinking of ways I could find a lead. How did Anya's father communicate with the killer? The image of his driver handing the suitcase to a shady man played in my mind, but it was a risky assumption to link it directly to the incident. It could have been for something completely unrelated. Perhaps the communication happened through the driver's phone, but it is kind of unlikely, because if her father cares so much about his reputation that he'd try to kill his own daughter, he would risk telling anyone about his evil plan. Maybe, he used a spare phone, one that can't be traced back to him. Yes, the idea of a spare phone seems plausible.

"Anya, I know it is really too much to ask you, especially in this condition, but could you try to find out if your father has a spare phone? It might be in his study or someplace where he usually keeps his files. I have the video of your accident from a nearby CCTV, and I think he wouldn't have taken the risk of using his main phone as it could be easily traced back to him. So, he probably has a spare phone which he used to contact the killer. But please don't take unnecessary risks. I'm mailing you the CCTV footage." I text her, then forward the RTI mail to her.

ᐅᐅᐅ

I try to reach for my phone to turn off the alarm as my eyes were reluctant to open. I press the button to stop the alarm with my half open eyes. The alarm screen closes and notifications start to appear. I scroll through them until I see a text from Anya and click on it.

"Stop treating me like I'm fragile. I can handle things on my own. I'll try to find the phone as soon as I get the chance." Her text read.

"I thought you enjoyed it when I treated you like you are delicate—picking you up and putting you on the bed you don't strain your legs." A smile of relief appears on my face as I send the text, then leaving the phone on the bed, I sit up to get ready for work.

As I was about to exit my apartment, my phone pings. A reply from Anya. "Don't say those things. I'm already frustrated that I won't be seeing you. Now don't text back and let me do my job here." I want to see her too, but I want her to be safe more.

ᐅᐅᐅ

My phone vibrates on the desk. I grab my phone and Anya's mail appear on the screen. "Found the phone. Check the attachments." I scroll down and click on the photos attached in the mail. The photos were screenshots of the call logs made to a number. There was a call on the night Anya went home to talk to her parents and it was pretty late, which just makes me surer of my guess about that shady deal of driver. There were another calls, some after the accident and a few in between.

I instantly search the number into truecaller, which returns the name of the killer as Arun and a photo of him, which looked familiar. He was the same man I saw the driver handing suitcase too and this was last bit of surety I needed to take a step further without risking Anya's life. The pieces are finally coming together, and the gravity of situation intensifying. I continue to stare at the screen, my mind consumed with preparing what to say to him on call, that would help in gathering some evidence. For all I know, he could be a member of some gang.

I bought a sim card on my way to the office, optimistic about my hunch. I couldn't afford to make any mistakes—one wrong move and I can put Anya's life back in immediate danger. With every passing moment, my anxiety kept growing, and the weight of the situation becoming more overbearing. If I wait any longer, I'm sure I'll mess up everything. I'll have to act fast, before it's too late.

So, I run to the basement parking. But by the time I reach the basement, I was breathing hard and that is because I just ran down six floors. Maybe, not waiting for the elevator wasn't a good idea after all. I take a few long breaths and exhale to calm my heart down, then dial the number with the new sim card.

He picks up the call in the fourth ring. "Arun." I say, lowering my voice, trying to pass off as the driver who facilitated the money exchange.

"Yes. Who this?" He replies.

"I'm the one who handed you the money for killing the girl." I keep up the pretence, hoping he takes the bait.

"Sir, you said this was a onetime thing. Please leave me alone. I did what you asked for." He replies, and I mentally congratulate myself because judging from the tone of his voice, he doesn't seem affiliated to some gang.

"No, you didn't. The girl was supposed to be dead, but she's not and we have a CCTV footage of you hitting her and running away. So, either meet me at the end of foot over bridge of Andheri west station in an hour, or you won't be able to meet anyone ever again. Got it?" My heartbeat increase tenfold. He has to agree or we are screwed because I've already handed him the smoking gun. Right now, we need all the luck in the world to be with us, so I squeeze my eyes shut and pray for god to help us.

"Okay," he says in a defeated tone.

ᐁᐁᐁ

It was our lunch time, so I excused myself out and head towards the Andheri west station.

I look around as I reach the spot. I kind of have an advantage here because he doesn't know me but I have seen him, and there he is. My eyes fall on him.

I dial his number without taking my eyes off him. "Walk ahead." I say, in the voice I've been trying to perfect all day. He walk. "Turn left." I walk a few steps behind him, and also carefully scanning the surroundings for anyone who might be with him. He takes the left street as I told him to.

It was a comparatively empty street. On being sure that no one was with him, I bridge the distance between us, and place my hand on his shoulder. He tries to turn around but I stop him. "Keep walking." I say, and he continues to walk ahead until we reach a completely isolated street.

He stops, then abruptly turns back with a pocket knife in his hand and tries to stab me with it. To be honest, I kind of was expecting it, thanks to the movies—I mean, I'd be a moron if I didn't think this was going to happen. I maintain my composure and duck, trying to hold his hand, but he pulls back quickly, giving a cut on my hand. He tries to stab again, and I dodge, but this time I get a hold of the wrist, then punch him right on his face. He stumbles back keep my hold on his wrist tightly, twisting it, then take the knife from his hand and throw it away.

I twist his arm to his back, holding the back of his neck, I shove his face on the wall. "Now, listen you asshole. Either you start talking fast or I have a person standing outside the police station who is gonna give all the proofs along with the video of you hitting her if he doesn't get a call from me within a minute. Try anything funny, and I'll bury you right here. Now start talking."

"I'm sorry. I needed money. Please... no police. My wife and my kids need me." He says, his voice forced because of my grip on his neck.

"The girl you tried to kill was my family. Why the hell should I care about yours? Don't waste my time. Why'd you try to kill her, and who told you to?" I shout at him, pressing his face harder against the wall. I had already started the recorder on my phone before confronting him. I know that Anya's dad asked him to, but I want it on record.

"Please, I'm sorry. I didn't want to kill her—boss did. I worked in his office as a clerk. My wife..." He groans out of pain but I still tighten my grip. "has cancer and I needed twenty lakhs. So when I asked him for help, he said he'd give it to me if I did this. My wife and I have three children, and I didn't want my kids to lose their mother. Please don't tell the police. I'm sorry."

My grip loosens a bit on hearing about his wife and his children but I tighten it again. "Don't you dare move. I am making a call first." I release his head, then twist his hands further, pressing him against the wall with the side of my shoulder, then reach for my phone in my pocket and pretend to talk to someone on the phone. "Don't leave just yet, but if I don't call you back within three minutes, go inside." I say.

"Where did you get those fake number plates?" I ask.

"There's a shop I knew who made it, and I got it from there." He replies.

"You were ready to kill someone for just twenty lakhs. What would your wife think if she finds out that the money you brought for her treatment came because you killed someone? Anyway, I'm not here to talk about you. Now listen very carefully. Here's what you're gonna do if you ever want to see your family again. You'll call your boss right now and say specifically that you tried to kill her because he told you to do so and then blackmail him for more money. Tell him that you'll go to police and tell them everything if he doesn't agree to you. Make him confess. Also tell him that the fake number plates you bastards used—you've taken it on his name, and tell him that you're gonna give every evidence you have to the police. Record everything and give it to me and I'll tell my person to stop. Try to double-cross me, you won't be seeing your family ever again, and your boss would still be going down anyway. You do this and I'll let you go and you can live with your family. I won't bother you again. Do we have a deal?"

"I'll do it."

32
Chapter Thirty Two

"You did what? Are you fucking out of your mind? What do you want me to say? Praise you because you think you're a hero or smack you right on your head for your stupidity?" Shruti yells at me as we sit in the cafeteria. She walked in when I was wrapping a bandage on the cut I got from the knife. "You escaped with just a minor cut Aahil. God knows what could've happened if he had been a criminal or had there been more than one person. I told you not to shut your brains and be an emotional moron, but here you are, doing the stupidest of things. What if something would've happened to you?" Her voice gets low as she says the last sentence.

"No... Shruti, I didn't go there blindly. I took a calculated risk. I told him over phone that I have a video of him hitting Anya, and he sounded scared. If he was a criminal, he wouldn't have been scared. When I reached there, I carefully checked the surrounding to make sure he's alone, and then I did what I did." I explain.

"What if you couldn't duck?" Her voice barely audible.

"I know that it was a huge risk, but this was my only chance to gather the evidence. When she was in the hospital, I was there with her all the time, and I wouldn't have let anything happen to her. But now, she's in her home, with the person who wanted to kill her, and after what I just did, I don't think she has much time left before he catches her lie. I'm scared for her. I'm really-really scared, and I know it was very risky, but I had to do it. And nothing happened to me, I am here, right?"

"You should've at least told be before doing something so reckless. I would've come with you."

"I know you would've, and that's exactly why I didn't tell you. I don't want your life to be in danger too."

She shakes her head. "But do it again, and I am never talking to you."

"Okay, I won't. But I need your help still." I say and sigh.

"What?"

"See, I got the recorded voice of Anya's dad confessing that he tried to kill her, and I'm gonna confront him today. I'm gonna tell him, how big of a douchebag he is. And I have a feeling that all the proofs that I have aren't enough and things could get worse out there. Frankly, if he can try to kill his own daughter, what stops him from crossing any other limits? Even if I could defend myself, Anya would still be in the room and I don't want anything else to happen to her. So, here, take this." I hand her the sim I had used to talk to the killer.

"Why this?"

"I'm gonna video call you on this number before I confront him. Keep yourself on mute, your camera off, and screen record everything. But no matter what happens, do not speak. I will send all the other evidence to you now and you'll also have a video of him form the screen recording. If anything happens to us, take it to the police."

"You shouldn't have had to face so much. You guys love each other—isn't that enough?" Her voice reflecting the genuine pain she feels.

"It's okay." I sigh. "If you ask me, I really wish things would've been different, but to be honest, right now, I wish Anya had a better father, even if she didn't have me. She doesn't deserve a father like him. Last night, all I kept thinking was how she would be. She must have been on alert all night. I don't want her to live like this. I want her to be happy, loved and safe." I pause for a moment. "You know, when I saw the man who tried to kill her, I was so enraged, that in that moment, all I wanted was to beat him so bad that he understands the pain Anya had to go through, and I almost did. You know when I shoved his face against the wall, he said that his wife has cancer, and he only did it because he needed money and he didn't want her children to be deprived of their mother. Anya had two parents but one was always busy. She always had her mother by her side. Her father, on the other hand was constantly occupied with work, and now this. I saw it in her eyes, how she felt when she told me this, and I don't want anyone to ever feel that way. And that's why, I let him go, you know, after he did what I asked him to."

"I'll do it." She declared with a new strength. "And you know what? All your struggles will end tonight and you guys will be together after this." Shruti comforts.

"Hope so. But there is one thing that we have to take care off first, and that is, bring back the real Shruti. I like it when you are all bubbly and savage, and all you've lately been is sentimental and dull."

"Okay, what do you want me to say then? Make fun of you?" Her lips curve in a small smile.

"Anything, but 'You both will be together'. You don't talk like that." I mimic her dull voice.

"Okay, how about—go get that son of a bitch and make him regret the money he loves so much." She laughs.

"Umm, not yet there, but I can work with it. And by the way, you just called Anya's grandmother a *bitch*." I chuckle.

"Sorry grandma." She laughs. "Be safe."

"Oh I can handle it with my eyes closed. Remember the bluff."

"That is exactly why, be safe."

ϷϷϷ

I press the doorbell, then take a step back, holding a bouquet in my hands. The door is opened by a maid who lets me in.

I walk in, feeling like I'm out of place. The floor's marble, glossy as hell, and everything looks way too perfect. The maid leads me down a hallway, and I'm just kind of following her.

We get into the living room. The maid walks inside to call Anya's mom, while I keep looking around. It's kind of hard to appear nonchalant, you know, because this place is huge. The whole room look like something straight out of a magazine. Dark leather sofas, big glass coffee table, and a giant TV on the wall. There are these abstract painting on the walls. Expensive, I'm guessing. Everything in this room is designed to scream money, and honestly, every time I come to this locality, it does a great job of humbling me to the last fibre of my being.

Anya's mom come in after a while. "Hello aunty." I greet her and hand her the bouquet. She takes it graciously and greets me back with a warm smile. She places the bouquet on the table in front of us gesture me to sit on the sofa. She sits on the one next to it. "How's Anya?" I ask.

"Still more or less the same but okay. Come with me, I'll take you to her room." She says, rising up from the sofa.

"I'm not sure she would want that." I say, trying to protect her lie.

"She wouldn't. Yesterday, she was asking about why you were there all the time and why did it not bother me?"

"Huh! What did you say?" I immediately blurt out, wanting to know. "I'm sorry—I didn't mean to say it like that. I just wanted to know."

"Don't worry. We are past that." She says waving a hand, starting to walk inside. I follow her. "Like I said it to you that I am proud of her that she chose you—I told her that I'm fine with both of you. She seems happy about it too. But I haven't talked to her dad, yet. So, don't get your hopes high just yet."

She knocks on the door. "Come in." A voice calls from inside. We walk inside and I see her lying on the bed inclined with pillows, too engrossed in her iPad to look up.

"Anya, there's someone I'd like you to meet."

"I don't wanna meet anyone mom." She protested, and I hold my laugh on her childlike innocence.

She walks ahead and sits next to her. "Aahil come inside." She says and Anya immediately looks up from her iPad, and as our eyes lock, my heart skips a beat. Even now, she manages to make my heart skip a beat. She's biting her lower lip right now, and I kind of want to stop her right now from biting, but I want to kiss that lip more. I should behave myself, or I'd be literally thrown out of this house.

Anya continues to look at me and then shift her gaze toward her mother, giving a puzzled look. "Aahil is here to check if you're okay?" her mom explains her.

"And you're really okay with that?" She asks.

She nods her head. "Yes," her mother replies.

"You mean, you're okay with him meeting me in my room." She asks again to her mom, while I continue to enjoy this conversation.

"I am okay with you being with him. I haven't talked to your father, but I will. Soon." She gently holds her daughter's cheeks and kisses her forehead, then straightens up.

I could visibly see Anya's face lighten up. "It took you three years mom to understand. I told you he's good." She says softly.

"Yes you did and now I understand." She gently caresses her daughter's hair. "I'll leave you two be. Call me if you need anything."

I close the door behind me, even if it didn't really need to be closed. "What if we asked her for a condom?" I blurt out stupidly again and she raises her eyebrows, glaring at me. "Oh, sorry-sorry. I'm being very stupid today. Actually, it is my first time here and I'm like... very tensed right now."

I then reach behind my shirt and take out a long-stemmed red rose. Her eyes softens and a blush spread across her cheeks as she holds the rose in her hand.

"What are you doing here?" She asks.

"You told me that you were frustrated that you didn't get to see this handsome face. So, I thought maybe I should surprise you." I say slowly walking towards her. "God, I was so worried for you. I missed you so much." I cup her face between my palms as I inch closer to kiss her. This has to be the best part of my day.

We pull away and her gaze falls on my bandaged hand. "What happened to you?"

"Ah, it nothing. So this is where you used to talk to me?" I try to change the topic.

"Yes it is. But don't change the topic, and tell me how'd you get that bandage?" She raises an eyebrow coupled with a tell-me-or-I'll-kill-you-stare.

I place my thumb on her forehead and bring her eyebrows back to where they should be. "You do that a lot. This bruise... is because I met the person who tried to kill you."

"Are you hurt anywhere else? Tell me" She says, leaning forward, trying to lift my shirt.

I hold her wrist, enveloping it in between my palms. "No, just this. And look at yourself. You should be worrying about yourself more." She places her other palm on my bandage, gently caressing it.

"I trust you, and I know you wouldn't have done it unless you thought it was the only way but if anything would've happened to you... I could go on living without you for the rest of my life, but I cannot live a single moment if the only place you exist is in my memories." She says in whispers.

"Nothing happened to me, and nothing's ever gonna happen to us. I have all the evidence we need and I have your father's confession saying that he was the one who ordered him to hit you with the car. He will have to admit every atrocious crime he did to you." I reassuringly squeeze her palm.

"I don't want my mother to get hurt." She whispers softly. "But today, we are gonna confront him. We won't be living in fear anymore." She touches my face with her palms. "I'm sorry, you got dragged into this because of me."

"Don't ever say that. And yes, we'll confront him today. That's why, I'm here."

"Can you promise me something?" She asks, her voice soft.

"Yeah, anything."

"Please never become my dad." She says and I shift closer to her, nodding my head. "I love you Aahil and I wanna spend the rest of my life with you, but please promise me that you'll never yell at me with anger. I know I do stupid things and I know I'll drive you crazy at time, but please scold at me with love. Never raise a hand on me. Love me like you love me now."

I bring her palm closer to my lips and kiss them. "Never. I won't ever do that. I love you Anya and I'll love you even after my death."

"Lock the door." She says.

"You sure?" I ask.

"Yes, lock the door. I want to kiss you as much as I can, until I'm so out of breath that I can't anymore." She demands and I oblige and lock the door.

33

Chapter Thirty Three

❦

I help Anya in sitting on a wheelchair, and then we make our way to the living room to wait for her dad. Anya had somehow convinced her mother to spend some time with her friends in the neighbourhood, saying that she needs a break, even if it is for a few hours, and since I am here, she didn't have to worry about her. Although her mother initially hesitated, but Anya was too persuasive, and she reluctantly agreed to it.

I was sitting on the sofa in the living room, with Anya next to me in her wheelchair, when we notice the door knob turning. The door swings open and her father walks inside. He looked at me with anger in his eyes, and then turned his gaze towards Anya. "Dad, I want to talk..." She begins to say, but he interrupts her.

In a stern voice, he says, "In my study," and then walk past us without bothering to look back. I grip the handles of Anya's wheelchair and begin to guide her in the direction her father was walking. He gets inside a room, but just as we were about to enter, I stop for a moment to video call Shruti.

We enter the room, her father standing on the other side of the desk. "What is this Anya? I thought you've gotten over him three years ago." His voice filled with anger.

"Yes, but he was there for me when I was in the hospital and why do you hate him anyway? He's been nothing but good to all of us." Anya's replies calmly. I stand behind her, silently, holding the

235

handle of her chair.

"You don't know people like him. And what is there to like about him? He wants money for being there—fine I'll give it to him. But these people are nothing more than that Anya. They cannot afford a good life, so they manipulate girls from wealthy families like ours for their own selfish motives. He doesn't love you. He's merely using you to gain access to our family's wealth." He shifts his gaze on me. "I shouldn't have left you when I held your collar. I should've thrown you out, back to that shithole, you and your family live in. My bad—I didn't make myself clear, the other day. Stay away from her or..."

"Or what?" Anya cuts him mid-sentence. My hands have started to twitch, my grip tightening around the handle. "Or what will you do? Kill him? Like you tried to kill me? Apologize to him, right now." She screams at the top of her voice. I place a palm on her shoulder, silently urging her to keep her cool.

He looks stunned for a second, before quickly masking it. "What did you just say? I tried to kill you? Are you out of your goddamn mind? Who told you that? You're my daughter. Why would I try to kill you? But this just proves that I was right about him all along. He has manipulated you so much against me that you're talking back to your own father. I won't let this happen. And what were you saying—apologize to him. Have you lost all your manners too? You should choose your next words wisely, young lady, or you both would be in a big trouble." He threatens.

"I haven't forgotten my manners but you've forgot how fathers are supposed to be. They are meant to protect their child and not try to harm them. And I too wanna see how far you'll go to stop us from being together. Oh wait, you'll try to kill us, right? Cause that's how you wanted to tear us apart when you tried to kill me. So go ahead, let me see with my own eyes how disgrace of a father can you be." She shouts back.

"You bastard. You've manipu..."

"He didn't do shit. You are highly mistaken to think that he manipulated me." She interrupts him again. "He never said anything bad about you in spite of you always behaving like a jerk to him. It was me who told him that you tried to kill me. And you know how I know? Why don't you ask your goddamn killer, that why the hell did he do such a poor job when he came back to check if I was dead or alive?" These weren't just words, these were every pent up emotions that she was holding back. His face turns red, clearly he was shaken up, and now he knows that Anya didn't lose her memories and he was the one who tried to kill her.

"So, this memory loss... was just a drama?" He asks.

"Excellent acting, right? Learnt it from you—how you've been acting so esteemed and entitled even though you are so rotten inside."

"You have nothing to prove it was me."

"Oh, wanna bet?" She opens the email I sent on her iPad and play the audio of his confession. "How'd you feel about when we show this to the police?"

"You bastard." He says looking at me. "You tricked me into this."

"Like you left me any choice." I reply. "After what you did, you don't even deserve to stand in front of your daughter and instead of being ashamed of yourself, you have the audacity to yell at her. Guess we all know, who's what."

He bursts into laughter, slumping on his desk. "Do you really think a bunch of amateurs like you can blackmail me with this? Let me tell you, you're not the first ones who've tried to blackmail me. So, what exactly do you want me to say? That I killed you? Okay, I'll say it. Yes, I tried to kill you because you were going to destroy my reputation by marrying a loser from some lower class and jeopardise my business deal. Why do you think I brought you up all these years? Certainly not for whatever the hell you're planning. And let me tell you something, morons, you can go to whoever you want, the police, the court—they won't do a thing. You simply don't get it that I've been in this business long before you were born. Do you really think I have all this money for nothing? But wait, why waste money for a bunch of losers like you. Go ahead, file a complaint. My lawyers are easily going to prove that the audio is fabricated or delay the proceedings indefinitely, and that would be a life time misery for you and your so-called lover and his family, but for them, it would be just another file in the pile of cases." He boasts.

"Dad!" Anya's voice breaking. "Why are you doing this to us? What have we done that you hate us so much."

"Yes dear. I'm not the one who started this—you both did. I'm just telling you what's gonna happen in the future. And you're asking what have you done? I was going to make a multi-crore deal by getting you marry Akash, but no—you just had to choose this loser. You've brought it upon yourself. You could've lived happily here, but you chose this life. Now don't blame it on me." Anya's face falls as he smirks. "Don't be sad, little girl. You did try your best—actually I'm impressed that you figured it out, got that audio—but it's not gonna help you at all. But since you're my daughter, I can do you a favour and as you already know that I am a really good father, and I don't want my daughter in a life-long misery."

He pulls out a gun from the drawer and point at us. I immediately walk and stand in front of Anya. "Well-well, look who decided to protect you Anya, your lover. So where was I? Ah... yes, I was about to free you from your life-long misery. So, who wants to be the first one to see his or her love die? Looks like the boy wants to die first. But before I shoot you boy, would you really want her to see you die in front of her. She'll be in real pain, even if it would be for a short while."

"I know you wouldn't do it or you too will be in a big trouble when the police finds out our bodies." I say, with a hint of stutter in my voice.

"I can sense fear. I like fear. Don't you worry about what will happen to your bodies once you both are dead. Taking care of that is very simple. I can make a call and they'll dispose your bodies, or I can call someone and they'll show it like some burglars entered the house and killed you. Which way would you prefer your bodies to be handled? Look, I'm being very generous today—giving you a lot of options. After all, it is about my daughter and her so called love."

"Dad, please stop. Don't do this to us?" Anya cries.

"Anya dear, I will not let anyone ruin my business and anyone who tries to tarnish it, I would take him out, even if it means taking out you, and about your lover—I don't give a damn about him. So boy, ready to die?"

"Look sir, we can talk this out and no one has to die. Please put the gun down? She's your daughter. She loves you so much, more than anything else in this world. She has time and again sacrificed her happiness because she wanted you to be happy. She never wished any harm upon you."

"What do you even see in him Anya? He is crying like a pussy. At least be a man and face it." He laughs.

My palms turns into fist. "A man... like you. No thanks." I take a step forward as he is taken aback in sudden change in my demeanour. "What makes you think every word you said won't leave this room?"

He gets his composure back. "I have a gun and you don't. You do get the situation, right? What will you do? Record another audio? I doesn't matter as you won't be alive to take it anywhere." He says, his gun still pointing towards me.

"And what makes you think that we wouldn't know that you have lawyers and how rich you are. I mean, I know that you're an idiot with an overblown ego, who thinks he's the smartest one in the room, but really? Do you think we are so naïve? C'mon pull the trigger and let's find out if you're the one who gets in trouble or not."

"What do you mean?"

"You were so full of yourself, that you didn't even notice that you've been on camera all along and there is someone who has recorded everything you've said. But am I smart enough to do that? Guess so. You were boasting about your lawyers, right? I hope they are really that good to prove a video fake, which has you holding a gun, admitting your attempted murder, threatening of murder, disposing bodies, bribery and what not." The smirk on his face is now completely gone and there's an expression of worry on his face.

"Now put that gun on the table and move back, because if you don't, that person is going to take this clip to the police along with your confession and several other evidence I gave him before I came here. And then, your so called reputation, which you love more that your daughter, will be ruined. Not to mention, all your business partners and all the people you seek approval from will know about your actions. What will they think about you? Would they shame you or they'd just kick you out? So, what do you say?"

"I... I don't trust you. You're bluffing. There's no one on the other side." His voice stumbling.

"Maybe or maybe not. Let's make a bet. What do you say Anya? Am I bluffing or not?" I look at her still keeping him in the peripheral vision. She is as clueless as her dad. "By the way, I can sense fear in your voice. Where's that egoistic smug voice of yours? But okay, since you've been extremely generous to us, I'll give you a proof. 'Hey there, other person can you clap,' how many times do you want him to clap—won't say. It's fine. 'Clap three times, and show us that you've recorded everything.' Fine?" I say, making sure not to reveal Shruti's name or she would be in danger too. Shruti claps thrice. "See, it is entirely your choice to put that gun away or not. But, I won't give you more than five seconds to decide, and when the countdown ends, the evidence will be sent to the police as well as uploaded on YouTube. Big businessman, threatens to kill his daughter because she loves someone else. Great title for views." I say then begin counting. "Five. Four. Three. Two..." he puts the gun down and slides it away. I take a step towards him and he grabs my collar. I hold his hands tightly. "Is this your patented threatening stance? Anyway, if you think you intimidate me, you're being naïve. Now get your hands off my shirt or this time I wouldn't care if you are her father, cause, certainly you've lost that right." I tighten my hands around his and take them away with force, then push him back. "Try to do something stupid, you know what can happen, and I do what I say. Now listen carefully what she has to say, and remember, I'm watching you and so is the camera."

I take a good look at him for anything he would be hiding before letting him walk towards Anya. I step aside as he takes slow and heavy steps towards her, while I walk towards where the gun was and pick it up using a handkerchief. Carefully, I unload all the bullets from the gun and hold it in my hand. Anya continues to stare at me. "What?" I ask, as she gives me a puzzled look. "I watch movies."

She sighs, then shift her gaze on her father. "Dad!" her voice soft. "If you want it so bad, we won't interfere in it again." She says, gesturing towards everything. "Everything that has happened until now, won't leave this room, ever."

"Anya." He whispers.

"Let me finish. We have a deal for you. Let me and Aahil marry. Keep mom happy, not like you treat her now, but really happy and never let her find out about this. Do it and we won't say a word to anyone. You have my word, but only if you stick to yours. We don't want your money or property or anything from you. This is our deal and it's non-negotiable. Take it or leave it." Her voice reflected the pain her heart felt.

He shifts his gaze on me. "She's speaks for both of us." I say. "But remember, if you try to hurt her, or her mom or our family, I'll tear you apart, and your so called mansion of filth to its last brick." He keeps looking at me, then shifts her gaze back to his daughter.

"Okay, I agree. You can marry him and I'll try to keep your mom happy." He sounds defeated.

"I did it for mom." She says, as a tear slides from the side of her eye.

<h1 style="text-align:center">Epilogue</h1>

"Hurry Anya, we'll miss our flight." I call her.

"Just a minute." She replies from inside while I wait for her at the door, having already moved our travel bags outside our apartment. She comes out of the room in a hurry, double checking things in her purse.

We walk out of the apartment and I lock the door behind us, and rush to the airport. It is an hour long flight from Mumbai to Goa, and I've already arranged for our pickup at the Goa airport.

I hold the door open for her as she slides in the cab, and then I get inside with her. The drives pulls the cab on the driveway and we head towards the resort. I gently wrap my arm around her whole she looked outside through the window, placing her chin on her knuckles, which rested on the frame of the window. The traffic of the city, slowly fading into tall trees standing on both sides of the road.

The cab stops at the entrance of the resort and a man opens the door for us. We climb out of the car, while he helps us with the luggage. The resort had cosy wooden cottages with a balcony and a sitting area, which offered a stupendous view of the Arabian Sea. The cottage was completely surrounded with trees and plantations, providing the freshest air. I hold her hand as we walk on the pathway towards out cottage.

The attendant opens the door for us and hand me the key, while Anya walks inside. As I enter the room, a delightful scent of roses greets us. I gently close the door behind us, while Anya looks around, barely able to control her happiness. I take a step towards her, wrapping my arms around, I gently move her hat and place a kiss on the top of her head. "You like it?" I ask, bushing my nose against hers.

"I love it." She mumbles on my chest, wrapping her arms around me. Then look up, into my eyes, with a smile, that could probably light up this whole town. I gently caress the strand of her hair and smile back.

"You are beautiful, Ana." I say, then lean towards her, until our lips brush against each other. Her lips curve into an arc as she smiles, and in that moment, we do not kiss. Instead, we remain locked in each other's arms, silent—breathing each other. The time stood still or maybe it was moving too fast or maybe it did whatever the hell it wants, but we didn't care. We were too lost in each other to care, and when it got too irresistible for us to keep holding each other's gaze, our eyes close and our lips meet.

She rests her face on my chest as she gasps for breath. "All this beautiful scents in the air, and I still want to breathe you." She whisper then look up. Her cheeks in beautiful shade of crimson.

ᐳᐳᐳ

My mouth drops open as she walks out of the bathroom, wearing a bikini. All the bruises that she had, have now healed, even though they left small scars as reminders. She walks towards me with a knowing grin on her face. "You look smoking..." I inhale, "hot. But you're not really thinking of going outside wearing this, right?"

"Why?" She asks.

"Because you're my treat. I don't wanna anyone laying eyes on you."

"Oh, c'mon, there's no one on the beach."

"There might be." When she realizes that I won't budge, she takes a step towards me, slow, placing her palm on my chest. "I know what you're trying to do. Stop."

She still walks closer, such that her skin brushes against mine. She slowly moves her fingers on my chest, "Please," she says batting her eyelashes.

My mouth goes dry. "Oka... no." I take a step back from her and shift my gaze on anything but her. "Don't mess with me like that. At least get something to cover yourself until we reach the beach."

"Okay." She grins, then turns around, walking towards the closet.

"It should be a crime to be you."

"Stop staring at me." She says with a mischievous grin in her voice.

"I can't help it." I holler back.

She puts on a cover up and her hat. "Okay?"

The cover up hug loosely around her, still showing her body. I walk towards her and hold the ends of the cover up and wrap it around her. "Now okay." I wrap my hands around her waist holding the cover up in place. "Let's go."

"Like this?" She asks.

"Like what?"

"You holding me like this."

"Oh, so now I can't even hold you like this."

"You do know why you're holding me now."

"Fine. But at least wrap it properly until we reach the beach."

"Uhuh!" As I was about to take my hands away, she swiftly grabs them, slowly guiding them across her waist, while her eyes holding my gaze. "You know, there's a hook here." She teasingly whispers, then guide my hand towards the hook.

She takes a step closer as I lock the hook, wrapping her arms around my neck, she lifts herself on her toes. "Do not kiss back." She says, then leans in, pressing her lips against mine. My eyes close instinctively.

"I like messing with you." She says as she steps back. "Let's go to the beach."

"I need water first."

There were very few people on the beach. The sun is starting to change its colour, painting the sky with hues of orange. But we still had some time before it gets dark.

I unfold the mat on a dry spot, then place the basket and her bag on it. She takes off her beach cover up, leaving it on the mat too. I hold her wrist and pull her towards me. She rests her hands on my shoulders and I hold her by her waist. "You ready?"

"Born ready." She says and we start running towards the sea and jump in the water. She dives in first, and I follow, diving right behind her. Underwater, it's quiet—just bubbles and the pull of ocean. I kick my feet, pushing down, and then when I swim back up, I'm laughing, wiping the salty water off my face.

"Cold!" I shout, shaking my head. She giggles beside me.

"Let's go further," she says, her voice full of excitement.

"Hold my hand," I reply, grinning, not even thinking twice. She grabs my hand, and we start swimming further in the sea.

The waves aren't too strong, just enough to keep it fun. I can't help but play around a little, splashing her or giving her a quick shove. She's quick though—always ready to tackle me when I least expect it.

"Ah, stop!" I laugh, trying to dodge her, but she's already on me, pushing me underwater. I come up a little away from her and we both just end up floating there, catching our breath.

We are both a little tired now, but the water feels too good to leave, so we just float in water. Her hand's still in mine, and everything feels... right.

The sun starts to slowly sink in the sea, casting its rays that made Anya's face look even more radiant. She looks at me, and I pull her closer to me, leaning in and kissing her softly. In the distance, a giant reflection of the sun appeared in the water, but we pay no attention to the breath-taking view. We were too lost, because you know, it felt... perfect.

ᗐᗐᗐ

"Feels like a dream." Anya says as I gently towel dry her hair. She was holding a mug of tea in her hands.

"It is as they say—Second time's a charm." I say and then place a kiss on her shoulder.

"They say the third time is a charm." She replies.

"You want a third time?"

"No. Second is better."

I lift her by her thigh, moving her to sit on my lap. Her back touches my chest as I envelope her in my arms. I gently shift her hair to a side then rest my chin on her shoulder, hugging her tightly. "You know, sometimes I think we have a really good story to tell.

All these ups and downs, breakups, fights, and you know, some romantic moments too."

"Now that I think of it, we did come a long way. From you sending that friend request to falling in love and now, sitting here. And-and, don't forget the late night talks." She says, her voice soft.

"Do you think it would make a good book?" I ask, my gaze on the sea in front of us.

"I don't know if it would make a good book but it sure as hell is the most special thing in my life." She says, then shifts on my lap, turning to her side, so that her cheeks rest on my chest. "You know, I would give up anything in this world for what we have now."

"I love you."

"I love you too."

ᖰᖰᖰ

"Wake up Ana, we'll get late." I gently place my palm on her cheeks, caressing it to wake her up.

"Why? It's so early. I wanna sleep." She mumbles.

"I wanna show you something."

"I don't wanna see anything. Let me sleep." She mutters but I slide my hand under her and make her sit. She tries to fall back on the pillow but I hold her.

"Anya, you can sleep in the car. Come with me."

"No, I wanna sleep on bed." She falls back on her pillow the instant I walk towards the closet to get her a hoodie. I help her sit up again, then slide the hoodie over her head, guiding her hand through the sleeves, and then pulling the hoodie down over to her body.

"Ana, this is something you really don't wanna miss babe. Please wake up. I'll do whatever you say."

"Fine. But it better be something worth it." She reluctantly wakes up.

We lock the door and get inside the car which was already waiting for us. "Where are we going? It's still dark out here." She asks.

"Surprise."

"Then wake me up when it comes." She says, laying her head on my lap. I tenderly place my palm on her head, caressing her hair as the driver drives us to the place.

"Babe, wakeup. We are here." I lean down and kiss her head. The car stops and I help her climb out of the car.

She rubs her eyes which were reluctant to open, but when they did, her sleep instantly fades away. "Hot air balloons." She says, her voice filled with excitement.

I nod, then tightly grasp her hand as we walk ahead towards the one we were supposed to ride in. The balloon was already up in the air and the only thing stopping it from flying away was the anchor it was hooked to and the operator who kept managing the flame.

We walk inside and settle ourselves, eagerly waiting for the ride to begin. The operator undoes the knot and within a few seconds we are flying up in the air. The ground beneath us slowly starts to fade away as the balloon carries us higher and higher into the sky.

There's a breath-taking view of green fields stretching out beneath us. Behind us is the gigantic Arabian Sea, glistening as the sunlight falls on the waves, and then there is a series of hills in front of us, completely covered in lush greenery. The sun is slowly rising behind the hills, casting a warm glow upon the surroundings.

I stand behind Anya, wrapping my arms around her. "You know, we've been together during dusk a couple of times. I wanted to chase the dawn with you." I gently brush my stubble against her cheek. "So is it worth it?" I ask as I leave her, getting down on one knee, and holding out the ring I've had in my pocket since the beginning of this trip.

She turns around towards me but before she could say anything, "Will you marry me?" I say.

She covers her mouth with the back of her hand, trying to contain her happiness. She too falls on her knees and wraps her hand around me, crying, overwhelmed with emotions. "*Yes, a thousand times yes.*"